Wild Hearts

MĀNOA 22:2   UNIVERSITY   HONOLULU
                   OF HAWAI'I
                   PRESS

LITERATURE,

ECOLOGY, AND

INCLUSION

Wild Hearts

EDITED BY

FRANK STEWART

AND ANJOLI ROY

Actors Ichikawa Kodanji VIII as Kōmori Yasu and Kawarazaki Gonjūrō I as Kirare Yoza

Artist: Utagawa Kunisada I (Toyokuni III), 1786–1864
Publisher: Maruya Jinpachi (Marujin, Enjudō)

Japanese, Edo period, 1860 (Ansei 7/Man'en 1), 7th month.
Woodblock print (nishiki-e); ink and color on paper;
vertical ōban. Museum of Fine Arts, Boston;
William Sturgis Bigelow Collection, 11.40179;
Photograph © 2010 Museum of Fine Arts, Boston

In a Kabuki play first performed in 1853, Kōmori Yasu, "Yasu the Bat," is a small-time criminal who looks sinister because of the bat tattoo on his face.

Editor Frank Stewart

Managing Editor Pat Matsueda

Designer and Art Editor Barbara Pope

Associate Editor Sonia Cabrera

Assistant Managing Editor Nicole Sawa

Abernethy Fellow Eleanor Svaton

Staff Kathleen Matsueda, Allegra Wilson

Corresponding Editors for North America
Barry Lopez, W. S. Merwin, Carol Moldaw, Michael Nye, Naomi Shihab Nye, Arthur Sze

Corresponding Editors for Asia and the Pacific
CAMBODIA Sharon May
CHINA Howard Goldblatt, Ding Zuxin
HONG KONG Shirley Geok-lin Lim
INDONESIA John H. McGlynn
JAPAN Leza Lowitz
KOREA Bruce Fulton
NEW ZEALAND AND SOUTH PACIFIC Vilsoni Hereniko
PACIFIC LATIN AMERICA H. E. Francis, James Hoggard
PHILIPPINES Alfred A. Yuson
SOUTH ASIA Sukrita Paul Kumar
WESTERN CANADA Charlene Gilmore

Advisory Group William H. Hamilton, Robert Shapard, Robert Bley-Vroman

Founded in 1988 by Robert Shapard and Frank Stewart.

Mānoa gratefully acknowledges the continuing support of the University of Hawai'i Administration and the University of Hawai'i College of Languages, Linguistics, and Literature; the grant support of the National Endowment for the Arts and the Hawai'i State Foundation on Culture and the Arts; and the assistance of the Mānoa Foundation.

NATIONAL
ENDOWMENT
FOR THE ARTS
A great nation
deserves great art.

HAWAI'I STATE
FOUNDATION
ON CULTURE
AND THE ARTS

Mānoa is published twice a year. Subscriptions: U.S.A. and International—individuals $30 one year, $54 two years; institutions $50 one year, $90 two years; international airmail add $24 per year. Single copies: U.S.A. and International—individuals $20; institutions $30; international airmail add $12 per copy. Call toll free 1-888-UHPRESS. We accept checks, money orders, Visa, or MasterCard, payable to University of Hawai'i Press, 2840 Kolowalu Street, Honolulu, HI 96822, U.S.A. Claims for issues not received will be honored until 180 days past the date of publication; thereafter, the single-copy rate will be charged.

http://manoajournal.hawaii.edu/
http://www.uhpress.hawaii.edu/journals/manoa/

CONTENTS

Editor's Note

For over two decades, the *Mānoa* series has been publishing uncommonly thoughtful and ethically committed literature from Asia, Oceania, and the Americas—often in new translations, and featuring authors and languages little known in the West. Frequently, we have anthologized new writers from a particular place, such as India, China, Japan, Cambodia, Indonesia, and French Polynesia. In addition to emphasizing translation and cosmopolitanism in our pages, we seek out writers who are most attuned to what literature, at its best, can do to prepare us for a world growing more crowded by the day (an estimated 9.5 billion souls by 2050), and at the same time increasingly divisive, intolerant, partitioned, and dangerous.

The role of literature in a time of crisis, it seems to us, is not to compose manifestos, propagandize, proselytize, or moralize. It's enough that words and stories restore our powers of ethical imagination—make us more understandable to ourselves, more explicable to others, and more capable of not merely tolerating but welcoming the differences and samenesses of other individuals and communities.

In *Wild Hearts* we blur the lines between geographical places, ways of knowing the world, and the uncontainable complexities of the human heart—which, as we have heard, has its own reasons and manners of reasoning. In *Wild Hearts* are, among others, fiction writers Barry Lopez, Leo Litwak, and Andrew Lam; South Asian playwright Manjula Padmanabhan; the preeminent American expert on Japanese cinema (and long-time expatriate) Donald Richie; contemporary poets Yang Zi, from the PRC, and Arthur Sze, from New Mexico; and filmmaker and director Aaron Woolfolk, interviewed by Honolulu artist Calvin Collins.

Some of the works here address the relationships between humans and non-humans, and the prehistory of their mingling; they re-draw reality in alternate and surprising ways. For example, Robert Bringhurst writes of the interstices between the local and the universal, naming and knowing, the here and there. "Home," he writes,

> is alive, like a tree, not skinned and dressed or cut and dried like the quarried stone and milled wood houses are made of, nor masticated and spat out like the particle board and plywood used for packaging prefabricated lives.... Home is

Onitsutaya Azamino and Gontarō, a Man of the World
(Onitsutaya Azamino, isami-tsū Gontarō), from the series
True Feelings Compared: The Founts of Love
(Jitsu kurabe iro no minakami)

Artist: Kitagawa Utamaro I, (?)–1806
Publisher: Nishimuraya Yohachi (Eijudō)

Japanese, Edo period, about 1798–1799 (Kansei 10–11).
Woodblock print (nishiki-e); ink and color on paper; vertical ōban.
Museum of Fine Arts, Boston. Gift of Mr. and Mrs. Frederic
Langenbach in memory of Charles Hovey Pepper, 54.1519.
Photograph © 2010 Museum of Fine Arts, Boston

the whole earth, everywhere and nowhere, but it always wears the masks of particular places, no matter how often it changes or moves.

Scientists Deborah Bird Rose, Anna Tsing, and Thom van Dooren question how we look at relationships among humans and those animals who are the "unloved others" among nature's kin, because they are often associated negatively with death. Each of these authors articulates a poetics of "inclusion," illuminating the crucial place of such creatures as vultures, fungi, and bats in multispecies communities. These and other essays on the same theme are forthcoming in an issue of the *Australian Humanities Review* in spring 2011.

Andrew Schelling writes about three *bhakti* (devotional) poets of South Asia, introducing a word from Sanskrit poetics, *sandhya-bhasha,* which means "twilight speech":

> Twilight speech is imagistic, paradoxical, a-logical, to counter the "logic" of the powerful. I also appreciate the term used of Kabir's baffling paradoxes: *ulat-bhamshi,* "upside-down speech."
>
> These kinds of non-rational speech communicate with immediacy. Lovers, children, and family members use them all the time. So do Zen teachers, poets, saints, and popular songwriters.

These words might also characterize the writing in *Wild Hearts.* Though many of the works don't resemble the epistemologies of Zen teachers and poet-saints, each author takes seriously the need to be comprehensible to others across the frontiers and partitions of unexamined ideas and manipulative political reasoning. Some of them show us our madness or cruelty; others show us the ecstatic heart.

The editors would like to thank the Museum of Fine Arts in Boston for permission to include Japanese woodblock prints from the exhibition *Under the Skin: Tattoos in Japanese Prints.* The exhibition is on display at the museum until January 2, 2011.

Andrew Schelling's translations of Jayadeva's *Gita-govinda* first appeared in 2008 in a limited-edition artist's book by Ken Botnick, of Emdash Editions; these translations are also forthcoming in an anthology from Oxford University Press, India, edited by Schelling.

Kazuko Shiraishi's essay first appeared in Japanese in *Landscape of Poetry: Portrait of the Poets,* for which she received the prestigious Yomiuri Literary Award in 2009. Yumiko Tsumura translated the essay especially for *Wild Hearts.*

We also wish to thank Leza Lowitz for her help in editing the selections from the journals of Donald Richie.

Donald Richie in a bookstore, Kanda, Tokyo, ca. 1955.

DONALD RICHIE

Where I Am Sitting, the
Light Falls Just Right

A Note About Donald Richie

In 2004, the preeminent expert on Japanese cinema Donald Richie published *The Japan Journals: 1947–2004*, extensive excerpts from the personal journals he kept while an expatriate in Japan. During those years, he became acquainted with all the major directors, actors, and critics of Japanese cinema, as well as international authors, poets, translators, and artists.

Richie dated the final entry in his book 18 April 2004—the day after his eightieth birthday—and considered it to be the last of his journal writing. But about a year later, he noted to himself, "I had thought the fit was finished, that everything lay safely dead on the page. But no, the urge remains." And so, to his surprise—and mine, as I had been permitted to edit *The Japan Journals*—he started again to record his careful observations of the daily moments of his life.

What follows here are excerpts from journals Richie kept from 2004 to 2009. They display the same candid manner of the earlier entries—a style that reveals Richie's care and masterfulness through a deceptively simple, almost off-handed prose. Richie is unsentimental and unassuming about his own life, yet tender and witty in his assessment of friends and critics. Readers come to know the mind of a fascinating man who has lived an extraordinary internal life, while witnessing and participating in one of the great social transformations of the twentieth century.

As I noted in my introduction to his book, Richie saw and described the remarkable changes that took place in postwar Japan, beginning with his arrival in Tokyo on 1 January 1947, as a journalist for the *Pacific Stars and Stripes*. What he recapitulates in his journals is both more and less than a large spectacle. He was more attracted to the private than to the public. He sometimes mentions big events, but more often he records the details. His emphasis is usually upon his reactions rather than the events themselves.

What was Richie's purpose in keeping his journals? Certainly, like anyone who keeps a journal, he wanted to intervene, to make lasting the ordinarily perishable, to save experience. Typical is the beginning of the entry for 18 December 1996: "I walk the windy streets of Shibuya, a territory completely given over to the young. Here they come in their hordes, driven by fashion. Let me describe them lest this motley show be lost forever."

There are other reasons for journal-keeping as well. Richie has been, like any foreigner in Japan, restricted to the role of spectator. Even though he has lived there most of his life, he has never become a citizen, merely a permanent resident. He pays full taxes, but he cannot vote. And, given Japan's peculiar attitude toward foreigners, he has been powerless in many other ways as well.

Richie's first fame came for his work on Japanese cinema. With Joseph Anderson, he wrote *The Japanese Film: Art and Industry,* which is regarded as the seminal study of Japanese film. He went on to write well-regarded books on Kurosawa Akira and Ozu Yasujirō, as well as further histories of Japanese film itself. In addition, he has written numerous essays on cinema, taught at various universities, served on many film-festival juries, and so on.

Whatever its other qualities, film demands observation. One sits in the dark and regards. Richie's detachment and the keenness of his attention are qualities that make his observations so valuable. In his journals, he can stand apart from himself and observe not only the context of his life but also its sensitive center—himself. This is something he learned to do.

Part of the fascination of these journals lies in just this: their rich immediacy, their passion for detail, and their impartiality. Each page is like a scene from the past, brought alive again and illuminated by the writer's intelligence and concern. Not that the tableau is ever complete. We always seem to be examining a corner, though in great detail. And with that we are aware of an attitude, a person, a style. We realize that we are being told something of great interest, something the writer was moved enough to record for posterity.

For many reasons, then, we can be grateful that Richie has continued to tell the story of himself and his times—and what it has been like to be a man neither entirely here nor there, in several worlds at once, some permissible and others less so, always present and yet apart. On 27 September 1998 he wrote:

> Smilingly excluded here in Japan, politely stigmatized, I can from my angle attempt only objectivity, since my subjective self will not fit the space I am allotted....So, how fortunate I am to occupy this niche with its lateral view. In America I would be denied this place. I would live on the flat surface of a plain. In Japan, from where I am sitting, the light falls just right—I can see the peaks and valleys, the crags and crevasses.

Outwardly content yet always seeking a home, Richie in his 5 December 1999 entry quotes Rilke: "We are born, so to speak, provisionally, it doesn't matter where; it is only gradually that we compose, within ourselves, our true place of origin, so that we may be born there retrospectively."

Leza Lowitz, Tokyo

31 JULY 2005

Reading Robert Moss's *Cleopatra's Wedding Present: Travels through Syria* (1997), I come across: "Being a foreigner in an alien culture is a way of institutionalizing your aloneness, of going public with it. You are no longer failing to meet the expectations and values of your own world, nor do you have to meet those of your adopted one—or if you do, no one expects you to do it perfectly."

This so well expresses what I have felt (and written about in these pages) that I am struck with a craving to begin again my journals. Once published [*The Japan Journals: 1947–2004*], I had thought the fit was finished, that everything lay safely dead on the page. But no, the urge remains. Time is passing, things are changing, and I must make some note of this. Also, nothing is quite real to me until I have committed it to writing, and hence my existence lacks shape until I have done so. Otherwise the days crowd together, today feels like yesterday, and life seems a series of breakfasts. Journals make dimensions.

So, begin once more I will, and hope that the application holds. Searching the files I find some fragments, pieces of a prior start. These shards I might as well include to shore up my new efforts.

7 DECEMBER 2004

Jean Silvestre, friend for near forty years, comes for dinner. We talk about his retirement. Soon sixty-five, he feels he no longer has a future. But he did back then. I remember him as a dashing French sailor in his twenties when he had the whole world before him. I say that things always look bad up ahead but when you get there it turns out not so bad as you thought.

Such banalities soon lead to a discussion of suicide, since retirement itself is a kind of suicide since many people at this point die. Over our curries we discuss the different ways, and I tell him about the recipes in my *Final Exit*. We decide that only sleeping medicine and carbon monoxide (though not together) are least messy, but that nonetheless the body will put up quite a fight. Then we go out sobered and strangely lightened into the cold night.

8 DECEMBER 2004

Called up by *Interview* magazine. They are doing a Japan issue and want me in it. This is the harvest of *The Japan Journals* being published. They had acquired a copy and apparently read it. Being in the celebrity publication of Andy Warhol was not among my ambitions, but I put on my good jacket and go anyway.

The shoot is held in the new Chanel Ginza Building, and the photographer is none other than the head of Chanel itself, Karl Lagerfeld. He stands in black in the center of a group of busy and beautiful young people, a ring on every finger, his hair in a ponytail.

It's powdered, you know. I always powder my hair, he says. Like George Washington, I say. Yes, but for different reasons. It is wild, my hair. I am Angela Davis but only dirty gray. With powder I am neat and platinum. But you...

He turns me around by the shoulders. I am the new assignment. Shakes his head at my good jacket, shouts an order, and soon I am in a form-hugging black Yohji Yamamoto coat. He nods approval: Just right. Takes off ten years, he says.

I am then draped over a black-leather and chrome chair, sat sidewise with one hand propping my chin, the other hanging useless. I try to imagine the results—tousled elegance is the best I can come up with. In the meantime, very professional, the photographer is snapping. The results are wired back to a large console where a group of the pretty people are gathered.

Splendid, oh, marvelous, fabulous, they say. Over and over again. They are not praising me. They are cheerleaders spurring on the star as he crouches and snaps. Coat, he snaps, and a lovely young woman rushes to my side and pulls hard, smoothing the lump that Yohji was apparently considering. Then, after a large number of pictures are taken, Karl comes closer, indicating that the session is over.

We briefly talk, and he says that they are splendid, marvelous, fabulous, then mentions the model just before me. Like a movie monster. This was a reference to Miike Takashi, now standing sullen in black leather and dark glasses at the other end of the room. The photographer had mentioned movie monsters because Miike is after all Japan's most famous maker of horror/violence pictures. He had mentioned it now to me as a graceful indication that he knew I was somehow also in the movies.

In the meantime the chorus at the console are exclaiming how fabulous the pictures are, but I am not invited to inspect them. So I sit and listen to this chorus of praise. It is not simple flattery, it is too urgent for that. I am reminded of a progressive school where the student must be encouraged by constant praise.

The editor comes in on the run. She has been busy with the big local film star Kaneshiro Takeshi. He was jetted in from Taiwan for the shoot along with, would I believe it, she wonders, three, yes, three Chinese minders who just took over. They answered his questions for him too. Big bruiser types, they were.

The editor is Ingrid Sischy, whom I had met twenty years before when she was with *Artforum*. So energetic, so smart, so skeptical. She is carrying a copy of my *Image Factory*. Maybe that book is among the reasons I was asked. Maybe their report on trendy Japan will allow for a bit of my welcoming bile. The book, she says, is absolutely fabulous, just so great. So are the pictures Karl took, just fantastic. So is my coat, absolutely great. I tell her it is a real Yohji Yamamoto and then regretfully go hang it back on the rack.

9 DECEMBER 2004

I am given my imperial award, *kunsho*—a *kyokujitsu shō*. It came in its lacquer case, rosette attached. Since I had missed the main ceremony (the third day of the eleventh month of the sixteenth year of Heisei, reads the official letter) having been in America, this was an impromptu affair. The scroll reads: "The Order of the Rising Sun, Gold Rays with Rosette, is hereby conferred upon Donald Steiner Richie, Citizen of the United States of America, by His Majesty the Emperor of Japan." This is stamped with the seal of his majesty and signed with the seal of the prime minister. I was photographed receiving this and admiring the order itself, then the minister and I sat down to talk about movies. This conversation was transcribed and will appear in their magazine—not perhaps so much of interest in itself as something to mark this ritual.

While chatting, another part of me was wondering how I felt about all of this. Earlier, I had often enough announced myself satisfied with exclusion, pleased that I would never be allowed admittance into the sacred circle. And here I sit, covered with chrysanthemums. Do I feel that I have been compromised? No, not at all. I like the attention, and while I will not much wear my decoration, I like the fact that it will be somewhere in a drawer.

And I wonder if everything we think we are is merely the result of some occasion. When I thought I was safe from being decorated, I was satisfied. Once decorated, I am satisfied.

10 DECEMBER 2004

It is Tomiyama Katsue to whom I owe this distinction. She worked on the cultural ministry and got me accepted. Part of her reason is that this ministry is now more interested in films, and so is she, having created Image Forum. Another part is that we have known each other for a long time, and I admire her and have always supported her work. And now I sit, decorated, as she, her staff, and I plan the party.

This is to be held at the International House, include drinks and lunch, and will be the official announcement of my honor. I enthusiastically go along with this until I think to wonder who will be paying for it. Then I am told what I should earlier have recognized, that the guests themselves would. And the ten thousand per head we had been discussing would be translated into one hundred dollars out of the pockets of each of my guests. Even though the CD of my films would be thrown in as a door prize, this is a lot of money just to go and congratulate someone.

So I refuse. I cannot ask people to pay for something like this. And indeed I myself usually refuse this kind of party. And this kind of party is all that there is now that no one can afford the big bashes of twenty years ago. And to ask broke Fumio and always-strapped Makiyo to pay this much money to shake hands with their friend is unthinkable.

Another thing about my refusal is how very un-Japanese I am being. Japanese do not find this kind of compulsory payment at all objectionable. Indeed, paying this much is a way of being included. Only sincere "members" would fork out such an amount. And my presumption in asking them to pay could and probably would be viewed as a kind of friendship. I know them so well that I can go and lean on them.

Katsue is treating me as a Japanese. I am invited in as a member of the *nakama*. I am asked inside this sacred circle. And anyone I ask to come and pay for the pleasure will do so. But I am worried not so much about these now uninvited guests as I am about Katsue herself. What will she think when she has made me such an offer only to have it rejected?

She relieves my suspense. Upon hearing of my decision she says, "Well, I guess that customs differ. You don't do this over there, right?"

1 AUGUST 2005

Another high summer—the lotuses now tall as a small man, their faint stale-water fragrance mingling with the oily odors of the homeless sitting hopeless on the shores. Some changes: the vagrants are older than they used to be, the mosquitoes have now learned to fly as high as my eighth-floor windows, and the *yukata* has returned.

About half of the young people in the park are in these summer *kimono*. And about half of these are male. A common sight, she and he on a date, each in a *yukata*, his only slightly less bright than hers. The cut is traditional, though the garment itself is brand new and synthetic—polyester, or something. These can be bought at boutiques now, complete with the belt-like *obi*. And they are cheap.

Obviously designed as an instant fashion statement, they have caught on. The youngsters do not know how to wear them, to be sure. Boys have the *obi* all the way down to their pubes, girls attach big ribboned bows never traditionally seen with *yukata*, and both are engagingly sloppy in appearance, though the whole role of the *yukata* was to look cool and collected.

But you don't question a fashion statement except, in this case, to wonder what something this retro means. A generation ago young folks would have died rather than appear in something as icky as a *kimono*. And now young folks all over the place are out in them.

I do not think that the renaissance of the *yukata* can be read as merely politically conservative. At least I do not think the kids read it that way. It is simply the rash of a new fashion that, like typhoons, comes along every season now. On the other hand, with half the youngsters in the city now back into feudal gear, it must mean something.

2 AUGUST 2005

The pendulum swings, the times change. Signs of a major reversal, country moving to the right. Prime Minister Koizumi Junichiro insisting that he visit Yasukuni Shrine despite all the criticism. Several hundred schoolteachers were forced into retirement or fired because they refused to stand when the anthem ("Kimigayo") was played, when the flag (Hinomaru) was displayed. The Self-Defense Forces have been deployed to Iraq on a "humanitarian" mission. Ishihara Shintarō, Tokyo's governor, says the French language is not fit for communication since "you cannot count in it." He also deplores the danger of all of these foreigners in Japan. Debate continues as to whether it is possible for Japan to have an empress since the future now devolves upon one small princess. Cartoonist Kobayashi Yoshinori sells millions of books, saying that apologizing for wartime atrocities is humiliating. New textbooks that do not mention the atrocities are now being used in more schools. Murakami Takashi, popular artist, says that

Japan has been "castrated" by losing the war and enduring the Occupation. "A pervasive impotence defines the culture of postwar Japan, where everything is peaceful, tranquil, lukewarm." One must do something about this. But the public is placid, a whole generation of drones created by the Ministry of Education. Nonetheless, the great popularity of Fukui Harutoshi, pop fictionist who writes war novels. One of them this week opens as a film, *Boukoku no Aegis*, about a plot to bomb Tokyo bravely foiled by a selfless hero. *Boukoku* means "lost country." Wake up, Japan. At the same time, I read that the museum showing the famous Hiroshima murals, which were painted by the Marukis, Toshi and Iri, and depict all the horrors of the bombing, is going to have to close. No visitors, no supporters, and I heard that Hiroshima itself wants to tear down its famous ruin because ruins are not good for the business prospects of the largest city in southern Japan.

3 AUGUST 2005

I go to the press showing of a new film about Mishima. It is called *Miyabi: Yukio Mishima* and is an hour and fifteen minutes of rehabilitation. The descriptive adjective is an old aesthetic term that means something like *furyu*, for which "elegance" will have to do as a translation. It consists of one interview after another, all attesting to Mishima's classical status, mixed in with shots of the rising sun (or the setting one) and close-ups of earnest young people who appreciate him. Only Mishima the writer is concerned—Mishima the singer, the actor, the bodybuilder are neglected.

The people interviewed are selected in a somewhat random fashion, the few foreigners as well. The film is quite artless and has no intentions other than those stated. It thus ignores the enormous political potential of a film about Mishima right now. We hear essays by young people who go on about *yamato damashii* in a manner as approving as Mishima himself could have desired. There is mention about how "surprising" the newspaper clipping of the severed head was. But nowhere is it even acknowledged that there is a political dimension to the story.

This has never occurred to the director, a pleasantly clueless film critic, Tanaka Chiseko, who has made a film on Noh and has included lots of Noh footage in this one. I suggest that the political dimension nonetheless exists and that, in fact, the picture might be viewed as a symptom of the new emergence of the right. "Oh no, not at all. Mishima-*sensei* loved the classics."

How bemused Yukio would have been with this. He would have liked the rehabilitation, if that is what it is, but would perhaps not have liked all the denials. I am reminded of the Mishima exhibition arranged by his wife after his death. There was Mishima, man of letters, and nothing else. And there was the larger-than-life naked statue he had had made of himself, but over the loins the family had put a mass of what looked like putty, smoothing out and also hiding the cock and balls.

Lunch with Oida Yoshi, the actor, in his early seventies but still looking like the old-fashioned craftsman, the master carpenter, the black bristled hair now turned to gray stubble. I have known him for forty years now—he was initially a friend of Mishima's, introduced to Meredith and hence to me. For decades he has been living in Paris, working with Peter Brook, coming back here sometimes to appear in something. This summer it is a new version of the old-fashioned favorite *Yotsuya Kaidan*. We talk about Mishima, and he tells me something I did not know.

Several years before he killed himself, Mishima came to Yoshi, much worried. Someone had gone to his wife, Yuko, with the story that her husband was queer and had some proof of it—a picture or something. At any rate, it convinced her.

But, as Mishima now told Yoshi, she'd heard the many rumors, but these hadn't made much difference. He and she enjoyed an active sex life, they had a family, two children, of whom he was very proud, and they had a real home. He told Yoshi how much importance he had given this home in his life.

Then this happened, and now, despite everything, a fact proven, she turned against him. He no longer had a home, was no longer the head of his household. Everything of which he was most proud was taken from him. By her. Many times he would try to talk with her to regain his position as husband and father, but she would not listen and, whenever he left the house, she was filled with innuendo about where he was going and whom he was meeting. When he came home, there was no greeting, only suspicion and sarcasm.

This conversation with Yoshi occurred numerous times, and Mishima seemed to be growing more and more desperate, trying to regain that domestic pride that had been his. Then came the Tatenokai, then came the suicide plans, and then came death.

6 AUGUST 2005

Dinner with Non-*chan* [Nogami Teruyo] at the Kurosawa, another theme restaurant named after the director, this one next to the Hyatt in Roppongi Hills. We eat country-style food and talk about the ways of film directors.

Mizoguchi Kenji was the worst, she says. He never made any comment, just criticized. Would not indicate what was wrong. Do it again, was all he would say. This used to send his actors mad, and Yoda Yoshishige, his scriptwriter, had breakdown after breakdown. Non-*chan* once visited the set of *Ugetsu* and said everyone was rigid with terror at what the awful director would do next. Naruse was bad too but not this bad. He too would never say what he wanted, but at least he would smile when he told people to do it over again. Kurosawa was, on the other hand, never this kind of problem. Oh, he would shout and carry on sometimes, but he would also endlessly assist and demonstrate and offer advice. Actors always learned something when they worked with him.

I also learn that there is a mass of unedited Kurosawa footage. He once spent all night at Hiraizumi, filming an outdoor torch-lit Noh drama. Four cameras—simultaneously. But then the sponsor did not like the results, and the rushes were bundled into boxes and there they sit at Kurosawa Productions.

At once Marty Gross, who was dining with us, turned to Non-*chan* and asked if he could edit this footage. Then he turned to me and asked if I thought this request was not a bit too ambitious. I said I thought it was, but if no one edited the footage it would stay in its boxes.

7 AUGUST 2005

A family gathers affectionately about a baby. Though in a stroller, the infant is quite young and has reached the age when it has tufts of unkempt hair, a tooth or two, that tousled look where smiles and frowns flit meaninglessly across the face and drool appears. The family laughs delightedly at this. The sorry sight is amusing because the future of the child is also apparent and all signs of incontinent babyhood will soon disappear.

This I observe in the park and, shortly thereafter in the men's room, happen to glance into a mirror: tufts of unkempt hair, a tooth or two, that confused look of the old, drool shortly to appear. No one laughs because the future of this person is apparent and all signs of him will soon disappear.

How symmetrical life is. You go out as you came in.

22 AUGUST 2005

Eric Rutledge invites a number of new foreign graduate students to have dinner with Ed [Seidensticker] and me. Young people, in their twenties, they are meeting their elders and are polite and subdued. Ed is gloriously opinionated and gratifies them with his iconoclasm. Eric tells them all about the Edward Seidensticker Center he is planning at his school. This means a lot to Ed, and I reflect upon how otherwise lonely his life is. When the young people turn to me, I am surprised by how much they have read of mine. They seem to know everything, and copies of *The Japan Journals* are produced for my signature. I should respond with pleasure and gratitude, and I hope I appeared to do just that. Really, however, all this talk about me, all these opinions asked, is not gratifying. It makes me nervous. I find I am gazing over their bright heads to the idiot eye of the television set in the corner, as though for relief. Yet, since I presumably write to reach just such a receptive audience, I do not know why I feel this way—embarrassed, tense. I know it is not modesty. I possess none. It is probably that moronic younger brother I carry along with me, always set to spoil my fun.

29 AUGUST 2005

I was called *omae,* on the street, by a stranger who thought I was in the way of his bicycle, and now I wonder at how seldom that term has been used against me, usual as it is among Japanese. It is the lowest of the common terms for "you." These are *otaku, anata, kimi, omae,* in descending order. It need not be abusive, it can even denote a kind of affection, but that is only if it is used by someone you know, and I have never been called *omae* by someone I knew.

Then I wonder about this land where "you" has so many grades of rank. *Tu/toi* and *du/sei*—that is one thing, a simple gauge of intimacy. But this four-part measuring machine is something else. Degrees of rank, status, class are so important that four separate and distinct words must be used.

6 SEPTEMBER 2005

Still reading. Boswell thought that there is more pleasure in reflecting on life than in living it. In any event, the life not recorded is always lost. A Boswell quote: "Sometimes it has occurred to me that a man should not live more than he can record, as a farmer should not have a larger crop than he can gather in."

2 OCTOBER 2005

I go to the used-book shop and find a small paperback on Foucault. Interested, I buy it. It seems one of those books for dummies, easy to understand. Home, I open it and on the title page find some page references done in pencil in my own inimitable hand. I had owned this book, had read it, had marked interesting passages, and remembered nothing of it. Perplexed and disturbed, I sit down to reread it. Not an echo. It is as though I read for the first time. I am used to varicose veins now, and sagging muscles and aching knees, but I am not prepared for this inner collapse, this eroding of my life—for what is life but memory?

29 NOVEMBER 2005

Go see the preview showing of *Brokeback Mountain.* Nice, tasteful movie; not a foot put wrong. Also a romance. If it were about a boy and a girl, it would not be very interesting, however, since it is banal, Romeo and Juliet on the ranch. If it were about two girls, it might be more interesting since it is all about emotion let uncommonly loose. But since it is about two men, both of them big butch sheep herders at that, it rivets attention because it breaks barriers and busts taboos. I look at one fucking the other in approved movie-sex style (flash pans, offscreen areas, glimpses of flesh but only that) and marvel at how the world has changed. Even five years ago this film would have been impossible, let alone up to win the Golden Lion at Venice. Now the same crowd that ate popcorn and watched another romance, *Pearl Harbor,* will be watching this one.

11 DECEMBER 2005

My computer is just like my brain—aging. This morning it would not turn on properly, kept sending signals of bomb threats. I had to kill it (turning off the current at the source) to make it behave. In the same way, I am having an increasing number of senior moments when I cannot remember what I just thought of. Short-term memory loss. In the newspaper today, I read that Margaret Thatcher can no longer read because she forgets the first of the sentence before she finishes with the rest. At the same time, she remembers in detail something fifty years old. That is because memories are packed in different places. Eric [Klestadt] lost almost all of his words after his stroke, but he remembered almost all of his numbers, and these he could rattle off—bank accounts, phone numbers, birthdays. Part of my problem will be solved when I get a new computer. Mine is five years old, and that is five millennia in computer time. The other part of my problem is, however, not so easily solved. How about, I wonder, turning off the current at the source.

15 JANUARY 2006

From Ueno, land of the old, I go to Shibuya, land of the young. Watching those parading about in their fashions, I ponder. They are at present all in distressed jeans, much darned over (by the factory, not by them), and they are given to playful incongruity—lace with leopard, both faux. It is too cold for belly buttons, which were all over the place last summer, but lots of flesh shows through the rents in the jeans. Looking at the products of fashion, that mindless pendulum, I am struck by a thought. These people are dressed like the people in *manga*. In fact they want to be like people in *manga*. In fact, they are.

Manga insists upon types, not individuals. Its appeal is that it seems to demonstrate that human variety is finite, that I am OK and you are OK because we conform to a known pattern. The useless complications of a true individuality hinder the happy message of *manga* from getting through. So fashion helps things along—girls in their endless imitation of cute children, boys in their decayed sports image, illustrating various stages of juvenile disrepair.

Then I watch those preying on them. I stand behind three older "scouts" on the street as they approach the girls and make their pitch. They want the girls to work in bars or sex parlors, or worse. The girls know all about them, and no one stops in the half hour I watch. The scouts seem philosophical about this. I gaze at these two types of humanity available on the streets of Shibuya—the beautiful Eloi and the ugly Morlocks.

31 JANUARY 2006

Imprecision of the media. Notices of the film *Brokeback Mountain* talk of these two "gay cowboys." In the first place, they are not cowboys but sheep herders. In the second, they are not "gay," a term that implies exclusivity—men only. These two are married, have children. Look at it this way: if a homosexual married a woman and had a child by her, would that make him straight?

9 MARCH 2006

I look on my computer at all the various versions of my memoirs that I had laid out like corpses in a charnel house. They have names. "Watching Myself: Japan Memoir" (a provisional title), "Jappaned" (not a success), "In Between" (not bad), "Family History: Sections of a Child" (covering the early years). They sound real, as though they were responsible histories. But they are not. Does anyone any longer believe that it is possible to write a factual, objective account of the past?

No, that I must choose among facts in order to write at all means that I am engaged in an interpretation. I pick a few facts, things I remember and believe, and around this I construct something like a story. I present the past, but that does not make it history in any definite, provable way. History is heuristic—it is an interpretation of itself.

Even as I write what I remember I am mindful of something like a theme. I think I discover it, but actually I make it. Just as I think I find patterns, figures in the carpet, but I am the one doing the weaving. It is then easy to find all of this arbitrary. Is that, then, why I have stopped every memoir? Because they are dead?

10 MAY 2006

I meet with Tomita Mikiko. The Kurosawa Academy has collapsed. She herself has been unfairly fired from her liaison job, Nogami has taken her collection and departed, Tatsuya Nakadai has quit. I guess I will too, though I was never hired. The story is still far from clear, and the dust and smoke are considerable from a collapse this large, but I gather that one of the partners was a software concern with ambitions. They wanted the Kurosawa films to imbed into a new product, a cell phone that can hold whole movies. And to enhance the product, they decided to colorize those, such as *Seven Samurai,* which were not already in color. This, presumably, the son Hisao—Kurosawa's son—went along with as he went along with the films from the extant scripts, with the restaurant chain, with the gift shops, and with the *Seven Samurai* "action figures." Learning all this, I call Nogami. She is upset enough to turn very Japanese, apologizing for implicating me in it. I could get no details from her whatsoever. I wonder now what uses they will find for the fine skyscraper in far Kita-Senju.

25 MAY 2006

More and more, people are wearing earphones, walking along and staring at their cell phones, standing solitary, smiling, bobbing, talking. They bump into each other, do not know where they are going, do not see what they are looking at, do not hear what is around them. And I think of one of the precepts of Japanese Zen Buddhist study. Do what you do and only that. When you tie your shoe, you tie your shoe. That alone. Well, maybe that is what they are doing. When you stare at your cell phone, stare at your cell phone.

4 JULY 2006

Taxied with Ed all across town to the American ambassador's residence, where the annual Independence Day reception was held. Embassy much changed now that the resident is President Bush's old Texas buddy— they once owned a baseball team together. In the foyer where guests were once received was a large sign thanking all of the corporate sponsors for their generosity, Coca-Cola, Avis, and the like. Just inside and blocking a doorway is a Starbucks counter with free coffee and grinning servers. On the terrace are burgers and frankfurters, and in a tent is a Marine band doing minimal Glenn Miller and, later, a soprano who sang the national anthem several times.

Milling about and trying to somehow help was the embassy staff, looking ludicrous in baseball uniforms, men and women alike. Marching around were groups of Marines in full dress who stopped by guests for photo opportunities. Also mingling were Disney employees dressed up as favorite cartoon characters. Goofy kept placing himself in front of me and, when I said that I did not want my picture taken with him, grew belligerent and glared at me to the extent that his false head permitted. There was also the strange figure of a person in a muddy clay-colored uniform with a dripping clay-colored mask, carrying a rifle. I asked if he represented the unknown soldier, and he said that, no, he was an emblem of our brave boys overseas.

Inside was ordinary fare and very ordinary it was—the turkey was dry, and the salmon had been ruined by a Tex-Mex topping. Among all the guests, there was no one I knew. I thought for a time that this was because of my hermit-like lifestyle, but one woman turned and said that our hosts did not know whom to invite, that was the problem. The invited were mainly the perceived movers and shovers. I talked with Mr. Mori and his wife—those kinds of people. How Ed and I were ever considered to be one of their number I do not know. I wandered around and noticed that all the pictures on the walls had been changed. Most were patriotic in nature (pensive Lincoln, earnest Wilson), and hung about were bunches of bunting—red, white, blue. I looked in the corner once occupied—in the more elegant days of Ambassador Mondale and Ambassador Baker—by a splendid, small Innes, but it was no longer there.

Wandering around, I did not mind this lack of social congress, but Ed was disturbed by it. I do not know a soul, he kept murmuring, looking sadly about. He, who formerly liked such gatherings as this and had criticized me for a perceived lack of patriotic feelings, was now close to losing his. What has happened, what has happened, he kept asking rhetorically. I said that what had happened was that our president had happened, that our values had changed, that we were politely bellicose and had neither time nor talent for social niceties. This would have usually brought a tart rejoinder, but now he only wagged his head and said, True, true. I said that we were not very good guests, going around criticizing everything like this, even neglecting to join the long line leading to a shake of the ambassadorial hand. He nodded mildly and said, True, true.

1 SEPTEMBER 2006

I read Richard Lloyd Parry's review of my journals in the *London Review of Books* [17 August 2006, vol. 28, no. 16], a mean-spirited piece, filled with ill will. The thesis is that no foreigner can write literature about Japan. I try but fail. Why should this be? He then discloses sections of my sexual life. At the end of the piece, he says that if foreigners cannot write literature about Japan, perhaps I have shown why. OK, why? Though this veiled attack is enough to send off my paranoia alarm, I am now experienced enough to ignore the racket and remember that I am the one who elected to disclose and that he is only quoting what I have written. What I object to is not the disclosure but the manner of the disclosure. There are the facts: he arranges them to implicate; I arranged them to exonerate. I have never met the man, but there are some reasons for an antipathy lying there on the page. One is jealousy: he who has himself written down few books claims mine. Another is that he who is holding up his hands in horror is much attracted by my disclosures.

30 SEPTEMBER 2006

It is like being with the devout. Everywhere, far as the eye can see, people are walking, standing, staring into their raised palms as though expecting benediction. Each hand contains a *keitai*, a cell phone now so elaborated that it has become a second life. It can not only phone, it can also take pictures, make movies, show films, surf the Internet, play games. I steal glances over shoulders. Games mostly, it would seem.

Eyes are not raised, the gaze is never diverted from the hand, no visual contact is made with the environment at all. Naturally, people therefore do not look at each other. They remain oblivious. I stare and stare, but the devout eyes do not waver; the profile is never raised. Each person is in a cocoon, suspended but diverted.

11 NOVEMBER 2006

Midmorning, a knock on the door. It is Mr. Kondo, one of the caretakers from the lobby office. He is accompanying and introduces a large man in a tie who is perspiring freely. The man is clutching a bag full of kitchen towels and begins apologizing at once. I learn that he is from the construction company tearing up the street below and has come to apologize and to ask for further tolerance. We humbly request your cooperation he says, bowing, sweating. He must already have done this dozens of times this morning. I take my towel and smile, like the good citizen I am. Probably the lady below me was not so cooperative, but I am impressed. In what other country would efforts this strenuous be made to avoid public conflict?

20 NOVEMBER 2006

I look at the first third of Béla Tarr's seven-hour *Sátántangó*. In the afternoon I had been to see all of Kiyoshi Kurosawa's new film, *Sakebi*, just under two hours. That is not the only difference. The Japanese film is very fast, filled with effects, seeks constantly to monitor the viewer, push his buttons. It is about this ghost…The Hungarian film is slow, has no effects, does not apparently care about the viewer, makes no attempts on his buttons.

One slow sequence after another. Opening ten minutes: watching cows. Later, another ten minutes: walking along a road. Later, two ten-minute segments: watching a drunk doctor sitting in his chair, falling down, going in search of more brandy. These could have been longer, but the 35mm magazine will only hold about ten minutes.

But—the magic of length. It takes time to really look. Otherwise you merely glimpse. Those distant cows. They slowly move, and the camera slowly pans, concerned about them. When buildings get in the way, the camera faithfully dollies along, following where it thinks the cows might be. And, sure enough, there they are, glimpsed between barn and silo. Then, just as they are clear in the center of the screen again, they turn, and we watch them walk away, mooing and tossing their heads. When the last disappears, the camera keeps on looking.

We have been shown a movement, an act of changing location, the way in which something shifts, something like the development in a long story or a novel, something like the cadence or rhythm of a poem—what something does over a period of time.

Every minute lasts less long, every second becomes valuable because it is fleeting. Looking at those cows—self and its concerns turned mute—I see that seeing depends upon understanding, and understanding depends upon length, the time something lasts or takes from beginning to end.

This makes me hungry for more. Fills me with a kind of satisfaction, as though my stomach has been filled, as though I have finally understood something, finally seen something.

21 DECEMBER 2006

The *Japan Times* has decided to do a page on me. I am their oldest columnist and have been there the longest. They want to do something about my sixty years here, Alex [Jacoby] has already done the interview, and today the photographer came. We decided to do a before-and-after kind of layout. I found an old snapshot of me at twenty-two posing on Nihonbashi Bridge, and so we went there and I took the same pose in the same place. We determined which dragon it was that I stood in front of, by the building glimpsed at one side. The building is no longer there, but I remembered where it was. There I stood in the same pose as over a half century earlier, and I stood on the ground of long ago. After sixty years, I had come to rest in the precise place where I had been before. This being so, I tried to feel something. But, of course, I felt nothing. The picture was taken. It will show much difference. Not only am I different, but the bridge is too. Then it was the navel of Japan, from where all distances were drawn, and it was dramatic—filled with dragons in the Meiji manner. Now it is squashed under an elevated highway, and no one pays any attention to it because it is practically invisible. The many people passing across the bridge also paid no attention to what they saw—merely an old gent having his picture taken against the past.

28 DECEMBER 2006

Cold better. Dinner with Nogami [Teruyo] and Marty Gross. They already had copies of the page about me in today's *Japan Times*. We talked about sixty years in the same place. Then we talked about Nogami's book, *Waiting on the Weather*, copies of which we had both brought to have signed. Such a good book—almost entirely anecdotal—about working with Kurosawa. And we were eating in his restaurant or, at any rate, one of several named Kurosawa and run by his son. Dessert came, a kind of caramelized ice-cream cake. I wondered what it was called since the names of Kurosawa's films are sometimes given to the dishes. I remember that *Ikiru* was a kind of pork stew, and that the ingredients of *The Hidden Fortress* were not listed—

they were hidden. "Oh, I just wonder what Kurosawa would have thought of all this," said Nogami, shaking her head.

21 JANUARY 2007

I am much concerned at being eighty-two. Was I this concerned at being twenty-eight? I don't think so. There was not so much to be concerned about. Also it wasn't as…interesting. There are many accounts of growing up, the passage from childhood to youth, and the reason is that it is interesting. There is a whole genre of literature devoted to it. There is the *bildungsroman* about being educated. Why is there not a like genre devoted to growing old, to fading slowly away? Maybe because it would not be very popular. There is a glorification of youth. But why not a glorification of old age as well?

22 JANUARY 2007

More thoughts while lying awake at 3:25 A.M. I have an idea and think that I must remember it to preserve it in these journals. Then I start thinking about the nature of memory. That idea is a part of me, a part of my life, I defined it and it defined me. When I forget, as I increasingly do (short-term memory span is its dull name), it is as though it never was. For someone who remembers nothing, then he was never there. Terrifying. Well, about that thought that woke me up…but I find that I have forgotten it.

24 JANUARY 2007

Thinking about *manga* and wondering where the attraction could possibly lie. This began when on the train I saw an attractive young woman deep into a *manga*. Not the magazine kind. One does not see them much anymore. Either the quality is finally too low for consumption or else they became so popular that not reading them becomes a kind of fashion statement. No, what young people now read is the bound-book kind. This is what she was reading, and I thought it was an actual book until I leaned over to look. I often do this, fascinated by what people are reading. In this case no ordering of *kanji* and *kana*, but rows of pictures—a *manga*, though now upgraded to "graphic novel."

I was thus led to wonder at the popularity of *manga* as a form. Decided that it was the ease of its comprehension. When you read type, you are troubled to imagine the scene. This is, of course, the delight of reading, but if you are lazy, I suppose you could come to resent it. If the scene is already there, then you do not have to imagine it, right? So one whole step is left out between comprehension and appreciating. In a way, *manga* are more efficient.

In another way, of course, they are disastrous. You are not really spared imagination. You are merely using someone else's.

29 JANUARY 2007

Publishing party for Hiroshi Tasogawa, whose book on Kurosawa versus Hollywood, the making and unmaking of *Tora! Tora! Tora!* has won both the Kodansha and the Osaragi Jirō prizes. Enormous gathering at the Peacock Room in the Imperial Hotel. I get my name tag, and oddly—since I am not important to the project—a red paper carnation. I find no one I know in that enormous throng, all drinking and eating, and wonder if I have wandered into the wrong gathering. Then someone whom I have never seen before comes up and starts talking about Japanese literature. When I get away, I am again stopped by someone who wants to talk about Columbia University. I say that that is my university, and he looks at me and says he knows that. So I say, thinking of Donald Keene's Center there, that he should be talking to Donald Keene about this. He stares at me. Up comes someone else, complete stranger, tells me in familiar fashion that I look younger, then talks about Japanese literature. I tell him that he should be talking to Keene. He frowns and then says, But you are Keene. No, I am not, I say. Yes, you are, he says, and points to my name tag. I look at it for the first time. It says "Donald Keene." Everything is finally straightened out. I go back to the counter, get my proper tag, turn in Donald's—who in fact never appears—and, much apologized to, rejoin the party, where, in fact, no one now talks to me.

13 MARCH 2007

Very early spring, quite cold. Wan sun, pale light. The color seems bleached out of everything except a pastel leaf or a blossom here and there. Early spring always looks so unfinished, like a sketch for the lush oil to follow. Still, little by little, color is on its way. A pink winter hat, a pink cheek here and there. People in March always look as though they had been ill, but are now turning convalescent. Is this what Eliot meant about April?

28 MARCH 2007

The *Journals* have been widely read, reviewed, and accepted. I get letters from strangers, and last night I was taking my walk in the park below my windows, and a young foreigner gave me a glance and said something to his girlfriend. I turned away, only to find him bearing down on me. Aren't you Donald Richie? Turns out he is reading the *Journals* and recognized me from a picture in them. He teaches here, is a *karate* master, already fourth *dan*. He wants to have a drink with me sometime and just talk. His girlfriend says that he talks about me all the time. On his card is his phone number. I would never have guessed him to be among my readers, and I still don't know why he is. But this is why we write—we reach out like this and are always surprised to find that we have reached someone.

20 APRIL 2007

I take a long walk around Ueno. Living in a place dulls you to it. You get used to it. Slowly, time cataracts your vision. Now, I make an effort to see. This means seeing the past as well. I look with care at the hole in the temple door made by a bullet during the Ueno War in the middle of the nineteenth century. I gaze at Shinobazu Pond and see it as a swamp in 1947, when I first saw it, then as a rice paddy during WWII, then as a racetrack, then as exposition grounds, then as a temple lake (as it is again now), peeling back layer after layer of time.

22 APRIL 2007

I wonder at my no longer being pleased at what used to please me. Here I am recognized on the street, recipient of grateful letters, two films being made on me, and I can publish anywhere I want. Why am I not thrilled by all of this? I certainly would have been before, would have turned this over and over, marveling at it. Proust says you can get anything you want but only on the understanding that you will no longer want it when you get it. Can this be true?

18 NOVEMBER 2007

Late Saturday night at the Ueno basement theater I saw leaning against the wall an attractive young foreigner in a workman's cap. I stood next to him, and though extending a hand would have been the most natural thing, I instead spoke to him. Our conversation went as follows:

>   Me: You come here often?
>   He: First time. I read about it.
>   Me: Your Japanese is that good?
>   He: No, I read about it in English.
>   Me: Wherever?
>   He: In this book.
>   Me: Some kind of guidebook?
>   He: No, it's by Donald Richie. I read a lot of him.
>   Me: Is he interesting?
>   He: Oh, yeah, real interesting. I like him a lot. He's honest, you see. And
>   he don't give a shit.

Me: He don't?

He: You ever read him?

Me: Well, I have.

He: I'd like to meet him sometime. He lives around here, he says. Has a picture of his place in that journal book of his. So, what do you do?

Me: Me? Oh, I write books.

He: So you write too. What's your name?

Me: Donald Richie.

Even in the dim theater I could see his surprise. I had thought maybe this meeting was some elaborate something-or-other, but his surprise was too real. And later, over hot chocolate at Starbucks, he said that he had had no idea. His name is Christian, and he is in film too—an animator.

One writes for many reasons, and one of them is for such rare, funny, warm coincidences as this.

28 JANUARY 2008

I notice that I am again being privileged. People in crowded public vehicles give me their seats, they stand aside to let me go by, they are unusually helpful. Trying to find an address, I stand there, map in hand, and a woman comes up with an offer of help. The last time people were so nice was in 1948, when the Occupation was still on, and though I was only twenty-five, I was a member of it, a sahib. Now it is 2008, and I am no longer twenty-five and no longer a sahib. But I am eighty-four, and nice people are being nicer to me. The reason is no longer what it was, it is much more human. It is not my eminence but my age.

29 JANUARY 2008

Now that I do e-mail, I am within easy reach of my friends and they of me. This is not something to be completely approving of, but it is, as they say, convenient. And more. Thanks to the wonders of electronic communication, Claudiu [Vinti] in far Bucharest can complete the translation of my *Different People* [aka *Japanese Portraits*] into Romanian, and I can accompany him on every step. It is out now and very handsome and I am very grateful to him, and have now gotten quite used to this form of communication with its "Hi, Donald" springing up from nowhere. Typical greeting. We are not going to be formal. We are not even going to be grammatical. We are going to be brief and preferably enthusiastic. I don't think e-mail is going to be a popular vehicle for bad news. I don't think the War Department is going to use it to report deaths to family members. I can see it now—Hi, Bereaved Family Member.

Invited to a somewhat mysterious meeting of something called the Blenheim Group. Named after Churchill's castle and, it turns out, the salon he there cultivated. I am to be the nucleus about which the members gather. Ed has already done this, so has Donald [Keene]. Reassured, I find my way to the designated apartment in the hills outside Yoyogi-Uehara.

The group turns out to be academics in universities and embassies, all of them young and interested. My host is Martin Laflamme from the Canadian Embassy, and I have been invited in my role as local historian. I have been in Japan for sixty years and have seen an enormous number of changes. They want to hear about these and my opinion of them—for, after all, I am one of the few left around to compare.

I have played this role before, and so run through my pieces—seeing Fuji from the Ginza, Tokyo as a water city, a Venice, etc. Then they add observations, and I begin to see my home through their eyes.

This is what a salon does, it makes opinion visible. I am reading the new edition of *The Goncourt Journals* and can compare Princess Mathilde's and Martin's. They are much alike, and I am tonight doing the noisy Flaubert role. No one shouts me down, as Gauthier did Flaubert, however. Everyone is respectful, even reverential. Age does this. If you are not abject, you are powerful.

I look through a book on the differences between them and us—in this case, the Japanese and the English. I read that the Japanese always change into the national costume upon coming home from work, and other unlikely stories. Yet this book was written in 1990, and even then such a "national custom" had long ceased. Why are differences considered consoling and similarities troubling?

I go to the National Film Center to see *David Copperfield,* the 1935 George Cukor version that I had not seen since I was eleven years old but remember liking. Now I again view it. A few recollections—Dora's dog, the sorts of things a child would remember. But the gates of memory fully opened only when little David walked all the way from London to Dover, an elaborate montage with signposts and Freddie Bartholomew getting more and more bedraggled. It was, I saw, the template for my own escape seven years later, when I left home and hitchhiked from Lima, Ohio, to New Orleans, Louisiana. Freddie was going somewhere and I was leaving somewhere, but the bridge of travel was the same. And now, seventy-three years later, I see in the carefully smudged Freddie my own travel-worn self, trudging those beautiful, empty, pregnant roads.

3 MARCH 2008

I carry around a small notebook and jot things down lest I forget. This notebook invokes on its cover (in two languages) Mnemosyne—ancient Greek goddess of memory. I do too, for without her, life is nothing at all. It is as though things never were. Recent evidence: in October I looked at the 1969 horror film by Teru Ishii, *Horrors of Malformed Men*. Now, since I will next month be showing it, I looked at it again… and remembered nothing of my former viewing. It was as though I had never seen it before. To be sure, it is so silly as to be forgettable but still, to forget everything—this is serious.

26 MARCH 2008

Leza has now edited *Botandoro*, my collection of short fiction, sixty years of it, everything that I want to save. Now it is being proofread, and then I will give it to Printed Matter, pay the bill, and have three thousand copies to dispose of. After that, get Stone Bridge to put out the essays, and I will have done it—saved what I could, almost everything in print. But why am I so interested in this? It is, I think, a bid for something as commonly desired as immortality. If they are here, then I will be here too, even if I am not. I think of Kafka, pleading in his final, pain-filled weeks that all his work be destroyed. Max Brod did no such thing, and we should all be grateful. But would Kafka be? Yet my wanting to save everything and Kafka's wanting to save nothing have the same root—truly excessive self-concern.

22 MAY 2008

I do another one of my Japanese Cinema Eclectics at the Roppongi Super-Deluxe. This time it is *Horrors of Malformed Men*. Big crowd of a hundred and fifty or so, all anxious to be frightened. But the film is not frightening, and I am showing it so I can indicate the various readings that are possible: title as content, example of J-horror, only commercial-screen appearance of father of Butoh, Hijikata Tatsumi, etc. There is some disappointment at the absence of promised horror, but then I remind that I never promised that. This the advertising hype ("Transgressive, Disturbing, Depraved") had, and I say that they should never believe things like that. Relieved, the audience decides the film is funny, and the general laughter is certainly healthier than the morbid wish to be scared.

R and T are thinking of making a movie on me. They filmed me last night at the showing. Their first film on Frank Lloyd Wright is good, but they have no real take on me yet. They really want me to come up with something. But that is just what I cannot do. Hence one aborted memoir after another.

9 AUGUST 2008

I go to the neighborhood theater to see *Ginrei no hate* (The Snow Trail [aka To the End of the Silver-Capped Mountains]), a 1947 Senkichi Taniguchi film now revived because it was Toshirō Mifune's second film.

Revived now because in these days of falling film attendance, distributors will try anything. This is part of a weeklong package featuring the early work of Shintarō Katsu, Yujiro Ishihara, and Mifune himself—all major stars, all petrified into legend, all dead.

I sit and watch the twenty-five-year-old actor in this sixty-one-year-old film. Mifune plays a tough ex-con with a foul mouth and violent ways, a role he would continue for a time—in Kurosawa's *Drunken Angel*, 1948, and *Rashomon*, 1950.

And as I sit and watch this melodrama unreel, I remember how different Mifune himself was. Far from violent, he always wanted to do the right thing in a world that was plainly wrong. He always tried to be the nice guy—his depreciating laugh, his big, wide, embracing smile, his concern for whatever you were talking about, and when talking about himself, that reasoned, guarded tone that some men use when talking about their sons.

But the world does not like nice guys—it prefers punks like in this picture. We say that nice guys finish last, and Japan thinks so too. Nice guys, like Mifune, are charming, fun to be with, absolutely trustworthy, and so what? So says the world.

So Mifune became the consummate actor (we never realized how good he was when he was alive) and impersonated all those people he wasn't. Oh, he had a self. He would raise his eyebrows and spread his fingers when he spoke of his career, then sigh—as though it were not his own. He was not taken in by this self. He was not vain, regarded his accomplishments seriously, but not too seriously, was quite willing to consider himself just another person, someone like—well—you and me.

He was the nicest man I ever met.

And he is the cavorting punk up on the silver screen, and in fifty-some years he will be dead—seventy-seven years old, suffering dementia, organ failure. And here, right in front of me, he is so young, so alive, so vital. The world is plainly wrong.

10 AUGUST 2008

In the subway, I look at the full row of seated people in front of me and think not *row* but *pew*. Why is that? Then, looking more closely, I understand. Each has in his or her folded hands, opened like a breviary, the cell phone that now contains their entire lives. Heads are bent as in study or in prayer, pious hands push buttons, and mysteries (*manga,* old photos, magic messages, voices from the beyond) are revealed.

13 AUGUST 2008

I am as conflicted at eighty-four as I ever was at fourteen, my vessel split on the very same rock. I cannot approve of who I am. This means that I must break myself apart or account for myself. I have to apportion things out and put them into boxes: sacred and profane, good and bad. Without embracing duality, there is no accountability—you cannot have a god without a devil. Oh, occasionally I experience the joy of unification when suddenly (music, alcohol, fast driving, sex) I am put together and, like the good book says, that which was sundered becomes whole. "I am a man, sitting in a boat." That sentence [from *The Inland Sea*] is about this, and never have I forgotten the bliss of being whole again.

10 OCTOBER 2008

Taken out with Ben Simmons by Eric Oey, our publisher for the new Tokyo book. Over the fine food and wine, we discuss it in a gentlemanly fashion. His point is that he must sell our product, and the potential readership is used to a certain kind of format. We, on the other hand, unconcerned with this, want a new take on the material, showing it as it is, not as some reader wants it to be. This argument is a familiar one, and each side understands the other's position. I look down into my reasoning and realize that my opposition is based on the fact that I do not want to be a popularizer. I was recently called that, in print, and it stung. Call me what you will, but not a popularizer.

28 OCTOBER 2008

Since so much is being made of my expatriation, my concern for the country I came to, my successful efforts at elucidation and, I suppose, popularization, I sometimes wonder at it. There is certainly the sense of inescapable estrangement that exiles are said to feel, but for me estrangement was what I was getting away from, that which I felt most in Ohio and have never felt in Japan. To be sure I am constantly being reminded of my foreignness, of the fact that I do not "belong" here, but this I find consoling because I have discovered that belonging is not the goal—being yourself is. And yourself is what you must have proper loam to cultivate. This, Japan has given me: my subject. I may sound as though I am a doctor with a very sick patient, a whole country, but actually I am an alert pupil listening to the final words of a dying teacher. My role is that of family friend.

13 NOVEMBER 2008

R and T have been snapping me for some time and filming me here and there. Lots of fine pictures of the back of my head. Today, however, was the first film interview. Sat down, faced toward camera, responded to questions and remarks for two hours. R was pleased with the results and so was I, because of the intelligence of her questions. She wanted to talk about big themes and so we did. But we got into this using the famous Proust questionnaire—the one he answered at thirteen and again at thirty. He tried to be honest, and I tried to be as honest as I could. And if you do not know how to be honest at eighty-four, you never will.

21 NOVEMBER 2008

I was eight when the Great Depression pressed down upon us. I was so young that I did not know about not having enough to eat. I am in my eighties when it again rolls around, and now, I am old enough to worry about not having enough money to spend.

I wonder why the narrative of growing old is not so popular as the story of growing up. It is just as filled with learning, with understanding, with epiphany. But—a possible reason—it does not have the charm of suspense. We already know the ending of the narrative. And the ending is not only the same for everyone, it is also not interesting. It resolves nothing, except life.

20 JANUARY 2009

I go to see the new James Bond. Stupid title—*Quantum of Solace*—but a strange film. It is constructed of so many ellipses, so much jump-cutting, such fast editing (many cuts but one second long) that it becomes incoherent. I could not follow all this, not being a fast film reader, and still do not know what those snow-encrusted ornaments in the final shots mean. But younger, faster readers would, probably. For me it was also vastly vulgar. By which I mean everything was sacrificed to satisfy a too-simple wish. Just as porno must forever search for the best angle from which to view the genitals, so must this film cut through everything to catch the action. Just action, all for its own sake. Bond jumps, but the cutting is so intent on the jump that we do not see where from or where to. And we care not, because we have got our shot of action adrenalin. This too-simple wish governs everything in this incomprehensible film. And no one complains.

23 FEBRUARY 2009

A country projects images of itself, and these images change as the country changes. The bellicose WWII Japan was discovered to be the mystic home of Zen, tea ceremony, formal martial arts, *wabi, sabi, ma,* and *wa.* Man and nature in symbiosis, etc. Nothing to do with the real Japan, but a very attractive projection.

Next came Japan's mercantile success, and the place became mystic home of massive auto and camera and TV sales. Then came the bubble years and their consequent big bang. Now, suddenly, Japan is all juvenile—*manga, otaku, anime,* the cults of the cute, the ascension of kitsch. Quite a distance from Zen and *sabi* and even more attractive.

This is the latest projection, and it sells well. Sells better than it wears. Part of the poor quality is that we are scraping the bottom of the economic barrel here. A perk is that anything excluded before as too cute, too kitsch, is now back and salable again. This includes the sudden pantheonizing of the pink film, the Nikkatsu action film—genres not considered worth watching before but now filled with fun.

5 MARCH 2009

Another mini stroke. I was crossing the park, on my way home from the station, when again this inner earthquake. That is what it is like. It is as though the ground is shaking. I lose my balance. I lurch and grab things. This time it was a stanchion, and I held on until the awful rocking subsided and I could make my way to home and bed.

The first one was about a year ago now, and several months after that, I woke up with a larger stroke, tongue unwilling, slurred speech. With lots of sleep, I woke recovered, lucky. Since then, blood thinners twice a day, and now this. It is like carrying a bomb with me wherever I go. I just hope that when it goes off, it does so with a bang that takes everything with it.

And now, having described it, I feel less afraid of it. The power of words.

7 MARCH 2009

A student of a colleague, another film scholar turned professor, wrote and told me it would be a great honor to meet me. He is studying Japanese film and is in Tokyo for several weeks. We agreed to meet at Starbucks in Ueno Station. I often do this: meet students, listen to their plans, offer suggestions. It is something that I should do.

Then I noticed that he was perspiring, a film at his temples, his forehead. And as he spoke, he squinted, and he stuttered. And I realized that I was doing this to him. He had read the books, he knew my age, my reputation, and that I was an authority. And the stuttering got so bad that he had to stop talking. He excused himself.

And I, to lessen an embarrassment that was now coloring him pink, said I knew he would forgive me if I told him that I too was a stammerer, at least until I was eighteen, and that leaving home had cured me. And that my condition had been caused by the school's attempts to change me from being left-handed to right-handed. He told me that his was, he thought, congenital, that he had always stuttered, from the first. As we talked, we went back to Japanese film, and he stammered much less.

16 MARCH 2009

Tomiyama Katsue of Image Forum comes over to talk about *Gisei,* the 1959 film with Hijikata and his troupe that has recently been restored. She wants to show it at her festival with my other films. This will help sales of the new DVD. We talk about Oshima Nagisa since this is his seventy-seventh birthday. Most days, she says, he does not know who anyone is, including himself. Then, like clouds clearing from the moon, he suddenly and heartbreakingly does. This, with references to the current economic plights of millions, brings us to a discussion of suicide. Nothing too messy—no knives or dives off high places—and I add, having had some experience, no drowning. This leaves little except pills, but then comes the difficulty of trying to get the proper ones. And keeping them down once they are taken, she darkly adds. In short, a completely rational discussion of a completely irrational subject. Then, among the many anecdotes of merciful sudden deaths, we remember *fukuyoshi.* This is death while screwing, a surprisingly frequent way of shuffling off the coil. There was this famous minister of finance, etc. She then tells me that one may use this term only if the other party is a mistress or a prostitute. If the gentleman expires on his wife, a different word must be used. It is things like this that make Japanese a difficult language.

20 JULY 2009

Approached at SuperDeluxe by a young man from Hokkaido. He wants to talk about my films. We meet today at the Ueno Starbucks. His name is Hirofumi Sakamoto, and he is a lecturer at the Wakkanai Hokusei Gakuen University. He is very well prepared, has written a book on experimental film, is still in early twenties. Wants to get the chronology straight. I reel off the years. He can barely believe that 1947 is when I first came, and 1953 when I returned. These must sound like Biblical dates to him, names of eras rather than years. And I knew Maya Deren (or at least met her) and Stan Brakhage. It sounds like the age of the gods to him. So many of them dead now. So many immortalized. I am on my way, I see. I am not used to being famous, even in the small way I now am.

12 AUGUST 2009

Occasionally, wandering through the forest of life I reach a place where the trees part and I am in a grove, able to see in several directions—my future path, my previous one. Today was such: looming ahead was Venice and after that Hawaii, and at the end, where it again gets dark, two weeks in hospital having an operation to repair a hernia, the complication being that my blood must be cleansed of thinner and that takes some time. Now, back into the brambles.

25 AUGUST 2009

My sister, Jean, called me on the phone yesterday, worried that I was traveling alone back here from Venice. Today I wrote her,

> And it was so touching, your thinking of coming to Venice to carry me off to safety. But that would have been expensive and impractical, besides which I am perfectly able to travel alone. It is just that I am spoiled and don't like to.
>
> Too, when you are eighty-five and the body begins to give out and you must contemplate the next five or ten years turning again into a mewling, puking infant (Shakespeare), the alternative begins to sound strangely attractive. For example, Venice. If it happened there, I could emulate a favorite book and accommodate the personal legend I have been so assiduously cultivating. One is not afraid of the fact. One is afraid of the process.
>
> But I know me. I will be perfectly all right. I have had a tremendous run for my money and will always land butter-side up except for that last time.

At the Love Leather

Mr. Le looked up one morning from mending a vest at the Love Leather and saw a very good-looking Asian kid, his oldest grandson's age, maybe, seventeen at the most, staring quizzically at him from the sidewalk. When their eyes met across the glass pane the boy's ruddy cheeks turned a deeper shade of red and Mr. Le had to look away.

Behind him, Steven commented, "Ooh, a hotty! If he comes in—baby, hide the dildos! We'll have to shoo our twink for browsing too long." Then he offered his trademark baritone Lou Rawls guffaw, "Hahha-hah hahr hahr."

"Personally, Mr. Lee, I wouldn't touch him with a ten-inch pole, know what I'm saying? Not 'less I want to be somebody's bitch in the slammer in a hurry."

Mr. Le turned around. "Slammer? Shoe?" he asked, adjusting his glasses. "Sorry. I don't know this slammer and this shoe you say, Steven."

"Oh, honey, don't be. *I'm* sorry," Steven said, slower this time, and with mild exasperation. "Shoo—S-H-O-O, as in, 'chase out somebody.' As in 'shoo, you crazy sex pig, shoo, get off me!' Slammer is 'jail.' You know, 'prison,' like your re-ed camp? And a 'twink' is someone too young, under age, you know? Hairless, smooth, smells like milk? And 'being somebody's bitch in jail' means…oh, never you mind what it means."

An inveterate note-taker by habit, Mr. Le committed "slammer" and "shoo, S-H-O-O," to his growing vocabulary, to be written down later in his spiral notebook during lunch break. When he looked back out the window, the twink was gone.

He already knew "twink." And "dildos" he learned right away that first day when he asked Roger Briggs, the storeowner, about them. In a controlled tone, and as he intermittently cleared his throat, Roger Briggs told Mr. Le about their usage, including those with batteries. When Roger left, Steven thanked Mr. Le profusely. "That was simply precious," he said, laughing, clasping his hands as if in prayer. "You made RB squirm."

Roger Briggs, a big, tall man, with most of his blond hair thinned out and a beer belly, once served in the 101st Airborne Division in Nam. He remembered enough Vietnamese to say, "Let's love each other in the bathroom,"

*Zhang Shun, the White Streak in the Waves
(Rōrihakuchō Chōjun), from the series One Hundred
and Eight Heroes of the Popular Shuihuzhuan
(Tsūzoku Suikoden gōketsu hyakuhachinin no hitori)*

Artist: Utagawa Kuniyoshi, 1797–1861
Publisher: Kagaya Kichiemon (Kichibei)

Japanese, Edo period, about 1827–1830 (Bunsei 10–Tenpō 1).
Woodblock print (nishiki-e); ink and color on paper; vertical ōban.
Museum of Fine Arts, Boston. Bequest of Maxim Karolik, 64.834.
Photograph © 2010 Museum of Fine Arts, Boston

and, "How much for the entire night?" When Roger said the latter in Vietnamese Mr. Le inevitably laughed, though why exactly he couldn't say. Most likely, it was because Roger said it in a toneless accent, and it sounded almost as if someone wanted to buy the night itself.

Still, whenever he listened to Roger Briggs talk of wartime Vietnam, Mr. Le would often get the feeling that another Saigon had gone on right under his nose. Were there many Vietnamese homosexuals? And were they finding one another in the dark alleys and behind tall, protective flame trees?

Roger—who was once very handsome and fit when he roamed the Saigon boulevards at night, read entire biographies, and concealed hunger from furtive glances in the moonlight—said yes. "There are many versions of any one city," he said, his eyes dreamy with memories. There was another Saigon that Mr. Le didn't know, a Vietnam of hurried, desperate sex, of bite marks, bruised lips, clawed backs, and salty-sweat night and punch-in-the-mouth morning denials, and of unrequited love between fighting men that was just as painful as shrapnel wounds. Just as there was another version of San Francisco that Mr. Le couldn't possibly have imagined when he was reading his *English for Today!* textbooks years ago, dreaming of the majestic Golden Gate Bridge and the cling-clanging cable cars climbing up fabled hills.

Mr. Le's last name is pronounced Ley, but Steven liked Lee better and somehow it stuck. If Roger Briggs corrected Steven half a dozen times since he hired Mr. Le, who had extensive experience working with leather, it was to no avail. Steven was "poz," he told Mr. Le right away that first day, and his mind was out of control half the time because of some "cocktail." It made him "a chatty-patty," and "so please, Mr. Lee, don't you mind my rambling roses." A few days later Steven mentioned AIDS again, but sounded oddly upbeat: "I'm kept alive by a drug cocktail! Imagine that, Honey Lee. Too many cocktails un-safed me. But now? Now, gotta have me three a day— that's three, to keep me a-go-goin'. Well, honey, make mine a cosmo, please!" Then he laughed his Lou Rawls laugh, "Hah-hah-haaa-hhaah."

Were Mr. Le to run the place, it'd be very different. For one thing, Steven was bad in math, and shouldn't be working the register, but peddling leather goods to customers. He would have an assistant make some of the leather pieces at the Love Leather rather than order everything from a factory. He would offer wallets and purses as well, and not just chaps and harnesses. If there was one thing he knew besides working with leather, it was running a business. Back in Vietnam, during the war, Mr. Le was considered prosperous. A two-story villa in District 3, two servants, a Citroën, two shops—the main one in Saigon, on Rue Catina, no less, the other near the Hoa Binh market in the lovely hill-town resort of Dalat—and a small factory making leather goods at the edge of town, employing over twenty workers. Not bad for a man in his late thirties. That was, of course, before he was deemed a member of the bourgeois class by the new regime and ended up spending close to four years in a reeducation camp after the war ended.

When he got out, almost everything he owned was gone. The villa, the factory, the two stores—along with his beloved gray Citroën—were replaced by two rusty bicycles and a small, one-room studio in a mold-infested building near Cho Lon, the old Chinatown section. His wife and three children peddled wonton noodles at a little stand, and the family worked tirelessly on the street to scrape together enough money to buy a seat on a fishing boat for their only son to escape. Vietnam had invaded Cambodia, and the boy was facing the draft. Older boys from the neighborhood were already coming back maimed or in coffins. Their son escaped and, three years and a few refugee camps later, managed to get to America. It took another dozen years after that for him to sponsor Mr. Le and his wife and one of their two daughters. The older, married with a family of her own in Vietnam, was ineligible to be sponsored by her brother.

If he could, even now at fifty-seven, Mr. Le would start his business again. He was saving money, taking notes, and talking to potential investors, including Mrs. Tu, their neighbor and landlord. Mrs. Tu was rich, owner of the popular Cicada Pavilion restaurant on Geary and 7th and a five-story apartment building. If he had a successful business, he could send his two grandsons in Vietnam to college in America. He could even fly his eldest daughter over for visits.

But to start all over again—what a dream! Still, he wasn't taking notes for nothing. It depended on the support of his family, especially Mrs. Le, and serious business backers. Alas, he was eyeing a clientele with an income as disposable as their penchant for kinky sex. His dream would make anyone he knew, with perhaps the exception of Mrs. Tu, who was eyeing him, more than a little queasy.

At home, his wife said in Vietnamese: "*Minh a,* how are those *lai cai?* They're fondling you?" Then she laughed her girlish laugh. Her hair was almost half gray, but Mrs. Le's laughter always had a certain twang which would send Mr. Le reeling back to the past, to a happier time before the war, before they were married, teenagers too shy to touch. He sat at the kitchen table in their San Francisco apartment with the partial view of the Bank of America building, but he was also walking down the tamarind-tree-lined boulevard near the high school when they first met. That was in Can Tho, a sizable town in the Mekong Delta where he'd spent two years courting her. Back then there was no hand holding, not even when you desperately wanted to. Mr. Le was extra shy. For about half a year he trailed a few meters behind her and her giggly girlfriends.

Then one day, opportunity knocked. She was alone. It had been raining, and the straw flower attached to the tip of her stylish purple umbrella fell off. She didn't see it and kept walking. Mr. Le picked up the fallen décor from the mud, cleaned it with his handkerchief, and went to her. In a stammering voice, he offered to tie the lotus back on. The future Mrs. Le blushed and nodded but couldn't manage a word. It didn't help very much that her first name is Hoa, which literally means flower, and there he was holding one in his hand, hers to be exact. Under the pouring rain he stood trying to put the flower back on, shivering. They started talking regularly, walking side by side, and, after months of courtship and enough bad love poetry to fill a small book, finally held hands.

"Why, what if they are? *Minh oi,* jealous?" Mr. Le teased as he looked at his wife, still thinking of her umbrella and that small straw flower that got them together. Then in a rather mischievous voice, he added: "So, what do you think, my little flower? Should I bring home one of those rubber things for you to play with?"

Mrs. Le shrieked and covered her mouth. She looked out the window to Mrs. Tu's apartment across the courtyard and drew the curtain. She had seen the rubber dildos from the shop, had in fact helped him with his work on the weekend when she could spare time from her garment factory job, but the idea of having a large rubber dildo in their apartment, even as a prank, was too hilarious and far too shocking to entertain. What if their son and his wife saw the thing, say in one of the drawers, by accident, when they visited from San Jose? What if their second daughter comes home from college in Houston? What if their long-dead ancestors who stared out from the faded black-and-white photographs on the altar could see the thing? And what if Mrs. Tu came over—uninvited as always?

When she calmed down, Mrs. Le deadpanned: "*Minh a,* it's called *dildo.* If you bring one back, I'll beat you with it." Mrs. Le found it liberating to slip in a few dirty words in English in the middle of her Vietnamese sentences. She could never swear in Vietnamese. Cuss words would not fall off her sober tongue. But since her husband started work at the Love Leather, she'd learned many dirty words from his notebook, and the two, like giggly teenagers, had been using them with each other with gusto when alone.

One day she found, at the bottom of a page on the subject of sado-masochism, her husband's meditation on the Vietnamese word *minh,* which both she and Mr. Le were fond of using.

Don't know why, but Steven's "sadomasochism" reminds me of the word *"minh."* It's a difficult word to explain. *"Minh oi"* literally means, "oh body." What it intends: "my dear husband," or "my dear wife," depending on who the speaker is. How to explain the usage of this word to Steven? The self, when loved, is shared, no longer singular, the self a bridge to another. *"Minh"* can be "us," *"minh"* can be "me," *"minh"* can be "you," all depending on the context— your body is mine is yours is ours, as long as we exist in an intimate circle. Also consider: *"Nha minh"*: "Our house," or "our family." You and I, through love, and its consequences, are connected in a way that bonds beyond sex, beyond shared flesh—a communion of souls.

When she read this passage, Mrs. Le was moved to tears and resolved not to read Mr. Le's notebook again. America—what a shock to the system! This whole subculture, its obsession with sex and youth and physical attributes and—more curiously—the penis, was all very perverse to her. Until her arrival in America she lived in a world where the genitals never hovered in the imagination beyond a curse word or a dirty joke. It seemed to her American culture forced one's eyes upon them, and now, she, who couldn't resist flipping Mr. Le's new pages to find out what he'd been up to at the shop, had been slowly poisoned by it.

Steven found out one day that the Asian kid's name was Douglas, Douglas Kim, and he was of legal age, barely. "He browsed and he browsed—*and* he browsed," Steven reported breathlessly. "In the end he bought some Liquid Silk. He's a talker, that one. He was afraid to talk before cuz you were around. Asked me if you were gay. I said, 'Pshaw, honey, Mr. Lee is as gay as Liberace is butch. But if you need him to fix your penis harness or chastity belt, well, he's your man.'"

"Liberty?" Asked Mr. Le and reached for his notebook. "Bush?"

"No. Liberace. And definitely not Bush. Butch. B-U-T-C-H. You know, macho, strong, like...I don't know...Barbara Stanwyck."

Mr. Le remembered Barbara Stanwyck. His favorite movie of hers was *Bitter Tea of General Yen*. In it she played a missionary captured by a powerful Chinese man and, despite her resentment and horror of his cruelty, fell in love with him. He even remembered the TV show *Big Valley* on the American television channel in Saigon during the war. Although dark skinned, Steven had her air, and the same dramatic flair. "Steven," Mr. Le offered, "I think you butch. You're too good teacher."

Steven waved his hand, pretending to be bashful. "Oh pshaw, Mr. Lee, I might be very, very beautiful, especially my Angie Dickenson legs, but I'm no teacher. And I'm certainly not butch. Just a burned-out queen sitting on the dock of the bay." Then he started humming and gyrating.

Mr. Le, befuddled, watched Steven perform behind the cash register, and wondered if too much freedom could lead you astray. This had been unimaginable to him as he hustled and bled and scrimped for enough money to buy passage on that rickety boat for his son to set out to sea many years ago, dreaming of another America. But back then the dream was vague, and defined by what Vietnam was not. America was safe. America was hope. America was where you don't step on landmines or disappear in the dark of night. It certainly did not take the form of the wanton, unmitigated desires of the Love Leather.

One afternoon a week later, Mr. Le turned around and saw Douglas Kim at the other end of the store, where the porn rags and dildos and leather toys were on display. Mr. Le could see the kid's hands in his jean pockets making fists as he leaned forward to study the dildos and magazine covers. The boy's clothing was so loose his blue boxer shorts were showing. And the way his pant legs draped over his tennis shoes seemed like an accident waiting to happen. Meanwhile, from behind the cash register, Steven pointed conspiratorially at the kid's back and mouthed silently to Mr. Le, "Hide the dildos!" then giggled into his hand.

Douglas Kim turned. Their eyes met briefly. The boy looked away immediately. In a fraction of a second Mr. Le saw resentment, shame, lust, and confusion all at once in the boy's eyes, and perhaps something else, too: defiance.

The kid avoided looking toward Mr. Le's direction after that, but Mr. Le intermittently glanced at his back. He imagined he could hear the boy's nervous breathing over Steven's palpitating music. He thought of his oldest grandson in Saigon and wondered if the boy was doing as well as he had boasted on the phone to him last week. He would, if he could, give Douglas Kim a scolding. No kid should come in a place like this. He contemplated talking to him, when Roger Briggs walked in and, instead of saying hello to his employees, immediately zeroed in on Douglas Kim. Mr. Le flipped through his notebook, trying to remember the words. As Roger's hand descended on the boy's small back, Mr. Le remembered the words. He stared at the boy's neck and whispered, "Shoo. Twink. Shoo."

In her living room one bright Sunday afternoon with the windows wide open, Mrs. Tu, whose satin peach pajamas matched her swaying curtains, popped the deal as she poured chrysanthemum tea for her neighbors and tenants. "Brother, sister, now listen. Mr. Ba in Salinas who runs a little factory making leather bags and jackets just told me he's very interested in helping out if we buy the Love Leather. What do you think: I put in eighty and you come up with twenty? We'll split fifty/fifty, counting your skills and labors as the other thirty percent. With your skills, brother, and Mr. Ba's, we will sell those knickknacks for half what those leather stores are paying from their distributors—it's a winner. Of course, I can easily put in the hundred, that's not a problem. But I want you to have a stake in it, you understand, so that you're co-owners, not my workers. We're like family, after all."

Mrs. Le paused from drinking her tea and looked at Mrs. Tu for a full second. Xing-Xing, Mrs. Tu's white cat, had leapt onto her owner's lap and was now purring under attentive, stroking fingers. "Sister, you're serious? What you offer us sounds very generous, but you know where he works, who the customers are, don't you?" It was a rhetorical question. It was Mrs. Tu, after all, who had bragged to Roger Briggs, a regular at her restaurant, about Mr. Le's skills with leather.

Mrs. Tu was ready. "*Lai cai* clientele? Their money is as good as anybody else's. There are *lai cai* and *lai duc* couples in this building, some of the best tenants I ever had. *Lai duc, lai cai.* Makes no difference in business, as long as the business is *lai loi*." Then she laughed at her own joke. *Lai duc* is Vietnamese slang for lesbian. *Lai loi*, on the other hand, means making a profit—Mrs. Tu's witty way of rhyming gays and lesbians with money.

Mr. Le started to laugh too, but stopped short when Mrs. Le gave him a look that could have frozen the chrysanthemum in his cup. Mrs. Le gestured to the big mahogany cabinet, which was graced by photos of Mrs. Tu's grandparents, her parents, and her two husbands, the last one an aged American who had left her the building. A large bowl full of burnt incense sticks sat in front. "Sister, I know you are modern, but you are at heart traditional. If you invest in that place, wouldn't it mean you and I both having to help my husband on a regular basis to keep the business going?"

"I look forward to it." Mrs. Tu took pride in the fact that she came to America not as a refugee but as the wife of a mid-level Vietnamese diplomat during the war. "As for modernity, I'm Vietnamese but I'm very modern. Must the two have to be contradictory? As you know, I studied French in Vietnam at Marie Curie and then Vietnamese literature at Saigon University. *Alors, moi, je m'en fous, ce qu'ils font, des homosexuels.*"

Mr. Le understood French but his wife's was at best rusty. He was about to explain to her what Mrs. Tu just said, but thought the better of it. He acted calm but he could feel his heart beating wildly in his chest. If he was half-consciously currying for Mrs. Tu's favor, he still hadn't expected this windfall of a proposal, this soon. Yet there it was, looming near the horizon, the Love Leather, soon to be his. He could see it—money for the grandchildren, the entire family in one place. He could taste this dream in the bittersweet aftertaste of the tea.

"I'm not as modern as you, sister," Mrs. Le said presently in a cold, slightly sarcastic tone. "But I'm open minded just the same. I'm not worried about *lai duc, lai cai* either. My husband and I love and trust each other. Why else would I agree to have him work with them when you told us about the job? If anyone can seduce my husband, let me tell you, that person must possess magic charms because our love—"

Mrs. Tu didn't let her finish. She clapped her hands once and Xing-Xing jerked his head up, eyes wide and alert. "Of course you are. Of course you're open minded, sister. Why else would I propose it?" Mrs. Tu smiled as if everything had been agreed upon, the business settled. But the smile stayed a bit too long on her face, which now blushed brightly.

Mrs. Tu's face reminded Mr. Le of people who felt the exact opposite—hurt and embarrassed. He felt sorry for her and quickly looked down to study his empty teacup. When he did so, however, he incurred the wrath of his landlord. "Brother," Mrs. Tu said, looking at him, "I hear they have some kind of *festival* next month. We should all go and see what it's like, the lifestyle of our clients. I believe it's quite sexually liberating." She was still smiling. "And afterward, I would love to treat you both to a fancy dinner at the Pavilion."

"It's called Folsom Street Fair," he said weakly. Though he hadn't seen the festival himself, he'd seen the photo album Steven kept from the previous years. Images swam in his head of near-naked women in leather bras and leather thongs and overweight men in leather chaps and harnesses, their butt cheeks showing. And then there were the photos of Steven, who had gone the year before as a Marilyn Monroe in a blond wig. "Not a good idea," he added.

"Oh? Why not?" Mrs. Tu feigned disappointment. She looked over to Mrs. Le as if they were chummy and Mr. Le was spoiling *their* fun. "If we are going to sell these knickknacks to them, we need to face these people sooner or later. They may be sex addicts but they are sex addicts with disposable income. I've seen them. Harmless fun, that's all." Then she dropped the clincher. "Trust me, you two, if there's one thing I know well, it's making money. Roger Briggs is inept. That store, well managed with cheap supplies and with good advertising, could bring the rest of your family over in three years, guaranteed."

Mrs. Le, who knew nothing of the fair, but was familiar with business dealings, put her teacup and saucer down so they wouldn't rattle. Then, her dark, steely eyes slowly met Mrs. Tu's. "Eighty-five/fifteen," she calmly announced.

"Goodness, sister, how marvelous! You never talked business to me before, but I can see, honestly, that you're good at it. But let's talk about details later, how we share," Mrs. Tu said and looked for a reaction from Mrs. Le. "In business, it's relationships that you've got to build. So first we should check out the clientele, *n'est-ce pas?*"

"*N'est-ce pas!*" replied Mrs. Le, her face flushed with emotions. For sometime now she had been staring at the well-mended tear in Mrs. Tu's fleshy leather couch, where the cat had caused much damage the month before, now barely visible. "It's a date," she said. Her voice was cold but her body trembled slightly. "It's not as if I haven't seen *dildos* and *butt plugs* and *cock rings* and *dykes on bikes*." When she said "dykes on bikes," Mrs. Le's voice rang out despite her effort to hold herself in. Mr. Le supposed it was his wife's version of French, for it caused Mrs. Tu to involuntarily clutch at Xing-Xing's neck and pull his face backward to reveal an expression he'd never seen before on a cat: that of utter astonishment.

My wife, he decided, shaking his head slightly, feeling strangely amorous, is very, very butch.

A week before the festival, however, Mr. Le fretted. He couldn't concentrate at work. The feud between the two women occupied him. He fretted about what his wife would see. Worse, he didn't know how to fend off Mrs. Tu, whose love seat now suddenly had a new tear that needed mending.

When Steven asked Mr. Le if he had been in the army, he could barely hear him. "Bet you were a stud," Steven said. "Yeah, you in uniform. Hmm hmm-hmm, I can see it now. All the girls in those pretty slit-up oriental dresses, and some of the boys in theirs, all hot and bothered when you parade by."

"My brother and me were soldiers, yes. I was soldier for three years. I get shot in leg, they let me out." Mr. Le paused from putting a new zipper onto a pair of leather pants and pointed at his right thigh. Then he added, choking, "My brother, not so lucky."

There was a long, awkward silence between them.

"You know, Mr. Lee, I've been thinking. I'm a refugee too," Steven said.

Mr. Le looked at him, fixing his glasses.

"Now, I'm serious now," Steven said. "I fled from my God-fearing old man's crazy Mississippi shit. It was not the beating; every kid I knew got whopped. Hell, I even fancied myself a preacher when I was young, if you can believe it. No, I ain't afraid of his belt, you know what I'm saying? Just that way he looked at me when he found me out and wished his faggot son was dead. So I ran. Then here, I made real good friends but lost half to AIDS, and they were more family to me than my family ever was. So I figured it's kind of like a war too, you know, what I went through. I'm serious now."

Steven's voice was sad and low, but Mr. Le only nodded and said nothing. AIDS is not the same as war, he was thinking, not even close. People with AIDS at least knew carnal pleasure, which in the end was what killed many of them. People who died under bombs died right away or soon thereafter from their wounds. They don't dance behind cash registers to trance music talking up a storm. They die without saying goodbye to loved ones, in horror and screaming and in anguish. Bombs and bullets give you no time.

"My brother was very young. He was just a twink," Mr. Le offered.

Steven stifled a giggle and Mr. Le looked at him sternly. He could tell when his co-worker was thinking something naughty. It was there in the eyes. "Well, that's a shame!" Steven said. "But maybe some of his army buddies gave him a good time before the end."

Mr. Le slammed the pair of scissors he was holding onto the worktable. "Not everything in life is sex, Steven," he said evenly.

"No," Steven's voice rose to meet his. "But everyone's ruled by some kind of desire."

Mr. Le frowned. Steven backed down, his voice barely a whisper, "Hey, Mr. Lee, listen, I didn't mean anything by it. Mr. Lee, you can write down in your little notebook there that Steven is a royal jackass. That's J-A-C-K-A-S-S. Honey, write down that his sorry-ass libido runs amok."

Mr. Le didn't say anything. He took off his glasses and turned to look out the window. For some reason, he half expected to see Douglas Kim looking in. But he saw nothing but a sun-drenched street. That was when he felt Steven's hands on his shoulders, the warmth passing through his shirt. Up close, Steven had a distinctive smell, not unpleasant exactly, but powerful and salty. It vaguely reminded Mr. Le of freshly turned earth. "Libido. L-I-B-I-D-O is sex drive, pure lust and desire, is what makes someone a fool of his old self," Steven murmured quietly above Mr. Le. "I never had any control, Mr. Lee. I've always been a fool. Fool for love. And look where it gets me."

With his mind's eye, Mr. Le checked himself. No arousal, no sexual feelings, no fear, no quickening rhythm of the heart. Rather, the opposite: lethargy settled in. Steven's kneading was comforting; he felt tired all of a sudden. He opened and closed his fists, his fingers aching. He wanted to laugh. He thought of how he struggled so hard all his life—of the horrors he'd seen, the war, the reeducation camp where real whipping tore many a dissident's flesh and left horrid scars, and now he found himself in a childish, ridiculously genitalia-obsessed world, where whips rarely leave a mark but the pain and suffering are hyperbolized, become theatrics—yet, how odd, that this was going to fulfill his hopes and dreams to reunite his family.

"Relax," cooed Steven. Mr. Le yawned instead and closed his eyes. "Relax." And Mr. Le saw that he'd somehow turned into a bird flying across a mysterious ocean, and there was no land in sight.

> The poetry of the flower
> 'Tis the hardest to write
> Her admirer sits at the dawn hour
> Beguiled by her beauty, fueled by her light

Wherever in the future he is now, Mr. Le remembers first and foremost the way he stood at the fair, in a white shirt with the sleeves rolled up at the elbows, his arms outstretched as if he were a traffic cop at an intersection. His glasses are gone in the scuffle. Behind him stands Roger Briggs in an opened black-leather vest, stomach protruding, his cat-o'-nine-tails raised high in the air. In front of him stands Mrs. Le, pressing close to Briggs, her face enraged, her folded parasol also raised, ready to counter Roger's attack. To his left, a naked Douglas Kim lies bent over a sawhorse, wrists bound to ankles, his buttocks striped with red marks. He is turning sideways and looking up at Mr. Le.

Farther out, Mrs. Tu stands with the staring crowd, her mouth agape, her eyes wide with fear. Most striking to Mr. Le, however, is Steven. He is wearing a sort of adult diaper, holding a bow and arrow, a pair of strapped-on wings protruding from behind his bony shoulders. Steven is jumping up and down and, in Mr. Le's memories, the tiny wings are flapping, as if they can somehow bear Steven, body and soul, toward the heavens.

Indeed, this riotous tableau seems to Mr. Le to have been tapped from some underground river of libidinous dreams, such that a part of him imagines, or rather wishes that it were so, that it was a modern pantomime of sort—until reason and shame step in and clear the fog of denial and remind him that it was all, alas, too real.

Mr. Le is forced to search again and again for a theme. How, after all, to explain himself, a quiet, dignified Vietnamese man, a participant, albeit unwillingly, in a public S & M ritual?

If one has never seen, say, a rose or a chrysanthemum, can he imagine it in full bloom by looking only at the bud? No, no more than he could imagine what would come at the fair. His mind repeats the scene until it turns, over time, into a sort of metaphysical flower in motion, each of its petals a different shade, and they, in their contentious ways, counterbalancing one another.

Nothing of the day belongs to the ordinary, and everything seems to lose its original meaning thereafter. Take, for example, his "Ode to Flower," which he penned onto the silk fabric of the parasol, a gift to his wife on her fifty-fifth birthday. Mrs. Le, who had wept upon reading it, had brought the parasol to the fair for an entirely different purpose than protecting herself from the sun, or as when she was younger, as a kind of beacon so that their rowdy children wouldn't get lost in the market place. Still, even in her wildest dream, how could his wife possibly foresee that it would end up repeatedly striking Roger's sunburned pate?

Take, for example, Folsom Street, transformed into a collective display of otherwise very private passions—a bazaar of flesh. Plenty of it, in fact, in various shapes and sizes, wrapped tightly or spilling over, all in a kind of pompous sexual overture. Stalls lined the middle of the street like a make-shift hamlet whose denizens were identifiable by their penchant for leather. Onlookers of all sorts came, too; there were even families with strollers, Japanese tourists with cameras. Eight blocks had been sectioned off and the air, veiled in barbeque smoke, was festive and oddly communal.

Two petals uncoil and turn.

Mr. Le sees again Mrs. Tu. She appears more "modern" than he'd ever seen her, in matching black leather jacket and pants; on the fairgrounds, a new personality emerges: vamp. She touches people's breasts when invited, and slaps men's buttocks even when not, laughing gaily afterwards. More than once, he catches her eying Mrs. Le, looking for a reaction.

In Mr. Le's memory, there is a sad and nervous quality to his own voice when he says, "*Minh oi*, let's leave," to his wife, who shakes her head. Since entering the fairgrounds, Mrs. Le's face had turned pallid and her fingers now grip the parasol's handle the way she would the metal bar in a crowded bus, knuckles turning white. Mrs. Tu's laughing banter with a blond dominatrix in a pair of red leather boots and a red leather thong that barely covered her groin has somehow given Mrs. Le the grim resolve to brave on.

Near-naked and sun-burnt Americans in leather harnesses and thongs moon them with their large behinds from every possible direction, and the few that recognize Mr. Le from the shop shake his hand or even hug him. Mr. Le trails slightly behind the women as they walk on, feeling miserable, trying to be invisible.

Then he hears his wife say in a surprisingly cheerful voice: "Sister Tu, mind holding my parasol for a minute?"

"Sure," answers Mrs. Tu and takes the parasol. "What's a neighbor for?"

"Thank you. My husband made it, pretty but heavy. Must be his sappy poetry that weighs it down."

Mrs. Tu glances up. Mr. Le's "Ode to Flower" casts a faint shadow. She mumbles the words, and the parasol wobbles. Mr. Le looks down and pretends to study his dry, opened palms, but not before glimpsing an unusual look on his wife's face as she retrieves the parasol: triumph tinged with a modicum of guilt. He feels immense love for his wife then, not for the cruel act but for what she is willing to do in order to protect what she has. In memories, his love is partially obfuscated by Mrs. Tu's face, however, for it seems to have infinitely aged. Her grin has reappeared and she now wears it vacantly. It must be his imagination, but has the widow's hair somehow turned grayer under the harsh sunlight?

"Sister," Mrs. Tu finally musters, "you're a very lucky woman."

Then—"Hah hah hah hahhh"—another petal unfolds.

There's Steven, unrecognizable at first to Mr. Le because he appears in a diaper and holds a bow and arrow. Steven laughs as he prances toward them. "I do declare, Scarlett, I just *adore* your parasol," he says to Mrs. Le, then to Mr. Le he adds, "I saw Douglas Kim stripping for some serious whipping at the Love Leather demonstration. You might want to check it out, Mr. Lee. Roger's doing a number on our twink."

Our twink?

Mr. Le does not see it at the moment, but in the recalling, he sees Steven in another light. Playful Steven of little self-control and three-a-day drug cocktails wants Mr. Le to save Douglas Kim. When Mr. Le shakes his head no, thinking it is too much for his wife to see, and turns, Steven places a hand on his shoulder and says in a slow, serious voice, "No, Mr. Lee, you didn't hear me. Our twink is this way."

Our twink. Perhaps the store could have been saved if Mr. Le did not respond. But Steven's hand would not leave Mr. Le's shoulder, and the trill in his voice stills Mr. Le's feet.

"You will want to see this," Steven says, his cupid arrow pointing toward a gathering crowd.

Three petals unfold and stretch.

In the middle of a large crowd stands Roger Briggs, the burly but sensitive man who deferred to Mr. Le as if he were the boss at the Love Leather.

Roger Briggs' motto, "There's always a different version of the same city, different version of the same story," applied most aptly to himself that day. Roger, who once cried in front of Mr. Le at the memories of a fallen comrade, is a leather daddy who has found a tasty morsel in a newly inducted masochist willing to be humiliated in public—a demonstration of equipment all available at the Love Leather.

Douglas Kim's alabaster skin glows under the sun.

Above Douglas stands Roger Briggs. The easygoing man is gone, replaced by a drunkard. "Who's your daddy?" Roger demands in a loud, slurred voice. "Tell me. Tell your daddy you love him."

"Please," cries Douglas Kim. Despite his discomfort he sports an erection. "Give it to me. I've been bad, sir. I deserve it."

The whip whirls in the air. Douglas Kim screeches. As the whip makes its impact, two things occur to Mr. Le: that this is the end of his dream of owning the store; that Roger Briggs is not faking. Blood trickles from the welts on the boy's buttocks.

He is slow to react, but his wife is not. She steps in and, with precision, brings her folded parasol down on Roger's head.

Twack!

"What!" Roger Briggs exclaims. He dazedly turns to look at Mrs. Le and promptly receives yet another hard blow—*twack!*—on the side of his head, which forces him to drop the whip and, out of his daddy character now, to squeal, "Ow!"

"*Minh oi*," yells Mr. Le, but it is much too late. Mrs. Le can no longer hear him.

The crowd roars with laughter.

"You horrible! You cocksucker!" yells Mrs. Le, her voice more ferocious than Roger's had been. "You hit a boy."

Something in Mrs. Le's voice gives weight to her accusation. Roger looks stricken, as if she is about to take away his toy. He looks down at Douglas Kim's naked back. Then he gathers up his courage and cries through his stupor, "I hit a *sex slave*. Not a boy. My *sex slave!* He's mine! And he loves me."

Mrs. Le ignores him and fumbles at Douglas Kim's shackles. "Oh, God!" says Douglas Kim when he sees her face. He starts to cry. This is not the humiliation he'd bargained for. Beads of sweat and blood run down his back and buttocks, a strand of saliva drips from his lower lip. "Oh, God! I can't believe…," he mutters and closes his eyes.

Roger meanwhile fumbles for his whip on the ground.

Mr. Le steps into center ring, outstretching his arms.

The flower blooms.

A *pas de six*.

…Behind him Roger raises his cat-o'-nine-tails. Mr. Le can smell the faint alcohol wafting from his employer's breath.

…Mrs. Le looks up, turns, and picks up her parasol once more. Then she rushes toward Roger as Mr. Le strengthens his arms to block her.

…Farther out, Mrs. Tu turns partially away, her hands go up to shield her eyes.

…Next to Mrs. Tu, Steven jumps up and down, aiming his fake arrow at the center stage, wings flapping.

…Douglas Kim looks up at Mr. Le and groans in pain. Mr. Le looks down. They hold each other's gaze. "You," says the boy, lips quivering, "you're my daddy."

In that fraction of a second before whip and parasol descend, the image that will become the New World is that of a mysterious and vast garden. In it each flower blooms from the commingling of a myriad of dreams and far-flung desires, its soil made fertile by love and its endless foibles. The descending sun washes the world in a fiery orange light; the air wavers. Further out, the crowd stares, their blurred faces aglow with expectations.

Mr. Le didn't see it before, but he sees it now: how far he has traveled. His dream has taken him farther from his homeland in a way that the jumbo-jet plane never could. How everything has changed, as if the skin, once broken, will in some way remain forever open to the larger world, just as the borders, once crossed, remain forever porous to the traveler.

In the kitchen his wife is moving about, the dishes clang and clatter, and the air smells of fish sauce and ground pepper. A cool breeze through the living room sways the curtains, and behind them the high-rises of San Francisco appear and disappear. *"Minh oi,"* yells Mrs. Le lovingly, "time for supper."

The Shuihuzhuan Hero Ruan Xiaowu Fighting Underwater, from the series Modern Lifesized Dolls (Tōsei iki ningyō)

Artist: Utagawa Kuniyoshi, 1797–1861
Publisher: Ise-Yoshi

Japanese, Edo period, 1856 (Ansei 3), 2nd month. Woodblock print (nishiki-e); ink and color on paper; vertical ōban. Museum of Fine Arts, Boston. William Sturgis Bigelow Collection, 11.36641. Photograph © 2010 Museum of Fine Arts, Boston.

Six Poems

RIDING A BUS HOME AT NIGHT

Riding a bus home at night,
I see erotic streetlights along the road,
giant buildings,
police in bulletproof vests.
A light smell of dust
and moldy food in the air.

I fall asleep on the bus.
I dream that all the vehicles in the world crash into one another,
all the police in the world blow their whistles.

The bus is filled with exhausted laborers,
their black faces ground shiny by misery,
their smiles
imitate the nonexistent heaven.

Passing the city's heart,
I wake up.
On both sides of the road, bulldozers roar
like lunatics shaking.

PEARL RIVER

Who will speak of it in reverent language?
Who will endear it "she"?
Every morning, every night,
tired buses carrying half-dead people
cross the twelve bridges.
Distracted, dull eyes were cast toward it,
without the slightest bit of love,
as if this motionless corpse

has sucked the spirit from their bodies.
Nobody pays attention to the ghostly white yacht
and the foolish "Waterside Shangri-la."
Lights on both banks are a spread of gold
like a field of rape flowers,
what an expensive beauty!
In summer, the suddenly risen river
will flood the white air roots of banyans
and the marble stairs of the Trade Center,
will flush the floating filth
to the feet of lovers.
Looking at it, at the half-dead people
swinging in the tired bus
sliding over the twelve bridges,
I want to shovel the shameless pride off those people's faces.
All we drink is this foul water.
The beautiful lyric in our body has long been replaced
by this devilish thing with nausea.
The beautiful dream we cannot realize,
the secret anguish we cannot swallow
will all flow in its arms
to the sea.

RAIN

Rain falls on the dry water pool,
on the crow-black pebbles,
on the dead pedestrians and the living statues.
Rain falls on the hard flowing water like smashed silver,
on the sunken chest of the end of the millennium,
on the bankrupt streets,
the colored lights like a cheap glass necklace on an old woman's neck.
Rain falls on my desk,
on my sad eye sockets.
Rain falls on the industry, the agriculture and the drug business
    hidden deep in dark hearts.
Rain falls on the innocent faces of children,
on the fat cloudy faces of shrewd men,
on the wasted farmland and forsaken factories.
Rain falls on the thousand rooms of a huge hotel.
Rain touches a young girl's breasts and thighs like an impudent hand.
She is the rented lover of the wrinkled old man.
He is cleaning himself up in the bathroom now.
Rain falls on the shiny iron bridge,

on the heads and bodies of pedestrians crossing the bridge.
Rain falls on the bonfire,
making *chi-chi* sounds.
Rain falls on blue, green and gold flames,
on the lovers' clinging bellies,
making *chi-chi* sounds.
Rain falls on the madhouse of the end of the millennium
and the supermarket of the poor
who are wholesaling toothpastes, soaps and toilet paper.
Rain falls on the necks of gentlemen and villains,
on tombstones of the great and grave mounds of the nameless.
Rain has an acid taste,
a raw iron taste,
a light fishy taste.
Yet in some places,
rain has a smell of tears and sperm,
a smell of sick birds,
a smell of filthy toilets,
a smell of damp corpses.
O crazy wild rain, O rain that ravages the land,
where are you flushing us?

RIPPLES

In this absurd city,
I've never heard
the rustling of leaves
as the wind blows by,
never seen
the ripples a pebble triggers on a pond
as it draws still,
never seen an angelic nurse
approaching me from the dark corridor's end,
never has she touched my face
and said to me:
Brother, you're okay, you're safe.

MY VILLAGE

One crosses the river on a horse.
One's hat is blown away by the wind.
One sucks at his thumb cut by a sickle.

One sits in the commune yard and curses the sky.
One is blown by the wind like a leaf
flying across the wheat field, across the cinema and the vet.
One talks about his sadness to a donkey, the wasteland and night sky.
One drank too much, keeps spitting, rolling his eyes, bragging about
    some fictitious romance.
One stares blankly by a post office counter, as if he's lost the address
    of an only relative.
Seized by heat, one runs wildly in the snow.
In the snow, a donkey's hideous penis droops heavily to the ground.
Upon thinking that life as such equals death, one shuts his eyes.
One digs a deep hole by the road and releases blood for the cattle.
One dozes in an oxcart.
One rides his horse up the mountain to chase the yellow goat.
One fakes madness when surrounded by women, talks dirty, until
    they drag his pants off and hang him on the tree.
One buys fertilizer at the general store.
One crosses the river on a horse, falls into the river,
stands up terrified, the water only to his knees…

THORN STUCK IN THE THROAT

Tonight, who pauses in his walk around the village,
looks at the lost hen and cold chimney,
thinks of his father's destiny, his and his children's destiny, eyes
    streaming with tears?

Tonight, who passes through the wheat field and ancestors' graves,
goes home with hands empty, like a specter,
afraid to be seen?

A strange halo rises above this grungy roof.
Field and pond are covered with omens.
Oh, even ghost fire won't visit this land!

Country! You're their embarrassment.
You let them wait in such a long queue
to collect poverty and shame!

Shimmering in the night
are the poor's teeth,
the poor's sickles.

He's home now, greeted by no one.
He steps in the dark room
like a lonely wild ghost.

The pond glows, a cold blue.
Muffled sobs crawl with him
into the icy quilt.

You're in his throat, country!
You're a thorn stuck in his throat,
making him suffer from head to toe!

Translations from Chinese by Ye Chun, Melissa Tuckey,
and Fiona Sze-Lorrain

Lu Zhishen, the Tattooed Priest (Kaoshō Rochishin)

Artist: Utagawa Kunisada I (Toyokuni III), 1786–1864

Japanese, Edo period, early 1830s. Woodblock print (surimono);
ink and color on paper; shikishiban. Museum of Fine Arts,
Boston. William Sturgis Bigelow Collection, 11.25969.
Photograph © 2010 Museum of Fine Arts, Boston.

A R T H U R   S Z E

Three Poems

SYNAPTIC

A peony unfolds in a green vase.
I sit to ripen: the mind is a fountain
brimming at the hub of emptiness.

Uncoiling a hose to irrigate
a quince tree in the orchard, I sense
water flow before it flows

through my hands. A pilot debriefs:
feeling like an irrational number,
he yearns to sail to Fiji

but knows fleeing is a mirage.
The word *artichoke* must have
accompanied an artichoke on the journey

from Arabic into English—
must have?—in a zoo, a yellow giraffe.
Inhaling, I focus on lifting

vertebrae, one by one, forming
new pathways up the spine. My hands
rub myrrh-scented oil on your skin.

THE INFINITY POOL

Someone snips barbed wire and gathers
yerba mansa in the field; the Great Red Spot

on Jupiter whirls counterclockwise;
sea turtles beach on white sand. In the sky,

a rose hue floats over a blue which limns
a deeper blue at the horizon. Unwrapping

chewing gum, a child asks, "Where is
the end to matter?" Over time, a puffer

fish evolved resistance to tetrodotoxin
and synthesized it. I try on T-shirts

from a shelf, but not, twenty months later,
your father's pajamas in the drawer.

Now the stiletto palm leaves are delineated,
a yellow-billed cardinal sips at a ledge.

By long count, a day's a drop in an infinity
pool. The rose tips of clouds whiten;

someone sprinkles crushed mica into clay
and sand before plastering an interior wall.

POINT-BLANK

Through the irregular mesh of a web,
you shove an inverted vase down
but, instead of trapping a black widow,
squash it when the glass strikes
the floor. In Medellín, a man recalls faces
but can't recall what he wrote or said
last night; fretting at the widening chasm,
he runs from *x* but does not know
if he lunges to his end. Put your fingers
on the mind's strings: in the silence,
you do not grasp silence—a thoughtless
thought permeates you. Lifting the vase,
you gaze at spider legs on the brick floor,
the bulk of the black widow smeared
inside the glass. *A yesterday like today,*
he wrote, and, in his point-blank gaze,
for a second, you are a spider in a web.

A View from North America:
Mirabai, Lal Ded, and Jayadeva

Author's Note

The following is based on a talk I gave on January 19, 2007, at Delhi University. I've incorporated a few thoughts from fellow artists: film-maker Kumar Shahani and *raga* singer Vidya Rao. The afternoon was organized by Ms. Ira Raja, and dedicated to the *bhakti* poetry of Mirabai (ca. 1498–1550). Translations of Mirabai are from my book *For Love of the Dark One: Songs of Mirabai* (Shambhala Publications, 1993; second edition, Hohm Press, 1998).

Mirabai

My work with the poetry of India has largely been through Sanskrit, a wide-ranging, elegant, and complicated language, connected long ago to Greek, Etruscan, and Old Irish. The Sanskrit word-hoard is a vast, archaic vocabulary, which anyone can access through a dictionary; it yields images from our nomadic past, compounded words of great subtlety, etymologies that transport you to far dimensions, and a seriously learned approach to wild nature and human nature. A trip to India in 1973 when I was a young man set me to the endless task of translation, and I have lived with Sanskrit's shapely old poems and its intimate vocabulary ever since. For ten or fifteen years I never gave a thought to working with India's medieval song traditions, which occur in languages related to Sanskrit but different enough to require a whole other set of skills.

In 1985 the United States government announced the year-long Festival of India. This was kicked off with an official series of events—culturally wide open, considering the temper of Washington, D.C., at the time, which was irrationally fearful of atheists, immigrants, communists, hippies, drug users, socialists, poor people, environmentalists, and artists. The festival began with a "street market" on the Mall. Musicians, jugglers, acrobats, camels, oxcarts, turban-wearing craftsmen, sari-clad dancers, even entire museum exhibits were brought from India. Musician Ravi Shankar gave the inaugural concert to an audience that included President Ronald Reagan, high-ranking senators, and lobbyists from inside what we call the Beltway.

Back in Berkeley where I was living at the time, my friend Philip Barry, manager of Shambhala Bookshop on Telegraph Avenue, pulled me inside the shop and asked what I knew of Indian poetry. The noise about India—full of art, images, and ideas unfamiliar to most Americans—had provoked a little flurry of interest in poetry. Nobody knew the name of any Indian poet, however, except Kabir, whose reputation in North America was based on two books. The first was *One Hundred Poems of Kabir,* translated many decades earlier by Rabindranath Tagore and Evelyn Underhill. That book carries the lingering scent of Victorian parlors, and is based on a manuscript that had surfaced in Bengal but disappeared shortly afterwards. Most likely none of its poems was composed by Kabir. The other collection was Robert Bly's *The Kabir Book.* Bly had taken forty-four of Tagore's translations and reworked them into colloquial American stanzas. There was a third small collection, but almost nobody was paying attention to Ezra Pound's stately translations of a handful of Kabir poems, done with Bengali poet Kali Mohan Ghosh and published in Calcutta in 1913. Beyond those three collections there was nearly nothing else in print.

That August the *raga* singer Lakshmi Shankar gave a concert at St. John's Church in Berkeley, concluding with *bandishes* (compositions) by Kabir, Mirabai, and Surdas, and with one of Tagore's own Bengali songs. I walked around the jasmine-scented fog-cool evening streets of the East Bay for days, high from her performance, and the following week wrote an essay. What I wanted to come to terms with was this tradition, *bhakti* or devotional song, so little heard in North America, so full of instantly recognizable sanity. Without knowing much about the lyrics, but with my head full of music, I could instinctively see a precise tradition of oppositional poetry, close to such American styles as gospel, hobo songs, and the blues.

By oppositional poetry I mean songs or poems showing—advocating, pioneering—a way of life that runs counter to prevailing civic good sense. Most social assumptions are in some fashion complicit in what Karl Marx called "false consciousness" and American poet Kenneth Rexroth bluntly termed "the social lie." American political reality in the mid-eighties had swung sharply right, and under President Reagan some real loonies were in charge of public policy. We know Ronald Reagan was a small-minded religious fundamentalist, that he consulted Hollywood-style astrologers, and watched B-grade war movies again and again to decide how he should proceed on the international front. He was dreaming up satellite-mounted lasers in space and talking to his cabinet about the Book of Revelations. One of poetry's enduring tasks, visible then as now, is to present alternatives to absurd ideas about the necessity of war and to point out inequities in wealth, political influence, and privilege.

However else you might characterize *bhakti* poetry—Mirabai's, Kabir's, and Tagore's, for example—at its base it is love poetry. It sings to a deity who might be a lover, who seems to have as much flesh as you or me. Its

Shi Jin, the Nine Dragoned (Kyūmonryū Shishin),
from the series One Hundred and Eight Heroes
of the Shuihuzhuan (Suikoden hyakuhachinin no uchi)

Artist: Totoya Hokkei, 1780–1850

Japanese, Edo period, 1853 (Kaei 6), 10th month. Woodblock print
(nishiki-e); ink and color on paper. Museum of Fine Arts,
Boston. William Sturgis Bigelow Collection, 11.39658.
Photograph © 2010 Museum of Fine Arts, Boston

premises are antiwar, it is indifferent to commerce, and it tends to expose sexism, racism, classism, and crippling religious authority. *Bhakti* poetry—which until modern times, and the democratization of literacy in India, was circulated through song—doesn't make its opposition through argument. It's more likely to circumvent debate and go directly to the human heart with a politics of eroticism and high-quality nonsense: the sort of nonsense that shows how feeble most social assumptions are. A term taken from Sanskrit poetics is useful: *sandhya-bhasha*, "twilight speech." Twilight speech is imagistic, paradoxical, a-logical, to counter the "logic" of the powerful. I also appreciate the term used of Kabir's baffling paradoxes: *ulatbhamshi*, "upside-down speech."

These kinds of non-rational speech can communicate with immediacy. Lovers, children, and family members use them all the time. So do Zen teachers, poets, saints, and popular songwriters.

These countertraditions—*bhakti* poetry being one of the world's longest lasting, originating certainly by the eighth century and still alive today—often come to us in the form of song. The *bhakti* poets' *padas* (lyrics) or *bandishes* get sung in *bhajan* style (when meant to sound religious), or as *thumri* (when meant to sound secular), or as folk song in villages. Quite malleable, they also move readily from language to language in India. They are not really poems at all, and seem, from at least the twelfth century, to have been sung to specified *ragas*. Music—we all know—has effects beyond what the accompanying words say. So does poetry, which can employ techniques similar to music. These have to do with sound, figures, and rhythmic patterns. Irony, playfulness, and teasing. "The meaning always exceeds the words" is the phrase I hold in mind. This is not anti-intellectualism, but a refusal of conventional thinking. And a bow to the old South Asian notion that spirits or intelligences live in human speech—whether we acknowledge them or not. With elegance, humor, passion, and other irrepressible human qualities, the songs of the *bhakti* poets turn the tables on hypocrisy and piety. That's why the songs sound vital today. The same pieties, assumptions, and power struggles that are wrecking our current world are the ones that tossed Mirabai's world into chaos. Only the cast of characters has changed.

When it came time in 1992 to gather a collection of my essays for a book on India's poetry, my editor, American poet Leslie Scalapino, asked if I would add some translations of Mirabai poems to the essay on *bhakti* I'd written back in 1985. She rightly assumed few Americans would know what the lyrics are like. I told her to reread my essay carefully. I was convinced that *bhakti* was really music, its performance outstripping what the words on their own could say. Go to the musicians, I'd urged:

> They are the ones, not the scholars and theologians (though these have performed fine and indispensable work), who risk themselves on each song. They

are the ones negotiating the delicate griefs and savage ecstasies you arrive at through Mirabai's music.

Leslie persisted, though. I admire her as a poet and publisher, and finally agreed to try some translation. I remember deciding I would stop at seven poems. My thought was to do ten, and stick with the best seven. I found a silk merchant who lived nearby. He had studied some medieval Hindi in school, and I was grounded in Sanskrit. Together we could converge on Mirabai from two directions. For a few weeks, in the winter of 1992, I would drive out to his rural Colorado neighborhood, park my Datsun below the bluff, and climb up through snow and Ponderosa pines to his house, with a rucksack stuffed with dictionaries. Between us, we collected a number of tapes of India's singers, including the great Mirabai recordings by M. S. Subhalakshmi, Kishori Amonkar's *bhakti* songs, and Lakshmi Shankar.

Once we got to work—I had managed to acquire several editions of Mirabai's *Padavali*—I saw it might be possible to do more than seven poems. At the time, there were really no viable books about Mirabai in English, the main one a literal and dishearteningly dry set of lyrics by A. J. Alston. With some further searching I found two other translations. They seemed to bear no resemblance whatever to Subhalakshmi's brave singing or Lakshmi Shankar's haunting *"Jogi mata jaa, mata jaa,"* which is almost an exact counterpart to the blues of "Baby, please don't go." What kind of mistranslation would you get if you took Blind Lemon Jefferson—this was the image that came to me—put his words to literal Hindi, justified them down the left margin, and printed them without his muffled smoky-torn voice and angry plaintive guitar strings?

Yet some of our poems began to work out.

> Binding my ankles with silver
> I danced—
> people in town called me crazy.
> She'll ruin the clan
> said my mother-in-law,
> and the prince
> had a cup of venom delivered.
> I laughed as I drank it.
> Can't they see?
> Body and mind aren't something to lose,
> the Dark One's already seized them.
> Mira's lord can lift mountains
> he is her refuge.

When my comrade the silk merchant dropped away from the project, I found someone nearby teaching Hindi and I took classes in earnest for a few months. That was an important part of the work, but only a part. The real task lay with my own language. I had to ask, why do the Mira *padas* look so dead on the page? What is the living heart of these things as songs? Take away the singer and what's left?

One of the most important cues came to me in the middle of the night. I woke with Mira's lyrics in my head and remembered an interview Miles Davis, American jazz virtuoso, gave to *Playboy* magazine back in the sixties. The interviewer, a dweller in the over-heated world of Hugh Hefner, just didn't get cool jazz at all. They were sitting in Miles' living room, where an Alexander Calder mobile hung from the ceiling. At one point Miles, exasperated, swept a hand toward the mobile—"If Calder can make sculpture like that, why can't I make songs move around?" That was a most important insight! Suddenly I saw why translating Mirabai's *text* didn't work. She never had a text, a set of lines strung one after another. The words, images, puns, rhythms were touchstones, to be set into motion, not fixed into place.

You see, such singing works by phrases, winding them around, testing their moods, repeating, varying, suggesting, threading them in delicate colorful ways for the night's performance. To line up Mirabai's *padas*, her "feet," one after another, simply didn't reveal them. Where was the high-quality nonsense of song? Now I had permission—from the singers, from Miles Davis—to weave lines into a vivid fabric, as performance. I might need to leave something out, or steal some gesture from a singer, or import the image from one song to another. Going back to the singers, I began to understand the mobility of images, of phrases, and could locate for each composition a central notion that had previously eluded me.

I want to discuss one other insight that came to me around that time. Every language has its own genius, what in India you call a *shakti*—a power, a living sinuous intelligence. "A snake-like beauty in the living changes of syntax," American poet Robert Duncan once wrote. A snake-like beauty! That's the feel you go for. Mirabai knew that the most powerful *shakti* is the one that animates your childhood language. That's the language where the snake-like beauty dwells. In what words do you make love? Speak to your children? Your parents? Your neighbors and friends? So I had to find the *shakti* of my own language. If a Mirabai song, in her Rajasthani-Gujerati-Hindi dialect, drives a shiver through you, it is only translated when the new poem makes you feel like you've stroked the hood of a cobra. There are beauties in poems that the translator has to leave behind with regret. But every language has its own splendors, powers, gifts of seduction, serpent-like thrills—and you can find "equivalents" to the original if you go deep enough into your own tongue. Again, the meaning exceeds the words.

I managed to turn eighty of Mirabai's lyrics into poems—out of around three hundred that modern scholars have established as authentically hers. That felt like a book. Each of those songs has at least one striking image I could locate at the center and try to animate with the powers of the spoken (and slightly literary) vernacular I've picked up in the American West.

My friend Vidya Rao, known for her *thumri* singing, points out that Mirabai has at least three types of "voice," each well defined. There is a defiant voice, a passionate voice, and then come the highly individuated *padas* of her late lyrics, which are smoldering and vulnerable. Vidya says, "There are many shades to Mira's person." She also demonstrates that by moving a lyric from one *raga* to another, or one style of song to another, you change shades of meaning. Are these lyrics ironic, vulnerable, passionate, seductive, defiant? Gesture and facial expressions in the *thumri* form of singing charge the words with complex overtones. Shift those same lyrics into the *bhajan,* or devotional style, and what was seductive may become entreating, or even pious.

When it came time to find a final poem—the "gateway" out of my Mirabai book, the taste that would linger in a reader's mouth as he or she took leave—I realized I had to determine which of the voices, which of the moods to select. This felt wide open to me: defiant, passionate, vulnerable, angry, seductive, rapturous. Nobody can establish a firm chronology for Mirabai's songs, so just as the order of lines in a song is malleable, the order of songs in a performance (or a book) is mutable according to a singer's mood. I decided to close my book on a poem of desolation—the raw vulnerability Vidya Rao suggests might be Mira's mature tone. Perhaps finishing with this voice casts a deeper, more believable shadow across the book. Perhaps it leaves the book an open question and protects it from anyone who wants to make Mirabai too holy, too slick. Who knows? Desolation is familiar to all of us.

> Drunk, turbulent clouds
> roll overhead
> no message.
> Listen!
> the cry of a peacock,
> a nightingale's faraway ballad,
> a cuckoo!
> Lightning
> flares in the darkness,
> a rejected girl shivers,
> thunder, sweet wind and rain.
> Lifetimes ago
> Mira's heart went with the Dark One,
> tonight in her solitude
> infidelity spits
>   like a snake—

Lal Ded

Almost certainly Lal Ded was born in the early 1300s in Kashmir, of Hindu parents. Her *vaakh* (verses, sayings) suggest an early education in the house of her father and eventual marriage into a Brahmin family of Pampor, where she was cruelly treated by her mother-in-law. She took to visiting the nearby river early each morning, crossing it to secretly worship Nata Keshava Bhairava, a form of Siva. Her mother-in-law suspected her of infidelity, rivers in Indian lore being invariably the site of clandestine trysts. One day when she returned with a pot of water on her head, her husband, in a fit of rage, struck it with a staff. The crock shattered, but the water remained "frozen" in place until Lal Ded had filled the household containers with it. The remaining water she tossed out the door where it formed a miraculous lake, said to exist in the early twentieth century, but dry today.

Word of her miracles spread. Crowds came to take *darshan* with her (to be blessed by being in the presence of a revered person), violating her love of solitude, and at some point she left the house of her in-laws to take up the homeless life. Legend has it she wandered naked, singing and dancing in ecstasy, like the "Hebrew *nabis* of old and the more modern Dervishes," as one Muslim chronicler tells it. Muslim chronicles are full of her encounters with their holy men, and Hindu texts speak of gurus. It's likely she regarded Siddha Shrikantha, a Saivite, as her teacher; she became known as a Saivite *yogini*, and in her *vaakh* calls herself Lalla. One of her *vaakh* begins:

> My guru gave a single precept:
> draw your gaze from outside to inside
> and fix on the inner self.
> I, Lalla, took this to heart,
> and naked set forth to dance—

Tales of her insight and magical powers outstripping those of her teachers circulated, though no records of her appear until centuries after her death. Even her death was a miraculous disappearance, when she dramatically climbed into an earthen pot, pulled another pot over herself, and vanished forever. In her day, Kashmir was the home of Buddhists, Nath *yogins*, Muslims, and Brahmin teachers, all of whom may have influenced her. The likelihood, though, from her own songs, is that she remained devoted to Nila-kantha, Siva, "the blue-throated god."

> Beneath you yawns a pit.
> How can you dance over it,
> how can you gather belongings?
> There's nothing you can take with you.
> How can you even
> savor food or drink?   3
>
> I have seen an educated man starve,
> a leaf blown off by bitter wind.
> Once I saw a thoughtless fool

beat his cook.
Lalla has been waiting
for the allure of the world
to fall away.   9

Ocean and the mind are alike.
Under the ocean
flames *vadvagni,* the world-destroying fire.
In man's heart twists the
flame of rage.
When that one bursts forth,
its searing words of wrath and abuse
scorch everything.
If you weigh the words
calmly, though, imperturbably,
you'll see they have no substance,
no weight.   41

It provides your body clothes.
It wards off the cold.
It needs only scrub & water to survive.
Who instructed you, O brahmin,
to cut this sheep's throat—
to placate a lifeless stone?   65

I might scatter the southern clouds,
drain the sea, or cure someone
hopelessly ill.
But to change the mind
of a fool
is beyond me.   19

I came by the public road
but won't return on it.
On the embankment I stand, halfway
through the journey.
Day is gone. Night has fallen.
I dig in my pockets but can't find a
cowrie shell.
What can I pay for the ferry?   5

The god is stone.
The temple is stone.
Top to bottom everything's stone.
What are you praying to,

learned man?
Can you harmonize
your five bodily breaths
with the mind?   66

You are the earth, the sky,
the air, the day, the night.
You are the grain
the sandalwood paste
the water, flowers, and all else.
What could I possibly bring
as an offering?   70

Solitary, I roamed the extent of Space,
leaving calculation behind.
The place of the hidden Self
opened and suddenly
out of the filth
bloomed a lotus.   103

O Blue-Throated God
I have the same six constituents as you,
yet separate from you
I'm miserable.
Here's the difference—
you have mastered the six *
I've been robbed by them.   128

I, Lalla, entered
the gate of the mind's garden and saw
Siva united with Sakti.
I was immersed in the lake of undying bliss.
Here, in this lifetime,
I've been unchained from the wheel
of birth and death.
What can the world do to me?   130

* The six *kancukas* ("husks" or "coverings" of existence in Kashmir Saivism):
  appearance, form, time, knowledge, passion, fate.

Jayadeva

The twelfth-century *Gita-govinda* of Jayadeva is widely regarded as the last great poem in the Sanskrit language. It holds two other distinctions. One is that it appears to be the first full-blown account in literature of Radha as the youthful Krishna's favorite among the *gopis,* or cowherding girls, of Vrindavana. Secondly, it seems to be the first historical instance of poetry being written with specified *ragas* to which its lyrics are to be sung. The poem presents the love affair of Krishna and Radha as a cycle, from initial "secret desires" and urgent lovemaking, to separation—nights of betrayal, mistrust, longing, feverish urges—and finally to a consummation that is spiritual as well as carnal. At this remove from Jayadeva's century, who can tell if he meant his poetry cycle as an allegory of the human spirit's dark night and final illumination? That is how it gets read, though.

Jayadeva's *Gita* (sacred song) has been called an opera. It is comprised of twelve cantos or chapters, with twenty-four songs distributed through them. Narrative verse, composed in Sanskrit *kavya* form and meter, connects the songs. The twenty-four songs, with their repeating refrains, resemble nothing from the earlier Sanskrit tradition. Jayadeva took their rhythms from folk sources; the songs occur in end-rhymed couplets (almost unknown to Sanskrit court tradition), each couplet then followed by a repeating line, a refrain that sums up the emotion or action of the entire song. In this way Jayadeva's *Gita* straddles high-art Sanskrit poetry and the local, vernacular traditions that would follow. For centuries the *Gita-govinda* has been performed, especially in Orissa, with dancers, costume, music, and stage settings. It is also considered a sacred text, and in the fifteenth century was instituted as the sole liturgy for the Sri Jagannatha Temple in Puri.

Jayadeva's birthplace is uncertain—some think Orissa, some Mithila, some Bengal. Accounts of his life say he was a carefully trained poet, in the Sanskrit mode, when he took a vow to wander as a homeless mendicant and sleep no more than a single night under any tree. On this endless pilgrimage he passed through Puri, where the chief administrator of the Jagannatha Temple had a vision that Jayadeva should marry his daughter—a dancer dedicated to the temple—settle down, and compose a devotional poem to Krishna. The daughter's name may have been Padmavati—a name that appears in one of the *Gita-govinda*'s opening verses. What we know is that Jayadeva complied. He renounced his vows, married the girl, and wrote his poem.

Meeting Padmavati wakened in Jayadeva the *rasa* of love. His poem never divides the *rasa* into erotic or spiritual modes. What might have seemed distant accounts of spiritual grace, a theme for poetry and folk song, or even an abstract religious doctrine, came alive in his own body: the merging of spiritual and erotic ecstasy. Later poets would sing of the *prem-bhakti-marg,* the path of love and devotion, and warn of its razor-sharp edge. But under Padmavati's hands Jayadeva learned that the old tales, the yogic teachings, were no abstract affair. They are an experience tasted through one's own senses, its rhythms and phrases available to anyone.

In Jayadeva's poem, Krishna appears desperately human. An underlying cadence suggests he is the driving force of wild nature—Eros incarnate—but his acutely human emotions give the poem poignance. In another sphere, the cosmic realm of Vaishnava devotion, Krishna remains the final resort for humans in the Kali Yuga, an era when older techniques of yoga, meditation, or worship may be out of human reach. One's own body, wracked as it is by desire and loneliness, is the sole vehicle for salvation, and Krishna is one's only refuge. Radha, meanwhile, may be something like a spirit of nature, dancing with anguish and ecstasy in our glands. For her, "erotic" or "spiritual" would be meaningless distinctions as she sets out, spurred by relentless desire, to the dark grove of tamala trees where her lover waits. She is pure life force, the spirit within us, that yearns to give love in a dark, cruel era.

The following verses, a selection mostly drawn from the more "classical" narrative stanzas, express the cycle of the poem as Jayadeva conceived it. Roman and Arabic numerals refer to chapter and stanza in the Sanskrit original.

JAYADEVA'S GITA-GOVINDA

I.1

"Clouds thicken the sky,
the forests are
dark with tamala trees.
He is afraid of night, Radha,
take him home."
They depart at Nanda's directive
passing on the way
thickets of trees.
But reaching Yamuna River, secret desires
overtake Radha and Krishna.

I.2

Jayadeva, chief poet on pilgrimage
to Padmavati's feet—
every craft of
Goddess Language
stored in his heart—
has assembled tales from the erotic encounters
of Krishna and Shri
to compose these cantos.

If thoughts of Krishna
   make your heart moody;
if arts of courtship
   stir something deep;
then listen to Jayadeva's songs
   flooded with tender music.

Krishna stirs every
creature on earth.
Archaic longing awakens.
He initiates Love's
holy rite with languorous blue
lotus limbs.
Cowherd girls like
splendid wild animals draw him into their
bodies for pleasure—
It is spring. Krishna at play
is Eros incarnate.

Krishna roamed the forest
taking the cowherdesses one after
another for love.
Radha's hold slackened,
jealousy drove her far off.
But over each refuge
in the vine-draped thickets
swarmed a loud circle of bees.
Miserable
she confided the secret
to her friend—

Radha speaks

My conflicted heart
treasures even his infidelities.
Won't admit anger.
Forgives the deceptions.
Secret desires rise in my breasts.
What can I do? Krishna
hungry for lovers
slips off without me.

This torn heart grows only
more ardent.

II.19

His hand loosens from the
bamboo flute.
A tangle of pretty
eyes draws him down.
Moist excitement on his cheeks.
Krishna catches me
eyeing him in a grove
swarmed by young women—
I stare at his smiling baffled face
and get aroused.

III.14

Krishna speaks

Every touch brought a new thrill.
Her eyes darted wildly.
From her mouth the
fragrance of lotus,
a rush of sweet forbidden words.
A droplet of juice
on her crimson lower lip.
My mind fixes these absent
sensations in a *samadhi*—
How is it that parted from her
the oldest
wound breaks open?

IV.10

Radha's messenger speaks

Her house has become
a pulsating jungle.
Her circle of girlfriends
a tightening snare.
Each time she breathes,
a sheet of flame
bursts above the trees.
Krishna, you have gone—
in your absence she takes shape
as a doe crying out—
while Love turns to Death

& closes in
on tiger paws.

IV.20

Sick with feverish
urges.
Only the poultice of your body
can heal her, holy physician of the heart.
Free her from torment, Krishna—
or are you
cruel as a thunderbolt?

V.7

The messenger speaks to Radha

Krishna lingers
in the thicket
where together you mastered the secrets
of lovemaking.
Fixed in meditation,
sleepless
he chants a sequence of mantras.
He has one burning desire—
to draw *amrita*
from your offered breasts.

V.16

Sighs, short repeated gasps—
he glances around helpless.
The thicket deserted.
He pushes back in, his breath
comes in a rasp.
He rebuilds the couch of blue floral branches.
Steps back and studies it.
Radha, precious Radha!
Your lover turns on a wheel,
image after
feverish image.

VI.11

She ornaments her limbs
if a single leaf stirs
in the forest.

She thinks it's you, folds back
the bedclothes and stares
in rapture for hours.
Her heart conceives a hundred
amorous games on the well-prepared bed.
But without you this
wisp of a girl
will fade
to nothing tonight.

VII.1

At nightfall
the crater-pocked moon as though
exposing a crime
slips onto the paths of
girls who seek lovers.
It casts a platinum web
over Vrindavan forest's dark hollows—
a sandalwood spot
on the proud face of sky.

VII.2

The brindled moon soars above.
Krishna waits underneath.
And Radha
wrenched with grief
is alone.

VII.21

The lonely moon
pale as Krishna's sad, far-off
lotus-face has
calmed my thoughts.
Oh but the moon is also Love's planet—
a wild desolation
strikes through my heart.

X.10

Let the old doubts go,
anguished Radha.
Your unfathomed breasts and
cavernous loins
are all I desire.

What other girl has the power?
Love is a ghost
that has slipped into my entrails.
When I reach to embrace your
deep breasts
may we fulfill the rite
we were born for—

Krishna for hours
entreated
the doe-eyed girl
then returned to his thicket bed and dressed.
Night fell again.
Radha, unseen, put on radiant gems.
A girlish voice pressed her—
go swiftly.

Her companion reports—

"She'll look into me—
tell love tales—
chafing with pleasure she'll draw me—
into her body—
drakshyati vakshyati ramsyate"
  —he's fearful,
he glances about. He shivers for you,
bristles, calls wildly, sweats, goes forward,
reels back.
The dark thicket closes
about him.

Eyes dark with kohl
ears bright with creamy tamala petals
a black lotus headdress & breasts
traced with musk-leaf—
In every thicket, friend,
Night's precious cloak wraps a girl's limbs.
The veiled affairs
  the racing heart…

Eager, fearful, ecstatic—
darting her eyes across Govinda she
enters the thicket.
      Ankles ringing with silver.

XII.1

Her friends have slipped off.
Her lower lip is moist
wistful, chaste, swollen, trembling, deep.
He sees her raw heart
sees her eyes rest on the couch of
fresh flowering twigs
& speaks.

XII.2, 3, 4

[Sung to Raga Vibhasa]

*Come, Radha, come. Krishna follows your
every desire.*

"Soil my bed with indigo footprints, *Kamini,*
lay waste the grove
savage it with your petal-soft feet.

"I take your feet in lotus hands, *Kamini,*
you have come far.
Lay these gold flaring anklets across my bed.

"Let *yes yes* flow from your mouth like *amrita.*
From your breasts, *Kamini,*
I draw off the *dukula*-cloth. We are no longer separate."

XII.12, 18, 19

[Sung to Raga Ramakari]

*She sings while Krishna plays, her heart drawn
into ecstasy—*

"On my breast, your hand, Krishna,
cool as sandalwood. Draw a leaf wet with deer musk here,
it is Love's sacramental jar.

Drape my loins with jeweled belts, fabric & gemstones.
My *mons venus* is brimming with nectar,
a cave mouth for thrusts of Desire."

XII.19

Reader, open your heart
to Jayadeva's well-
crafted poem.
Krishna's deeds lie in your memory now—
amrita to salve
      a Dark Age's pestilence.

XII.20

On my breast draw a leaf
paint my cheeks
lay a silk scarf across these dark loins.
Wind into my heavy black braid
white petals,
fit gemstones onto my wrists,
anklets over my feet.
And each thing she desired
her saffron-robed lover
fulfilled.

Konjin Chōgorō, from the series Sagas of Beauty and Bravery (Biyū Suikoden)

Artist: Tsukioka Yoshitoshi, Japanese, 1839–1892
Publisher: Ōmiya Kyūsuke (Sawa Kyūjirō)

Japanese, Edo period, 1866 (Keiō 2), 12th month. Woodblock print (nishiki-e); ink and color on paper; vertical chūban. Museum of Fine Arts, Boston. William Sturgis Bigelow Collection, 11.35892. Photograph © 2010 Museum of Fine Arts, Boston

Hidden Fires and Other Monologues

Author's Note

The following monologues were written during the time of the Gujarat riots in 2002. I began with the intention of making a record of what was happening in Gujarat, but by the time I finished *Invocations,* the last of five pieces [four of which are printed here], I realized it was pointless to tie them down to specific dates or personalities or governments. The despair I felt in 2002 was no different from what I had felt during the anti-Sikh riots of 1984 or while reading about the pogroms against the Jews in Hitler's Germany. There is a sameness about violent mobs that transcends nations, communities, religions, politics. We go to war because of imagined differences between ourselves and our enemies, but we are all much more the same than we are different. It was in the name of that sameness that I wrote these pieces.

Hidden Fires

The stage is dark. A red spotlight snaps on. A man is standing under it … He appears disheveled. He looks over his shoulder a couple of times before he starts to speak. He is calm, but taut.

MAN   Yes … yes! I can talk about it. Why not? I'm not ashamed. I am not afraid. Let me tell you how it was, in that first week. I was there at the beginning.

Yes—ten! That was my score. I refuse to be ashamed of it. I can explain it all—you see, they weren't really … people. Yes, ten or ten and a half—depending on how you count the one who was pregnant. In such a situation, do we count one … or one and a half? Or two? Anyway! The point is, ten … *cases* were involved.

It started without warning. I was standing in my shop. One moment I was thinking about my nephew's engagement, and the next moment … there was a sound. A customer in the shop, a woman—she heard the sound before me. She said, *What's that?* Then I heard it too.

We both stepped out. We saw someone running. Behind him were seven others, maybe eight. They were carrying sticks. The one in front was running towards me. His mouth was open, no sound coming out. I knew what I had to do.

I stood in his path. He swerved to avoid me, but I held him. In that instant the boys caught up. They leapt at the man, jumped straight at him! And stamped him out.

I heard the crunch of his bones as they broke him. Scorching red juice spurted from his nose. In his final moment, he looked straight at me. The heat of his life was like a blaze in my face! And then…he was out.

Others like this one had begun running in the streets. Some of them were female. If you want to—yes, you could call them people. I don't, of course. There's no point. That's what you don't understand. They *looked* like men, they *looked* like women. But in reality…well…

You have to understand. Some people are not…people. They share the street with you and me…but inside, deep inside…they're not *people*…

How else can I say it? There are some things you just know. And once you know it, you can't stop knowing it. It's like red-hot coal—it takes only one lesson to know everything you need to about getting burnt.

You call them people? I call them red-hot coals. From an ancient fire. Not people at all. So long as they remain cool and unmoved, they're all right. But the moment they begin to smoke, the moment they show that ancient heat—then! Ah, then. That's when we—we who can get burnt from that distant fire—that's when we must take action.

Who fanned those coals back to life—was it Them? Was it Us? Who set the streets aflame with them? Was it Them or was it Us? Frankly, I don't care. When a fire is raging out of control, there is only one rule for dealing with it: put it out.

Here, there, everywhere…fires were running this way and that, threatening our city, destroying our country. Some were actually aflame; others were just barely smoking. But all were burning from within, lit by their own…otherness.

When your life's in danger, you'll do anything to defend it, won't you? When your country's in danger, you'll do anything to protect it, won't you? That's what we did. Defended ourselves. Saved our country. We saw fires and we—stamped them out.

I see it in your face—you think I did something wrong. I tell you, it was not wrong. It was right. It was the only thing to do. You would do it yourself, believe me, if you saw a fire coming your way. If you thought there was no other way to save yourself from getting burnt.

At the end of that first day, we heard the news. Two hundred dead. At the end of the next day, we heard the news. Three hundred dead. At the end of the month, we heard the news. Two thousand dead. At the end of six months, ten thousand dead.

The fire of otherness. A deadly scourge. But there's a simple rule to follow: when you see a fire, stamp it out. That first day, I counted ten. But after that day, I stopped counting. I don't know how many I killed. It became routine. Nothing very special. Like pest control. Like firefighting.

You mustn't allow yourself to be confused. Some people—you for instance—want to know: but how could I, anyone, actually kill people? So many people? I keep telling you: I didn't kill anyone. Nobody killed anybody. We saw fires and we put them out.

It's a useful approach, this one. Before, when I was still just an ordinary shopkeeper, looking after the store, minding my business, I didn't realize how simple life could be. All these years, I used to think there were many laws, rules, regulations. I did as I was told. I obeyed all the rules. But now I understand: there is only one rule. When you see a fire, stamp it out.

Don't wait for help, or call for the police. When you see a fire, stamp it out.

And there are a lot of fires around, believe me. Not so easy to see all of them. Some of them are hidden. Even from the people in whom they burn. It takes special eyes to see them. My eyes for instance…but I am starting to doubt them. At one time, everyone I saw—I knew exactly who they were. Where they came from. No longer. Now everyone wears the same clothes, the same marks on their foreheads, the same spectacles and ties…Sometimes I have trouble guessing: is that one of Them or one of Us?

I used to think, *If I don't see, immediately, from your expression, or the clothes you wear, or the style of jewelry around your neck or the colour of your bangles, or the cut of*

*your blouse that you are one of Us, the chances are I will
assume that you're one of Them.* That's how I used to think.

It's like that amongst the animals. There are lions, there
are deer: does anyone say, *Oh, the lions are the same as
the deer, and the deer are the same as the lions?* No, of
course not! Of course we say they are each of them
different from the other!

Similarly with us. Some of us are deer, and some of us are
lions. That's all there is to it. Very simple. It's normal for
lions to eat the deer. It's normal for the deer to run from the
lions. After all, no one wants to be eaten. Even when it's just
their…how shall I call it? Their destiny. As deer. As prey.

It's the law of the jungle. And when the law of the jungle
is broken, there is Chaos. That's what. And no one
wants Chaos. Not even the deer. Ask me. I should know!
I don't want Chaos. That's why I'm talking to you.
Because I want to help you—to avoid Chaos, that is.

I'm sure you don't want Chaos either. You just want to get
on with your life. That's true, isn't it? It's true for me too.
I'm sure you can see that. Of course you do. I am sure you'll
understand then, why I've come to you now. Why I'm
standing here today. I just need a little of your time and…

Please—no—don't turn away: just listen to me. Please.

Till yesterday…it was all so clear. Like I've described to
you. Everything was simple. It was the law of the jungle,
and I was a lion. Till yesterday. That's when they came to
my house and—no, wait, please! Don't turn away!

They didn't even ask questions. They just began to beat
me up. Then they threw me out of my house and set fire
to my wife. She was not yet forty. They took away my
sisters and their daughters. They strangled my son in
front of me and pissed inside his dead mouth.

I screamed! I cried! I said, *I am one of you!* All they said
was, *Hidden fires. You have hidden fires. And we've got
to put them out.*

I said, *No! No! You're wrong! I have no hidden fires! I have
nothing you don't have!* But they were deaf. They were
blind. *Hidden fires,* they said, *we've got to put them out.*

Show me! I begged them. *Show me one sign that I am
different from you!* But all they said was, *We need no reasons,*

don't you see? That's the law of the jungle. You believe it too, don't you? Just like we do. You say you're a lion, but your great-grandmother, three generations ago, SHE was a deer—someone told us—and that makes you a deer! And that's your hidden fire. So we've got to put you out. Then they told me they would be kind to me. They would spare my life. Then they told me to go far away and never come back. They told me to forget about my shop, my house, my property. And that was all they said.

Don't you think it's unfair? Don't you—no! Please! Why are you turning away? Why don't you understand? There's been a mistake—isn't it obvious? Why don't you listen? They had NO REASON for beating me up! I have NO HIDDEN FIRES! If they could beat me up, they could beat you up—no, no, no! You must listen, you must! Please! It's for your own sake—believe me! If it could happen to me, it could happen to you—

Red spotlight starts to fade.

Please! Listen to me! Please! For your own sake, never mind about me—don't turn away—don't laugh and shake your head—please—listen to me—please—

While he talks, light and sound dim till all that remains is a small, red, flickering pinpoint of light on the front of the man's chest.

—I take back what I said earlier—I see that I was wrong, I was blind—I was intolerant—but it was all because I didn't understand! That's why I'm pleading with you—listen to me—it's for your own good—no! Don't turn away—don't…please…

The small, flickering light goes out too.

Know the Truth!

The stage is dark. A spotlight snaps on. A young woman is sitting in the posture of a newscaster…Behind her is a screen. Except when indicated, the screen displays scenic sights or abstract patterns.

YOUNG WOMAN   Good evening and thank you for joining us on *Know the Truth!* My name is Pranam Shanti, and I will be answering your questions tonight. The topic for tonight's program is the problems affecting a few regions of our country. No one has been seriously injured! Nevertheless, our film crew will be reporting live from those areas that have been affected. We call upon ordinary citizens to share their grievances with the nation! And, as you know, operators are standing by to receive calls at this easy-to-remember number: 100-100-100.

Needless to say, our advice to all those of you who are concerned for your loved ones is: Please do not worry! The government is doing its utmost to contain the violence. From all reports, it is succeeding very well— ah, here is our first caller…

[*Speaking to caller*] Yes—madam—yes, I can hear you clearly, please go ahead—[*Listening*] Ahh…yes…okay.

[*To the viewers*] All right, we have a caller from…uh… the outskirts of a Particular City. Her name is…well…as you know, here at the Happy News Network, we use Normal Names to protect our callers' identities—Okay, so, Mrs…uh…Jyoti…if I have understood your question correctly, what you want to know is, *What regions are still facing conflicts? And why can't we name the regions?*

[*Smiles charmingly*]…Well! That's certainly a leading question, isn't it, folks? And I'm sure some of you already have the answer…The reason we cannot identify any of the areas where the army has been called out is, of course, that the situation is still a little uncertain. We cannot risk further instability by drawing attention to those states and towns in which a few unrelated incidents of violence have occurred. In the past, when we followed the policy of revealing everything there is to know about a situation, it only resulted in prolonging the chaos. Nevertheless, in our bid to bring The Truth home to you, in a few seconds, we will show you live footage from one of the affected areas. Here it is now—live coverage—a simple rural scene …no sign of any disturbance…

Screen shows a crowded marketplace in Rajasthan. It is the Pushkar Fair, and colourful Rajasthani villagers are shown haggling over camels. It is a standard tourist-brochure shot, and there is no sign of any disturbance anywhere.

As you can see, everyone looks perfectly healthy and there is no longer any sign of the bloodshed—except for this one person, a child of ten, who has a minor cut on his elbow—

Screen shows a studio shot of a child actor dressed in Rajasthani peasant clothes. He is holding up his elbow, which has been covered in a white bedsheet, splashed with red ink to suggest blood.

[*To the caller*]—I hope that satisfies you, Mrs…uhhh… Jyoti! Thank you for your call—and—here's our next caller —yes, sir, yes—please go ahead, I can hear you perfectly well—[*Listens*]—yes—okay—I think I understand what

you want to know—okay, okay, please be patient, sir—it
takes a little time to…uh…to understand the
nature of your concern. Yes—please, okay—okay—
I'll get back to you, sir—

[*Slightly ruffled*] Well…that was Mr…Mr…Haz—uh—
Anand…and his question is, *What…what is the
Government doing about the…the disturbance on the
street where I live?* He…he wanted me to say that he lives
in a…Particular City…on the West Coast of India and
that he's had a…uhhh…small problem with the…
uhhh…water supply for the past few…uh…hours.

[*Facing the viewers, but as if also speaking to "Mr. Anand"*]
Now—you see, Mr. Anand, I understand your problem,
but the fact is, according to our sources, there is practically
no disruption of vital supplies happening in your area of
the country! So I am at a loss to explain what the matter is
in your house. Is it possible that there is some absolutely…
you know…LOCAL problem? A car accident or something
like that? Because that too can, you know, cause situations
in which citizens can be inconvenienced.

So…I hope that answers your query, Mr. Anand—and
I'm sure your wife and children will be returned to you
very shortly—after all, the Government has given an
absolute assurance that no violence will be tolerated after
8 P.M. on weekdays. Thank you for calling! And here's
our next caller now—

A loud crackling noise and the sound of static. Abrupt cessation of the call.

[*Looking startled*] Oh! Well—that was sudden—and now
we seem to have lost our connection briefly—no problem!
We'll just wait till our engineers restore it! And while we
wait, let me play for you a message direct from one of our
leaders:

Screen shows a politician speaking into a microphone.

POLITICIAN
—inform the people of our beloved country that there is
ABSOLUTELY NOTHING TO FEAR! The Government
has been completely successful in its campaign to end
the terror within the nation's borders. There have been
no live burnings or gang rapes in any of the disputed
territories in the past six hours. Telecasts and radio broad-
casts from foreign news agencies MUST BE IGNORED.
As we know, they have for centuries followed a policy of
maligning the people and culture of our nation. It is of
utmost importance that we resist their vile propaganda and

remain faithful to The Real Truth—which is that there is nothing bad happening within our borders at all. We are committed to the path of peaceful and nonviolent suppression of all anti-national behaviour. We ask only for a little patience—after all, such disturbances are a natural part of Nation Building. We are determined to bring the situation under control in the shortest possible time. So long as all our citizens avoid overreacting when they are faced with mobs or rapist-gangs, so long as they maintain patriotic silence when approached by foreign news agencies, we are certain that complete normalcy will be restored in less than half a year. *Jai Hind!*

YOUNG WOMAN —and that message was from one of our leaders, speaking from an undisclosed location somewhere in the world. Now! Back to our regular broadcast of calls from around the nation! Yes—and there's a caller—that's—okay, Puja Arora—hello, Puja! Thank you for calling! I recognize your voice from last week. Why don't you share your good news again with all our listeners today?

Screen shows a saccharine-sweet girl of about eleven years.

CHILD Auntie, I want to share my experience today with your audience! My name is Puja, and I am fifteen years old. The Particular City in which I am living is absolutely safe, and totally quiet! Nothing goes wrong, and we are all living in communal harmony! We have no problems with power or water! Only happy people are walking in the streets, and in the morning we read only good news in the newspaper! Every day, when I go to school, I am very happy to see my teacher and my friends! We have a lot to eat, and we study very hard! All my friends in my city are happy and healthy, and we are very proud of our country. My teacher says there is no country better than our country, and when I grow up, I'll be a teacher too! Or a doctor or a nurse or an engineer, so that I can serve my country better. I will be glad to give my life for my country if I get the chance. Thank you, Auntie, thank you for giving me the opportnity to share my real, true feelings with all my fellow citizens in the world's best country!

YOUNG WOMAN Awww! Wasn't that sweet? Wasn't that heartwarming? Thank you, Puja. I am certain all our viewers were deeply touched by your emotional message! We all need to hear the good news too—that's what we feel, here at *Know the Truth!*—after all, let's not forget: for every riot or rape, there's still some sunshine somewhere! Yes, my friends!

Let's concentrate on the cheers, not the tears! That's our motto! Forget the sadness of the past and focus on the gladness of the future!

[*Speaking to a caller*] And here's our next caller—yes, madam, please go ahead—Yes, I can hear you—of course, please keep talking—

[*Looking sympathetic*] Okay…and that's Ms. Khush Boo calling from a—uhhh—Particular City! Yes, Ms. Khush Boo—keep talking, I can hear you—what's that? Are those …uhh…firecrackers I hear? What? Oh…well, how can you be sure, Ms. Boo? Sometimes firecrackers DO sound like bombs! Ah well—just keep smiling and try to stay positive —I'm sure the police will come soon—or the army—whatever—the main point is, KEEP SMILING! Okay?

[*Nodding her head understandingly*] I know, I know—it's very difficult in these troubled times, Ms. Boo, to keep your spirits high—what's that? They're breaking down your neighbour's door? Ohh…I'm sure you're only imagining it! It can't be happening—really, it can't! The Government has ASSURED us there is no violence in your Particular City! Really, Ms. Khush Boo, perhaps you're just imagining it? After all, young people like you DO have very active minds! Awww…well, don't feel too bad…okay, Ms. Khush Boo—remember what I said: think positive thoughts! And maybe the bad men will go away…Sorry, no, I can't keep you on the line, as I need to get on with the show—bye-bye now—thanks for calling—

[*Smiling at her viewers*] That was a young caller complaining about some recurring nightmares she has! Poor thing— she imagines that all the young women on her street have been raped and/or murdered—now isn't that just impossible, folks? That can't happen in our country, am I right? And now she thinks there's a mob at her door! Poor thing! Ohh…delusions can be terrible, can't they? We at *Know the Truth!* are always keen to keep our delusions at bay. We just keep on smiling and telling people the truth, and though it's not always easy, as we all know, in the end, the truth DOES prevail!

And that's all for today! Thank you for watching! Tune in again every hour on the hour for the next edition of… *Know the Truth!*

Quick fade out and END.

Famous Last Words

A long, horizontal board on which twelve blank cards are displayed is center stage. Each card can be easily flipped over to expose another card underneath. Each hidden card bears one letter. Each letter, when exposed, is big enough to be read from the back of the hall. At the rear of the stage is a large, dark screen. A young man appears.

YOUNG MAN

Ah—thank you for joining me in a game of…"Famous Last Words"! Most of us have, at some time or another in our lives, played board games involving words and vocabulary. But tonight's game, ladies and gentlemen, isn't for the "bored"—*hahaha!*—no, it's for serious game-players. Deadly serious. For tonight's game, I am going to ask members of the audience to call out letters. Each correct guess will register on this board. Each mistake will result in random termination of members of the audience.

Now, some of you might think that this is a cruel sort of game. You will be telling yourselves that you don't want to play. And therefore, you'll remain silent. Bad news! That's not an option! Because for every minute of silence, someone belonging to the weaker sections of our society will be burnt to death. Naturally, I wouldn't want to offend the sensibilities of this audience! So I will spare you the sight of these minority deaths—and as for sound, you'll hear a small scream to punctuate each execution. As the seconds tick by, you'll see that screen at the back begin to fill up with small fires. Once the entire screen is covered in flame, your time as an audience is up: you'll ALL go up in flames.

Well, not me of course! This is MY show. So I get to survive. And yes—I can hear some of you asking the question, Is there any way out of this disaster? Yes, there is—hey! It's a game, right? The only way out of it is to guess the right word!

So, folks—are we ready? At the sound of the tone…[*Pauses, as if listening to a response from the audience*] What's that? Yes, sir? What's that you said? You want to leave now, before we begin? Sorry! Not an option! Didn't they tell you—before you signed up for this show—leaving was not an option? Because—hey! It wouldn't be much like real life, would it? I mean in real life, we don't even get to decide whether or not we'll be born—never mind whether or not we'll agree to slaughter our fellow citizens when we come of age.

So this game's a little bit like real life in that sense. You don't get to make the choices when it comes to fundamental freedoms—such as who gets to live and who gets to die.

That's fixed, right? Either you're born into a society that believes in the sanctity of human life or you're not. If not… then…you don't have the freedom to be squeamish! You just have to go along with whatever deck of cards is handed to you at the moment of your birth.

If you're one of the lucky ones, you're sitting in this audience and you have the right to remain alive and the right to stand by as your fellow citizens get slaughtered. If you're not so lucky, even though you're one of the lucky ones sitting in this audience tonight, you'll take the bullet for tonight's missed catches. If you're just naturally unlucky, you'll have been born into one of the countless weaker sections of our society and might be picked off at any time and for any reason.

So! We're going to begin! The word we're looking for today is ten letters long…There's the starting tone—

Sound of STARTER TONE; a loud ticking commences.

—and we're off! Time's ticking away, friends—don't forget! For each minute of inaction, one person from the weaker sections is bumped off the register of life. It could be any young woman at any time, of any age—a divorcee or a widow or a mistress! It could be a *dalit,* or someone in a mixed-caste, mixed-race, mixed-community marriage! It could be an old person, or an orphan, or a leper! It could be an AIDS patient, a *hijra,* or a prostitute! It could be a disabled person, a war veteran, or a diabetic! It could be anyone who has a secret, anyone who is insecure, anyone who doesn't have friends or family in government service— anyone at all! So don't waste time! Don't be shy! Don't be silent! Don't be—

Sound of BELL.

Oops! There's the bell—

A loud, pathetic shriek. On the screen at the back of the stage, one flame flickers.

And there's the first victim's voice! All right, folks, now you know we're not kidding! This is for real: the stakes are real, the deaths are real, the pain is real. Who's gonna take a shot at that word now, huh? Anyone? Someone? No one? So? That's how it's going to be then, people? You're going to sit back and be silent? Fine. Play it that way if you want. Because—like I told you from the start—you don't have choices. Either you let someone else burn—or you take a

chance with your own skin—or you get the answers right—
and if you don't make any moves at all, then, once the
screen at the back fills up, you get cooked anyway! 'Coz
that's the nature of the game. Only four choices. They die,
you die, we all die, or nobody dies—okay? That's what I
told you at the outset—that's the way it's fixed—though of
course I don't die 'coz I'm the one who sets the game up
and I've got to remain around, right? To see that there's
always an audience for the next game. And of course
there's always a—

Sound of BELL.

Oops! There's the bell!

Loud shriek; new flame on the screen.

Another poor soul down the hatch of eternity! Never to be
seen again! Never to be heard again! And you're the ones
doing it, folks! It's all up to you: stay silent, and they'll keep
popping! Stay silent and—don't tell me I didn't warn you,
okay? 'Coz I can tell you right now: there's no way of
predicting when that screen at the back is going to fill up
with flames. I know that some of you are sitting in the
audience, telling yourselves: *Someone else will speak up.
Someone else will lose nerve—and call out a letter. It doesn't
have to be me—and there's a lot of space left on that screen
at the back—no way it'll fill up before someone else guesses
the word!* Well, let me tell you, people, you have no way of
knowing how soon that screen in the back will fill up
because—you know what? Fire is an unpredictable thing.
Once you ignite a few flames, there's no saying where the
sparks will fly. No saying when, suddenly, before you're
prepared for it with your water cannons and your heat-
proof suits—suddenly, it's YOUR roof that's on fire, YOUR
daughter that's sizzling out there on the streets, YOUR
parents and children and—ah! Do I see a hand? Is someone
standing up back there? Is someone going to make a guess?

Silence.

Okay—okay—that's a hand I see. The gentleman in the
back—what's that? Will you repeat yourself, sir? Okay!
There's a guess coming in, folks! The guess is…the letter E!
The letter E. And…ohhhh dear! That letter is NOT one of
those that's on my list, folks! So, alas…for making one silly
mistake…guess what? One of you is going to die. Yes, folks,

that's the rules of the game. Sometimes, for no reason at all—other than making the wrong guess—someone in the audience gets to die. But don't worry. Unlike the unfortunate members of our target group—hahaha! little pun there, folks!—the audience dies by random selection. A quick, neat bullet. Don't bother ducking, anyone. It won't make the least bit of difference. If no one gets hit the first time, there'll always be a second time and a third and a fourth—until someone gets eliminated! And there's the warning buzzer—

BUZZZZZZ!

And there's the shot!

BOOM!

And that's one member of the audience eliminated! Hah! Isn't this exciting? It's just like real life! Well, onward, onward—keep those guesses coming, folks—keep those guesses coming—don't be slow, don't be callous—it's all up to you in the end, it's a game show after all—a deadly one, a heady one—come on, come on, come on—where's those guesses, where's those hands—time's running out, folks, the clock keeps ticking and—

Sound of BELL.

There's the bell!

Loud shriek; new flame on the screen.

Oh! What a shame! Another little life dispatched forever! Gone to the celestial dead-letter box! Gone to Valhalla! No reruns! No refunds! Over and out! And the ball's back in your court, people—time to speak out, time to share—just one letter, just one try—come on, folks—don't make me cry—come on, come on—where's that community spirit— where's that bleeding heart—come on, come on—time's ticking by—Ah! There you go! That's a hand! Up with that hand! Yes, madam—what's that you said? Did I hear you right? Yes! The letter O! Ladies and gentlemen, the letter O is…[*Going to the display board*] RIGHT! Here we go—here we go—not just one instance, but two! Hear that, people? This word includes two instances of the letter O—second from the beginning, and second from the end—and what does that tell you, people, what does that tell you about the likely construction of this word, huh?

Are you wracking your brains, folks? Are you straining every nerve, now that you know your actions can result in saving lives? Yes—is that a hand I see? Over on the right—yes, madam, speak up—what's that? Yes! N it is! Yes! Yes—and here's the N right here—right at the end of this word! Very good! Moving along, moving along! An O and an N, people—what does that tell you—what does that say to you—yes—there's a hand—very good, I'm glad to see it happening, folks—I knew I could trust in you— What's that you said? YES! S is the next one. Very good! I think you're getting the hang of it—yes, that's two S's in our word—and do I hear it from anyone else? Anyone willing to hazard a guess? Save some lives? That's all you need to do, folks—not very much—just stand up and make your voice heard—stand up and show that you care—stand up and try out a letter—yes! There we go! The lady in the front! Yes—what's that you said? What? T? Ohhhhh. No. Ohhh. What a shame. What a shame. It isn't enough just to guess, is it? Ah, no. We've got to get our guesses right, after all. Sorry about that—but you were warned—this game is for keeps, folks, and that means—yes—there's the buzzer—

BUZZZZZZZ!

Another shot!

BOOM!

Another unnecessary death! Another wasted life—Oh dear, oh dear—well, onward, onward—let's keep it going, let's keep guessing, folks—I like your spirit! Yes—there's another hand! And—yes! That's the correct letter! Give him a big hand, people—let him know you appreciate his spirit—the letter P—it's right here—right in the middle of this lovely word—yes, here we go—time's ticking away, folks, no time to spare—can't allow your mind to wander— hope you're thinking of your next letter and—yes! That's another one! Yes! The letter A! Right here! Right next to the P! Very good! Excellent! And look at that, folks! Look at that word! It's almost in front of you! It's almost complete! Just three more letters and you're home and dry! Just keep trying! Just keep playing—and there's a new hand—yes, I see you—yes, I hear you—yes, there's a C—and here it is, right in the beginning, right at the start, and there's your word, everybody—can you see it? Let me complete it for you—yes, let me give you that bonus, let me help you— here it is!

DING! DING! DING! DING! DING!

C-O-M-P-A-S-S-I-O-N—COMPASSION, everybody, yes
that's the word, a good word for these bad times—yes! And
now—

DING!

[*Returning to the display board and beginning to flip the
letters up so that the board is blank once more*]—back to
the display board for our NEXT word! Yes, ladies and
gentlemen! The game isn't over—it's not that kind of
game!—Frankly, folks, did you believe that one word was
going to do the trick? Can it ever be just one word, just one
cure-all magic bullet? Of course not! Can there ever be just
one solution? Of course not! Can we ever hope to sit back
and be complacent? Of course not! So…here we are again,
people, a new word, a new set of choices…And we'll reset
that screen at the back—get ready for the bell, and all the
same rules…

Sound and light fade out.

Thanks for playing with us tonight, folks—and stay right
where you are, for the next edition of "Famous Last
Words"—which is about to begin…RIGHT NOW! Okay
…an eight-letter word—there's the starting tone—

Fade out completely.

Invocation

*The stage is bare except for a board at center on which a thousand fairy lights are
visible. A figure appears, walks in front of the display of lights, and stops when
she is framed midway between the ends of the board. She addresses the audience
directly. Each time she reads a group of names, forty lights go out, until at last
she is left in darkness.*

FIGURE   I am going to read out a list of one thousand names.
Anyone who hears his or her name is welcome to raise his
or her hand for a few moments. That way, we'll know
who's with us today.

Here are the first forty:

*Duggal Jaiswal Sabharwal Vimal Rawail Kapil Savitri
Jethari Nathani Banwari Jhalani Watwani Sati Srichand
Choria Shakalaya Suneja Palwa Rantela Durga Kuswaha
Racchoya Vidya Bahuguna Arora Rajan Mohan Sarjan
Cabrihan Harbans Maggu Brijesh Ashif Fanthome Gaur
Nahar Attar Kuldip Amarjeet Upadhyay*

I got the majority out of the New Delhi telephone directory.

I opened each of the two volumes in the middle, then I used a needle to pierce all the way through one side of the directory, then the other side. Perhaps some of you are wondering how I managed to push a needle all the way through a telephone directory?

But first, another forty names:

Babar Johar Amar Brar Bansal Uppal Karnal Sabal
Shakuntala Srivastava Arneja Paharia Mobina Mukundan
Dutta Jana Samanta Chanana Nazrul Virmani Faridi
Ghazi Jaswati Virji Bhagwani Sawhney Sabir Quanungo
Madho Arun Hardev Ehtesham Ismail Jitender Mulk
Rawat Ussan Kalhan Sunil Raj

Well, the answer to the mystery of the needle is that I used a small hammer. I drove the needle in twenty or thirty pages at a time until there was a tiny puncture mark through every page. Then I just noted down the names that appeared closest to the puncture marks.

Now another forty names:

Arjan Haridasan Karan Ebraham Jaskaran Madan Sanan
Allen Stephen Saxena Charia Gainda Sunita Usha Bora
Virgotra Murasha Valsa Chaliha Bhageria Jindal Mittal Joel
Nimwal Satyarthi Elawadi Qureshi Banerjee Sachdev Rais
Girdhar Vishwamitter Opinder Jat Tambe Sukhatme Azad
Anwar Reginold Kulwant

I ignored names that had already been entered in my list, preferring, as far as possible, not to repeat any. It's not always easy to do that: sometimes a name will appear several times, in different places in the directory, with alternate spellings.

And here's another forty names:

Jiva Chhabra Raheja Mishra Qudsia Wadia Banarsi Vadami
Upretti Bhaduri Ansari Alamelu Sadhu Anu Francis Biswas
Jaswant Sawant Dushyant Suraj Om Lynnus Nitin Wad
Harjinder Kashal Gopal Santhanam Venkatraman Kumar
Chajjer Shanker Avdesh Ralhan Scott Subhash Johnson Jatav
Virk Mustak

That takes us up to 160 names.

So anyway…I wrote down the names in columns of forty, allowing five columns per sheet of A4 paper. That meant five sheets of paper. Once I had my basic list, I redistributed the names so that they were no longer in strict alphabetical order. I did this by copying them out from the columns onto visiting cards—twenty-five blank visiting cards. I entered the names onto the cards, reading across the columns, line by line.

Time for another forty names!

Gambhir Mir Sarup Anoop Ajmer Sagar Sharma Suresh Asirvathan Vijaraghavan Sudan Johan Balwan Harkrishan Benjamin Vaijayanti Padmini Udhani Doji Piplani Kundra Luthra Seetha Kathuria Nalkha Budhiraja Anita Wahal Bisht Charanjit Gopinath Inyat Jose Vendil Rajpal Sehgal Jay Chet Raghubir Oberoi

Once they were on the cards, I began copying them into my computer. It wasn't possible to pull out one thousand unique names using the needle system alone. So I chose a further ninety names by just searching through the directory for those that weren't already on my list. Once the names were in my computer, I rearranged them slightly, so that they would be easier to read out loud.

And now, another forty:

Chawla Birla Sudha Walia Ira Goyanka Kushwala Thadani Wahi Patni Gandhi Bedi Rizvi Sembhi Balmiki Varandani Nizami Mighlani Lohri Seistani Jolly Sahai Jhun Surgian Udyan Paliwal Patel Harpal Katyal Nagpal Mangal Dobriyal Anil Wasif Animesh Pinto Joy Sarkar Ajit Radhe

I looked only for surnames, and for the most part, I used the directory's main entries, the ones that appear in bold letters. So even though some names on my list appear to be first names, I included them because that's how they appeared in the directory. Wherever I made errors or found names that I had mistakenly entered twice, I substituted for them the names of my friends—being careful, of course, to include my own.

Another forty coming up:

Ganga Juneja Dudeja Nirmala Kapurthala Nagia Pincha Kaila Manchanda Bawa Aneja Gangoli Bali Haveli Suri Puthi Likhari Irani Gulani Dakshini Rohatgi Jit Menon Panwar Shahid Yad Bindlish Sujjan Padmanabhan Chauhan Kaushal Pathak Shat Serwat Vaseem Ajay Ugrasen Xavier Sahu Thakur

It's important that you know by what method I chose the

names on my list because, if I didn't tell you, you'd want to know what my selection criterion was when I explain WHY I made this effort.

But first, another forty names:

Dua Mehta Batra Lata Ahuja Sheila Bimla Chamalia Zatharia Thapa Wasuja Purshottam Niranjan Saini Vasi Roopwati Shakti Yogi Guliani Hemrajani Passi Kawal Olak Kanith Amrit Toshiwal Nag Namgain Anand Seth Sukhesh Chaudhary Kailash Baldev Ganjoo Garg Hinwar Parihar Joginder Surinder

Well, and that takes us to 320. Another 680 to go. Another seventeen pauses.

Now I am going to discuss the three reasons for which I put this list together. The first reason is that I wanted to make an invocation. By invocation, I mean, just as we invoke the gods by reciting their thousand names, I am reciting the names of one thousand real people, in order to invoke the gods of a democracy—that is, the people. The gods of a democracy are the people. I am invoking the power of the people to listen—listen to this protest.

Here's another forty names:

Gauba Dora Sakhuja Mehra Lamba Thimmaiyya Tota Chaturvedi Puri Bihari Chari Oli Kalawati Hingorani Joshi Shetty Kamat Balbir Ahmed Nigam Zubir Amrit Shansuddin Hisamuddin Gulwinder Abhyankar Kehar Mutatkar Basrar Jokhar Yadav Parvesh Malik Amrik Surjeet Parmjeet Roy Shadab Sultan Vats

The protest is my second reason for putting this list together. My protest concerns the names that are missing from the public record. Do you notice how, when there's a riot, we are rarely told who died? Instead, we are given numbers. We're given details of the property that was damaged. We are offered glimpses of who may have been responsible. But we are rarely shown the names of those who died.

Meanwhile, here's another forty names:

Toteja Bejana Bala Sharda Dogra Julka Malhotra Barua Rungta Gauri Negi Chatterjee Amrohi Kalsi Murli Kansal Dyal Kewal Chaswal Thukral Ahlawat Salman Shiv Sushil Ved Puran Mehar Lalit Permananad Bhowmick Oliver

*Gurbaksh Hiroo Yag Parveen Ambesh Shah Summan
Gautam Human*

A name is a powerful thing. It's the first thing we get when we are born. It's one of the few things that survive us when we die, continuing to exert an influence through wills and land records and tombstones. It's a handle by which we can be controlled as well as a tool with which some of us control others. To invoke the name of a powerful bureaucrat, for example, is to invoke the powers of that bureaucrat's office. A name is a passport across the borders of reality that shows who we are, where we came from, and to whom we belong.

Now here are more names:

*Bhojwani Nihalani Ghai Dimpi Phoolwati Kamini Bakshi
Ali Kapadia Saluja Sushma Charkha Veena Meena Hoda
Handa Dehalla Pundlik Neelkandhan Malkan Bishan
Shivrajan Aggarwal Lal Munjal Sheelawant Dixit
Imamuddin Khalid Noor Gurcharanjeet Sualaheen Tilak
Parshant Yesh Harish Keshav George Kad Chansarkar*

We speak of people being "twice born": the first is their physical birth into this world, and the second is their birth into their faith. The victims of riots, by contrast, might be called "twice dead": they die a physical death in the streets and a second death in the public record. We know of them only as statistics. Unlike soldiers who die in a war, unlike passengers who die in aircraft accidents, these victims of violence pass out of our consciousness as if their deaths were of no account.

Here's another forty names:

*Dhuna Daya Chandra Bhayana Maknotra Gullah Adlakha
Venugopal Pritpal Nonihal Pratipal Kariwal Iqbal
Bakhtawar Mazhar Kakar Swaran Khan Sampuran Kanan
Binani Khattari Shri Damani Mulseri Naveen Lakshmi
Ghasi Shenoy Dil Aklesh Chatrath Gurmeet Subendu Tokas
Yusaf Parkash Karjit Haradhat Ghose*

I'm sure that if you or I were killed in mob violence, we would hope, in our final moments, that we would at the very least be remembered by our fellow citizens. A victim of mob violence dies defending his or her right to exist. He or she becomes a martyr to the cause of human dignity. But unlike other martyrs, riot victims are not memorialized: at the very most, the few who have surviving family members are referred to in passing, in press interviews, after the event.

Time for more names:

Gian Pritam Subhan Dhiwan Jayan Kalia Verma Khera Bishwa Kanojia Shriniwas Prithviraj Dhir Kartar Majumdar Dawar Bajaj Ishwardas Hemraj Khandelwal Gurpal Abrol Chandhok Syed Sandhu Nathu Matoo Toor Shish Vakil Zamruddin Parikh Bijlani Gingee Lakhi Barti Airy Nomani Hari Mukherjee

State authorities and governments are not likely to publicize the names of those who died in violent riots, or to make an effort to inscribe their names in granite, or to create memorial sites to them. Why? Because a riot is a disgrace to the nation in which it occurs. By refusing to acknowledge those who die, we are, in effect, trying to keep the record clean.

Yet more names:

Kalra Khanna Dasgupta Bismillah Kanta Ladda Trikha Shukla Kataria Dhingra Baikunth Abdul Mathur Sangi Pulyani Vidyawati Maini Hothi Bhutani Prem Naseem Shokeen Bhanot Agyakar Tahir Issar Gurvinder Gullu Ranjodh Haryal Pardeep Rakesh Mukesh Harisharan Girijan Khimanand Mirjan Dhiman Gobind Chander

So that brings me to my third reason for putting together this list of one thousand names: to take the place of those we will never know. Since the names of those who really died are not revealed, I have created this list of recorded names, chosen randomly, to take the place of the unrecorded ones. The names of the living in the place of those who are dead.

Here's another forty names:

Bissa Rabiya Talla Gogia Kharbanda Preeta Narula Katnala Chopra Goel Bahl Kamal Dhanwal Kanwar Dhawan Darshan Bhushan Jagan Bhajan Modak Mrinal Harnam Ram Shyam Chand Sanjay Somani Farshori Rantri Indrawati Trilokhi Vij Khursheed Hakim Rajveer Paramjit Tikkoo Mathur Aganpul Jacob

Some of you may feel this is unfair: substituting names from a telephone directory, randomly and without permission, for the names of riot victims. But look at it this way: violent riots are unfair too. The deaths that occur are random too—names and identities suddenly turning poisonous, suddenly becoming weapons in the hands of oppressors.

Here's another forty names:

Gopalan Chaman Sugan Mannon Morrison Bhagwan Gonga Bagha Sidana Lanka Raina Dhameja Adkana Papna Hadija Dareja Bhupendra Rajpal Khattar Talwar Prasad Kamlesh Dhaundiyal Kaul Kiran Ramadurai Vijay Maheshwari Sansi Jaggi Massey Narsingh Mobin Islamuddin Rohtash Thomas Dagar Balwinder Birgu Triyug

And that brings us to 640. Another 360 to go.

Some of you may feel, with particular reference to the riots in Gujarat, that these names I've been reading out are especially inappropriate. After all, you might point out, the majority of those who died in Gujarat were poor Muslims, whose names would be unlikely to appear in any telephone directory. Meanwhile, the majority of names on my list, chosen randomly, are of Hindus who are at least wealthy enough to have a telephone connection.

Before you jump to hasty conclusions, however, here's another forty names:

Monga Bhola Tibrewala Dhalia Tamta Vijendra Anchalia Hina Marwah Letha Gostwal Kanhayalal Dharamvir Jagveer Chakrabarti Sidhwani Bagai Tuseer Jagdeep Ramavatar Ketarpal Lambardar Manzar Santosh Pramod Navinder Rajeshwari Sukhcharan Bhagat Gosain Kaushik Abraham Kishore Roshan Dabas Balasubramaniam Rajnish Pannu Mahesh Dang

It's true that when I started compiling these names, my aim was to protest specifically against the riots in Gujarat. To protest the deaths in the train compartment in Godhra equally with the deaths on the streets of Ahmedabad and elsewhere. But as my list began to fill out, I asked myself, *Why should this be a protest only against those particular riots?* Why discriminate among riots?

Here's another forty names:

Kanwal Sappal Dhanda Chadha Simha Bariwala Durga Lohia Kotia Sukija Baby Ramesh Tandon Vinay Prabhu Naresh Maqsood Rajeet Deveshwar Jainti Jagdish Khullar Anchan Langan Balkishan Mayal Sachan Rajgopalan Irkey Christy Tyagi Maharishi Govil Grover Pandit Daljit Mohsin Kazim Ibrahim Bhim

So, I began to think of all the violence we have heard about and been a witness to: the bomb blasts in Bombay and the riots that followed them. The anti-Sikh riots and the violence in Kashmir; the riots in Assam and the killings by and of Naxalites, the decimation of tribals, and the horror of Partition.

Here's another forty names:

Gulabrani Popli Bakshi Ubhi Bhattacharjee Jaitley Bablani Raniji Chiranjiv Bumrah Khurana Sadana Behura Dutta Gulia Taneja Saraf Mahajan Dhall Singhal Andhiwal Narang Manoj Vinod Magazine Khainiddin Sumer Tomar Deshraj Krishnan Raman Mehan Langoo Kapoor Rajesh Pande Mohinder Jagirdar Inderjeet Dalel

Then I began to think of all the other deaths that have occurred, elsewhere in the world, of people whose names have passed out of the sunlight of life and into the black night of unmemory. The victims in Bangladesh, in Kosovo, in Sri Lanka, in Afghanistan, in Iran, Iraq, Indonesia and the Philippines, in China, in Argentina, in Rwanda, Nigeria, the Congo and South Africa, in Vietnam, in Cambodia, in the plains of North America, in the jungles of South America, in the deserts of Australia…how endless is this list! How heavy with unremembered blood!

Here's another forty names:

Lekwani Mangi Bajpai Gulati Karakothi Viranwali Kulkarni Ramdevi Sarat Singh Tanveer Safiq Narain Manohar Chhibbar Rajender Podar Baba Rana Kindra Dahuja Palta Malgotra Surekha Bawalia Ekka Anotra Khangwal Umarwal Jaman Jagnandan Trehan Gurbachan Dewan Mohammed Mahabeer Isaac Bhatt Dev Budh

That brings us to 800. Another 200 to go.

If there is one lesson that the Jews of Hitler's Germany have taught us, it is the value of remembrance. Six million died in Europe, but their names have not been forgotten. Their deaths continue to resonate amongst our lives, as a remembrance of what must not be allowed to happen again. Their names have become the capital from which a currency of justice has been minted.

Here's another forty names:

Gulshan Kashyap Devrajan Brij Awasthi Ranbir Sarat Desai Tapar Virender Mahar Randhawa Nangia Manocha Phutela

Daya Batheja Bahuguna Khemka Midha Saha Ratha
Sushant Farooqi Sohani Jaisinghani Madhyani Jang
Kumbhat Zakir Trilok Chattar Bharathan Ashok Satbir Jad
Kishan Dabas Bhatnagar Gurdial

My list of one thousand names is as nothing compared to the list that would be generated if all the names that belonged on it were to be uttered. It is tedious enough to listen to one thousand names being recited. Imagine if we could hear the complete list. My list is a fragile audio-memorial to all those whose own names became their death sentence, all those whose names we will not hear. It is meant to be a reminder, and a warning.

Here's another forty names:

Solomon Gurmukh Rangroo Gupta Batliwala Nanda Bhatia
Tulika Kathpalia Asha Fuloria Mahna Khosla Sinha
Satinder Devinder Vishamber Avtar Bouns Sarin Tarsem
Ravindran Takhat Dave Bashal Jaspal Manmohan Kunti
Zakiuddin Nakar Kohli Chuni Sahi Chandwani Peshwari
Bahi Bharadwaj Rathor Jalan Jagdish

Because, in case we don't realize it, let me also point out that my list, which I compiled from the New Delhi telephone directory, could in a moment of blindness and misjudgment—one nuclear bomb, for instance—turn into a list of victims.

Here's another forty names:

Hafiz Gurbir Katyayan Devi Kirplani Sirohi Atri
Namboodari Rehmani Taragi Zalani Jasbi Koshy Sondi
Ranjit Vivekanand Pawar Bhanwar Bhasker Dar Manju
Mam Gajanand Javed Kuthiala Ojha Mittar Bodhan Sailaja
Chandola Bagga Arya Sarla Baria Tayal Ujlayan Rattan
Satish Sitaram Chugh

Only eighty names left to go, by the way.

The comfort and security you and I know at this moment might be shattered by factors that have little to do with our personal choice. An unfortunate choice of residence, a quirk of spelling, may result in your body being reduced to a charred husk, with all your futures and your pasts laid to waste.

Here's another forty names:

Hans Bisht Ganpat Kutar Wattan Pawan Unnikrishnan
Chanderen Gurkirpal Deswal Kocchar Assudaney

Tekchandani Tawdey Damyanti Bansi Qudri Bhandari Ravi
Soni Jai Rao Saroj Skariah Saira Vohra Kaushalya D'Souza
Renuka Nair Manjit Jaraman Mor Badlu Arvind Satwant
Jaswinder Godrej Ray Bhasin

Against such a circumstance and as a prayer that such a moment will not be visited upon you, or me, or any one of these thousand names—and the thousand, million, billion other names that might be on this list—I make this invocation. In the names of ourselves, in the powers invested in us as citizens of a free nation, I make this invocation. In the names of those who have already died, I make this invocation.

Here are my final forty names:

Harbhajan Gurusharan Wadhwan Bishan Kaval Dehall
Ashwani Rastogi Sodhi Tewari Nahid Manglam Manmeet
Rohella Tejan Paul Dal Banik Garib Jha Kuti Qadri
Krishnamurthy Watts Moulik Babu Saryu Arshad Sood
Ravinder Johar Jain Bhargava Bhambra Salarpuria Urmila
Chandela Kukreja Chittkara Satya

Let us be done with violence. Let those who have indulged in violence be named and punished. Let those who have died in violence be named and remembered.

With this, I end my invocation.

The Museum of Game Balls

On the afternoon of March 17, 1997, a small DHL express package from Savannah, Georgia, arrives at the estate of Patma Loomalatma Quirquawaddis—if you're a guest there, he prefers that you call him Patti—a few miles north of Yangon, Myanmar. The estate grounds comprise fourteen hectares of landscaped lawns and formal gardens and include about a dozen outbuildings in addition to the two-story, Tudor-style manse. The property is almost entirely surrounded by rice fields, and in 1993 Mr. Quirquawaddis made it his principal residence.

The package has come from Yangon by pedicab. A member of the household staff, I could see, received it and signed for it. He comes into the room where I am seated right away, to alert Mr. Quirquawaddis. It seems from my host's reaction that the arrival of the package is something he has been anticipating, but he gestures the servant away and continues our conversation.

As we greeted each other that afternoon, Mr. Quirquawaddis informed me, politely but directly, just to be clear, that he does not share details of his business dealings or investment strategies with anyone. I took this to mean that he assumed I knew of his reputation as an analyst of stocks and bonds trading on the Asian exchanges, but that this would form no part of our conversation. Mr. Quirquawaddis—lean, short, barely five feet tall—was born in 1910 but is still quite agile. An incongruous haircut, a roached crest, gives his ferretlike movements a slight edge of menace. In conversation he is quick to make a disruptive inquiry or a pointed observation.

The spacious room in which my host apparently receives all his visitors is furnished with uncomfortable Louis the Fourteenth chairs, rigid chaise lounges upholstered in brocade, and gilt-and-lacquered tables bearing porcelain vases filled with cut flowers. The walls are hung with large tapestries and paintings in the same seventeenth-century style. Mr. Quirquawaddis seems ironically amused by what appear to me to be these pretensions of his to Western *noblesse,* or perhaps it is how uncertain the decor has made me feel that amuses him.

"What is your race?" he had inquired bluntly, almost immediately, but with a bland smile. My grandparents, I answered, were Basque on my mother's side, Nigerian on my father's. My parents were both born in Port-au-Prince, during the First World War. I was born shortly after the Second World War, in a small town in Connecticut—Danbury, I said. This all seemed to please him.

My long-time professional interest in Mr. Quirquawaddis had been renewed by an article I had read recently in *Architectural Digest*. In describing my host's distinguished estate, the writer had referred to Mr. Quirquawaddis' obsession with balls of various sorts, especially those used in sporting activities. The largest of the estate's outbuildings, in fact, had been built primarily to house and display this collection, though it also included, the article said, a small stage fronted by theater seating for guests to observe plays, performance art, and choreography, some of which, according to the story, Mr. Quirquawaddis had himself written or designed.

When I contacted the writer of the article, he suggested I take my inquiry about the collection to a Mr. Bao-Ding, who was its curator. In response to my note, Mr. Bao-Ding sent me an annotated list of Mr. Quirquawaddis' holdings. Among the 641 items actually on display—that is, not including items kept in storage—were cricket balls, volleyballs, American and European footballs, golf balls, medicine balls, tetherballs, and balls from scores of games I'd never heard of. They appeared to be variations on croquet, on bocce, on polo, the last of these games played by riders on different breeds of domestic animals—all, I presumed, less tractable than horses.

I have no real familiarity with sports, but I marveled at the list. *Desali,* a kind of Uygar rugby, was played with a ball so small that a participant could hide it in his clothing. *Xchutel,* a Uruguayan style of billiards, was played on a surface that is uneven rather than flat, suggesting the relief of a hilly country. From Guinea-Bissau, a game called *Kat* used a leather ball with four protruding steel spikes, which a contestant hurled at a larger, hardwood ball sent hurtling over a rocky field of packed earth by the thrower's opponent.

After a page or two, Mr. Bao-Ding's list seemed merely exotic, a finger pointing directly at Mr. Quirquawaddis' eccentricity. I feigned great enthusiasm for the collection in a follow-up e-mail message to Mr. Bao-Ding, hoping my interest might lead to an invitation to visit and, with that, a chance to speak with Mr. Quirquawaddis himself. Mr. Quirquawaddis' notoriety and legendary guardedness had not so much to do, I thought, with his status as a highly successful Asian investor but rather served primarily to obscure his early personal history. He was well known to me and other Second World War historians for his traitorous and self-serving behavior in Burma during the war, not for any reputed skills that might have put him on a par, in Southeast Asia at that time, with the American billionaire Warren Buffett.

In 1930, following a severe earthquake and tsunami that leveled much of Rangoon, Mr. Quirquawaddis, newly hired at the Bank of Rangoon with a

Madaramaru, from the series Sagas of Beauty and Bravery (Biyū Suikoden)

Artist: Tsukioka Yoshitoshi, Japanese, 1839–1892
Publisher: Ōmiya Kyūsuke (Sawa Kyūjirō)

Japanese, Edo period, 1867 (Keiō 3), 4th month. Woodblock print (nishiki-e); ink and color on paper; vertical chūban. Museum of Fine Arts, Boston. William Sturgis Bigelow Collection, 11.35897. Photograph © 2010 Museum of Fine Arts, Boston.

degree in economics from Oxford, created and then supervised a plan that granted emergency loans for the rebuilding of the city. Many years later, it was revealed that there had been a pattern of favoritism to the lending and that the successful and timely retirement of all the loans had dramatically increased the financial standing of the bank in Burma. The strategy behind the loan policy was a gambit of sorts, but at the time not an illegal one. Certain people got loans, others didn't. By the time the Japanese took over the city in March 1942, Mr. Quirquawaddis was a vice-president at the bank. The Japanese general in charge of the occupation, Nanao Hirai, appointed him its president, and, with Nanao's support and approval, Mr. Quirquawaddis also took over the management of several large Burmese shipping firms. The British forced the Japanese out of Rangoon in May 1945. Amazingly, in a matter of just a few weeks, Mr. Quirquawaddis was able completely to transform the perception most people had of him. No longer a war profiteer, he was now seen as an indispensable liaison between the British military and what was left of the Burmese national government. Though publicly excoriated by some Burmese officials for his collaboration with the Japanese, he was never formally indicted. By the mid-fifties, he was respected as the most influential broker of business deals in Rangoon, which is to say in Burma. Mr. Quirquawaddis' unusual obsession with balls apparently dates from the period of Japanese occupation. He became keenly interested in Japanese methods of torture and mutilation, it is said, after reading about the emasculation of large numbers of Chinese soldiers by the Japanese in Nanking in 1937.

I wanted, as a war historian, to tell his entire story. All I needed was an entrée, which for me meant a ploy. At Mr. Bao-Ding's suggestion, I wrote directly to Mr. Quirquawaddis in my effort to secure an audience. I apprised him of my curiosity—quite sincere, actually—about his collection, told him I was a historian at Clemson University, and that I had a special interest in the folklore of hand games, card games in particular, which was also true. I emphasized as well a bit of history I thought might get his attention. My maternal grandfather, Estevan Garcia-Pocacho, I said, had been one of the principal figures behind the growth of jai alai in the United States and, later, its development in the Philippines, first as a player, then as an owner. As a well-known collector of *pelotas* (the hard rubber balls used in this Basque game), Mr. Quirquawaddis perhaps knew of him. Finally, I said I was going to deliver a paper in Delhi in March of the coming year and wondered if I might call on him on my way home. I could show him some versions of pinochle and rouge et noir he'd probably never seen, if he'd like that.

A member of Mr. Quirquawaddis' household staff met me at the airport in Yangon on March 15 and took me to a hotel close to the famous Shwedagon Buddhist pagoda. The escort suggested a full day of rest before I met with Mr. Quirquawaddis. I didn't feel any such need, but of course agreed. I spent the time sightseeing and traveling across the city by rickshaw, in order to observe people at their daily tasks, and I sampled the markets.

At 1 P.M. on the appointed day, I was driven to the estate in what the hotel doorman informed me, as it pulled up, was a 1953 Rolls Royce Silver Dawn. A pewter vase, set into a folding walnut table cantilevered above a footrest, held a bouquet of tropical flowers, of what sort I didn't know. They were all the same, the colors in each petal ranging from vivid yellow through apricot to ruby and pale pink.

Mr. Quirquawaddis met me at his front door with a bow and a gracious gesture of welcome. I did not extend my hand. I'd been told not to attempt to touch him and never to move out of his line of sight. He led me to the salon room furnished with Louis Quatorze pieces and requested pekoe tea for both of us.

"The tea the British coveted," he said archly, "and traded the Chinese all that surplus Indian opium for."

The ostensible reason for my requesting a visit with Mr. Quirquawaddis, as I've said, was our mutual interest in certain games. Mr. Bao-Ding had sent me a list of websites and suggested that I familiarize myself with some of the games for which Mr. Quirquawaddis had collected balls, so I would be a better conversationalist. I felt reasonably well prepared but, of course, knew Patti, as he kept insisting I call him, might easily trip me up. I was counting on pleasant banter and social courtesy to carry the first part of our conversation, our common interest in something ultimately of no great importance. From the beginning, however, Mr. Quirquawaddis took the discussion earnestly in another direction. He focused on mechanical engineering, specifically on the multiple ways in which ball-bearing races had increased the efficiency of various machines during the twentieth century. He went on to describe, with an impressive range of erudition, the way in which, for example, machined steel balls were used to crush terra rossa and other friable earths to create the finely pulverized pigments used in oil paint. On the way to lunch in another part of the house, we passed through a gallery of paintings. He gestured around the room, indicating several seascapes, each of which comprised a great and subtle range of blues and greens. His *quod erat demonstrandum.*

Much of his ball collection, Mr. Quirquawaddis clarified for me as we walked along, was actually devoted not to sporting balls but to cast and machined balls—the lead beads used in shotgun shells, the weights used as counterbalances in some small sets of scales. He seemed eager to convey, in case I might have arrived at his home with the wrong idea, that the objects he had collected were revealing in ways I might not have considered. He wanted me to understand that he was not an eccentric.

During lunch—which we ate in the convivial setting of a large and immaculate modern kitchen—Patti seemed to grow less suspicious, no longer considering, I assumed, that I might be someone who had arrived with ulterior motives. He was more the raconteur, less the interrogator now. He asked me whether I knew that table tennis balls were made of celluloid, the same material from which motion picture film is made, and told me that one reason it's so hard to hit carnival targets with a baseball is that the ball is sometimes asymmetrically weighted, the imbalance all but undetectable. He waved off as annoying my question about whether he collected Wiffle or Nerf balls. He said he found it hard to develop an affinity for synthetic balls. He favored metal, leather, stone, glass. A copper BB, a cat's-eye marble, an American hardball bound in horsehide—natural materials interested him most. As a competitive collector, however, he conceded the need to be informed about and to purchase French beach balls, modern billiard balls made of Bakelite, and so on.

Before dessert was served, Patti called for his butler to bring him something. The servant returned with a small silver box the size of a snuffbox. Patti pushed it across the table to me.

"Open it," he said.

Inside, on a bed of red crushed velvet, was a dark-blue ball slightly smaller than a pea.

"A *penin*. From Romania. I believe it is the smallest of all game balls, but of course one never knows."

"What was the game? How was it played?"

"It's for a confined space, the inside of a closet, let us say. Two players sitting on the floor face each other with small paddles, held between the thumb and forefinger. The court is a few lines drawn or maybe scratched on the floor. It is quite recent. Second World War."

He reached across for the *penin* and fired it straight down at the kitchen floor. It rebounded to a height of about four feet. He gave me a squinty smile, having shown how very lively the ball was and having also provoked, he knew, the question of what it was made of. Just then the cook brought a dessert of fresh, sliced mangoes and papayas. Patti took his with heavy cream. As he poured, his head came forward into a shaft of sunlight, and I saw reddish highlights in the gray spikes of his hair. The hair was cut close at the sides of his head to emphasize the narrow sagittal ridge that rose like a cockscomb from a pronounced widow's peak. The gelled, quill-like hairs of the crest dwindled in length from a few inches to less than an inch at the nape of his neck. He reached for everything—the cream pitcher, his silverware, the *penin*—with quick, assured movements. They reminded me of snake strikes. His agility, his short stature, the rows of small, even incisors—all of it accentuated something unpleasant in him. The red highlights in his hair disappeared when he pulled his head back out of the sunlight.

"So, tell me about your grandfather, Garcia-Pocacho."

"I'm surprised you recall his name."

"Yes. From your letter."

"I don't actually know much," I told him. "His family was from Navarre, near Pamplona I believe. He grew up in the twenties in the Caribbean. The family moved to Florida just before the war. He was a boy when he started playing jai alai, and right after the war he became very popular. People bet a lot of money on him. Then he had some kind of accident—a broken hand, I believe. Afterward, he couldn't play as well, but he'd saved a lot of money, so he bought one of the jai alai courts in Miami. I guess he was very successful. Later he moved to Manila and helped popularize the game there."

"How did he die?"

"Car accident, I think."

"No. Not at all. He was killed, Mr. Balewa. I arranged for him to be killed. Your grandfather was a thief. He stole a lot of money from the people who set him up in business in Manila."

"You are saying—are you saying that you killed my grandfather?"

"I do not kill people, Mr. Balewa. Surely you must intuit that. When things are not going well, I simply request that those things be taken care of."

I sat stunned, unsure of what to do with the conversation. Mr. Quirquawaddis motioned for the table to be cleared.

"You are surprised by this, but it was a long time ago—1956, I believe. And, of course, I have no bad feelings toward you. I have welcomed you into my home. But to be successful in life, Mr. Balewa, a person should look closely into the history of every situation before he acts. Your grandfather was a careless gambler. He was seriously in debt, and he chose the wrong way to solve the problem."

"I met him only a few times," I countered, "in Florida and Connecticut, when I was young. My father had him flown home when we got the news from the Philippines. The coffin I remember was closed, because of the accident."

"No accident. Only a story the police told your parents."

I wanted to get him off the subject.

"I had some interests in Manila after the war," Patti continued. "Your letter prompted me to remember the details of that history." He inclined his head toward me. "Are you all right? Your grandfather was something of a hero for you, I can see that now. What is the word in English? Swashbuckler, that's it. Your grandfather thought he was a swashbuckler."

I needed time to absorb what he'd said. To move us in another direction, I asked Mr. Quirquawaddis how he had built up the game-ball collection. How had it grown? Did he have specific goals, an end plan? Did he send out requests based on what his research revealed?

"I have many agents looking into things for me, Mr. Balewa. Historians, anthropologists. They advise me, they send me things to look at, and then I choose. Just today, someone has sent me something."

I began to wonder now whether he might suspect the real reason behind my visit.

"When did you begin your collection?"

"During the Japanese occupation."

"What got you started?"

"It started the way everything starts. Curiosity."

I thought by the reflective tone of this remark that he might be opening a door for me. If I handled things correctly, perhaps he would talk about how the many changes in his life had unfolded. I was trying to frame an appropriate question about the Japanese occupation when Mr. Bao-Ding entered the room. He said something to Mr. Quirquawaddis in a deferential manner, in Burmese. "We are ready for you to see the collection," said Patti brightly.

I hadn't requested any such tour but more or less assumed it might be offered, considering the great distance I had traveled, if I proved to be a respectful and engaged guest. I was glad for the quiet interval during our walk to the outbuilding. I wanted to consider how to pursue the conversation, once I was alone again with my host.

The museum was airy, well lit, climate controlled, with electronic surveillance cameras and laser beams barely detectable here and there. The balls were displayed in freestanding Plexiglas cases and on shelves along the walls behind plate glass. Texts of descriptive information floated in the air alongside them—holograms, something I had never seen before. If you shifted your point of view, the hologram disappeared. Modern technology gave the displays a sharp, clean edge. Here before me was a case with twenty-five or so different balls used in different games of ninepins and tenpins—duck pins, candle pins, barrel pins—even a stone ball from a pin game played in pre-dynastic Egypt. Red letters suspended in the air beside it read "5200 BP."

Mr. Quirquawaddis, accompanied by Mr. Bao-Ding, gave me free rein to browse. One or the other would occasionally make a remark as we went along, but mostly they conversed privately. I was standing before a case of what appeared to be balls bound in animal skin when I felt Mr. Quirquawaddis at my back.

"These are perhaps not for you today," he said. I nodded my understanding and moved ahead, though the vulgarity and size of the display was not lost on me. Human skin was part of it, I was sure. I caught some words in the holograms about Second World War POW camps before turning away. I was prepared, with this, to be ushered past several other exhibits—a display of balls made from the scrota of various animals, pairs of eyes in clear vials of formalin. Mr. Quirquawaddis wasn't hurrying me along. I had, however, the sense he had other appointments pending. I took the initiative and asked if I might come back the next day. The collection was overwhelming. Perhaps I could go through it with Mr. Bao-Ding, and thus not take up too much of his time. Perhaps he and I could then have tea again, and continue our conversation.

Mr. Quirquawaddis accepted my suggestion with his familiar mannered bow. We returned to the house, and he had the silver Rolls brought around.

As he walked me to the car, I noticed that he had the small DHL package of that afternoon in the crook of his arm.

"This is for you, Mr. Balewa. Maybe you will open it later. A custom-made jai alai ball. Very dangerous game, jai alai. Sometimes, on the return, the ball is moving one hundred fifty miles per hour."

The chauffeur held the car door open. I saw that a fresh bouquet of flowers had been set in the walnut table.

I made a slight formal bow to Mr. Quirquawaddis that he did not return.

"People are greedy, Mr. Balewa. When they try to be clever about it, they amuse me. Before you come back, please remind yourself why you came here in the first place, and what it is you expect to gain by coming back to see me."

I opened the package on the road to the hotel. The pasteboard box inside was packed with tissue. Nestled in it was the *pelota*, a ball a couple of inches in diameter, covered with two pieces of thin hide, sewn tightly together with red thread. It looked like parchment.

In the Mood, a Prologue and Finale

Mom said to me, "Dad isn't feeling well. He didn't sleep last night."

I heard the pacing. The boards squeaked. He moved from bathroom to kitchen. He set off the dismal pipes that girdled our walls.

But he looked good to me in the morning. No evidence of hard nights.

Eyes wide open, even though shadowed. On his feet, talking. He'd already finished the newspaper. He celebrated his heroes—Ted Williams, finishing a big season; FDR, warning the Japanese not to push us in the Pacific; John L. Lewis, demanding a living wage for coal miners.

He should have been down opening the store, but he was having a great time releasing the voices that had raced in his head all night. He swayed back on his heels, his arms swinging free, his head pulled back for laughs, the big Adam's apple bobbing.

Mom said, "Time to open up. Delivery men due at seven, Eph."

He said to us, eyes glittering, the swarthy face illuminated, "I wait to be delivered," an explosion of laughter. "The day comes," he said, "when I shall be elevated to my station and its duties. Meanwhile"—he bowed to Mom—"the grocery, my dear Ruth."

She warned me, "It's going to change. Don't be disappointed. Enjoy him while he's in the mood."

She called it "being in the mood." I knew what she meant, and resented her not speaking plainly.

When I left for school, he was outside on the walk, ushering customers into the store. Mom later came down to take over the register and check the orders. While in the mood, he was too exalted to tend to business and messed up the charge book and botched the orders.

At the same time, he was full of joy and invention. He lighted up, the mouth supple, his smile flowering, the extravagant beaked nose somehow appropriate to the spirit of the brimming eyes. He looked skinny but he had a powerful grip.

He claimed to be preparing a history of the Smiths. It was time, he said, we made ourselves known. We were a remarkable people. Ancient, he said. And then giving up his apparent seriousness, he worked out a genealogy that led to Homer and Ancient Greece. He derived *Smith* from *Zeus*,

Actor Nakamura Shikan IV as the Wrestler
(Keiriki) Tomigoō, from the series A Modern Shuhuzhuan
(Kinsei suikoden)

Artist: Utagawa Kunisada I (Toyokuni III), 1786–1864
Publisher: Iseya Kanekichi

Japanese, Edo period, 1861 (Man'en 2/Bunkyū 1), 6th month.
Woodblock print (nishiki-e); ink and color on paper; vertical ōban.
Museum of Fine Arts, Boston. William Sturgis Bigelow Collection,
11.29906. Photograph © 2010 Museum of Fine Arts, Boston

the *Z* speeding up and collapsing into *Sm* by a rule he called the "Smith sibilant," the *eu* losing its voice when the tongue slackened in grief at our fall and idled on the floor of the mouth, barely managing the almost mute *i* of *Smith*. He called that process the "Smith elision." He found permutations of our name in the lists of Trojans. He appeared again in the *Aeneid*. The joke was elaborated; it went on and on, and when it seemed as if he was stuck in the posture of a clown, he changed tone and there he was, again the true believer.

Mom insisted on straightening me out. We had no history. We were anonymous. There was no trace of us in any book. We had no one to mourn, nothing to recall. They were both born in Chicago. Her family was wiped out in the flu epidemic of nineteen eighteen. His family had drifted out of sight. That was the true Smith elision.

She wanted to prepare me for the shift in mood when he was no longer a source of energy and pleasure. He would begin drawing everything back into himself, leaching the air of joy, sucking us into his abysmal suspicions.

When he finally peaked and was looking down, bound to his rock by a spiderweb conspiracy, he could trace any event to cosmic origins.

I was only ten years old, already wise about Dad, and knew these matters better than she did. She spoke her warnings to arm herself against vain hope. She received no profit from his exaltation.

At the end of summer he took me to Boston to see the Red Sox and Ted Williams. We stood above the dugout after the ball game among the crowd greeting Williams, and Dad called out, "Mr. Williams! Congratulations, Sir! You have had a magnificent season! You have given us all great pleasure!" Williams was impressed by the regal tone and stretched over the dugout to shake Dad's hand. Dad said, "I brought my son from Syracuse, New York, to witness this memorable occasion." We were invited to the locker room. The rarely gracious Williams autographed a ball for me, confessed to Dad that this had been for him a magical season. Bat and ball and arm and heart and eye and the field were all linked, and almost every time at bat was a perfect realization. He confessed he'd never talked like this before. "You pushed my button, Ephraim. You've got a way with words."

Dad heard the news of Pearl Harbor on our Philco. The next day he put on his doughboy outfit. I didn't know he'd been a soldier.

Nineteen seventeen to nineteen nineteen.

He meant to enlist on the spot.

Mom asked, "Who'll take care of the store?"

"It's war, Ruth!"

She appealed to his fatherly obligations, but he couldn't be stopped. She told me to go along. I found him in the Ford, ready to take off.

"There'll be time later for goodbyes, son." It was a tremendous opportunity for him. He would make his way through Officer Candidate School and rise to the top. We would be stationed in California, quartered near the ocean. Friday-night dances at the Officers Club, partying in Hollywood. It was a joke and not a joke, and I couldn't decipher what was serious in his understanding.

I joined Mom upstairs.

"He'd leave me with the store if he could. It's not fair."

It wasn't fair. She looked older than Dad though he had a ten-year advantage. While he was in the mood, she was aged by anxiety, scrambling to be ahead of him or behind, wherever the obstacle might appear, clearing the path, trying to prolong his season of joy—her season of grief—knowing any event might be the trigger for his transformation. She was the keeper—so she supposed—of the monster—so she imagined him. His bleak time was better for her. Once he was down, she knew where to find him—hiding behind a newspaper in the store, sitting for hours at the kitchen table. She didn't have to fear cunning stories, extravagant orders, wrong entries, offended customers.

He was rejected out of hand by the army, and he returned home subdued.

Mom insisted that we close the store and take a drive into the countryside while it was still light. We passed denuded apple orchards, cornfields with dead stalks skewed by weather, grazing animals, wonderful barns, groves of willow that traced streams.

"What kind of cows are they, Eph?"

"Guernsey." Perhaps they were.

In our '39 Ford, springs bouncing at a steady forty-mile-an-hour clip, we were together and yet parted. He was off on a journey we couldn't share. Mom prodded him to answer her questions. He answered grudgingly. Then we passed an enormous oak. Blackbirds had settled on every twig. Dad said—it came from nowhere—*Les oiseaux du bois.*

Mom asked, "What?"

"Birds of the wood."

"But what did you say?"

He'd picked up French during the war.

I asked him if he'd seen men die. He told me in a documentary voice, not his flamboyant "in the mood" manner, that he'd been at Château-Thierry and Belleau Woods. He was an engineer. He dug trenches. He crept on his belly through no-man's-land. He laid pipefuls of dynamite beneath coils of barbed wire and wiggled away fast while the fuse burned. I recall his experience as vividly as if it were an old movie I'd seen.

Mom was surprised that he could speak French. He'd never spoken French to her. She was puzzled by the sober tone of his revelations. Where had he learned French?

From a nurse, in a Paris hospital, named Katya.

What was he doing in a Paris hospital? Her questioning was sharp now.

"You know. When I was gassed. Chlorine in the lungs," he explained.

"What kind of name is Katya?"

"She was a Russian. Her people were chased out by the Bolsheviks."

"Oh, come on!" She tried to egg him into his ordinary flamboyance so she could deny his invention.

"She worked for a princess."

"Eph, she was telling you a story."

"Maybe. It was a long time ago." She asked him to speak more French and he spoke the words of a song.

> *A quoi bon entendre*
> *les oiseaux du bois?*
> *L'Oiseau la plus tendre*
> *Chante dans ton voix.*

> Why listen to
> the birds of the wood?
> The sweetest bird
> sings in your voice.

"Was she pretty?"

"Who remembered?"

"Was she young?"

"Who wasn't?"

"Well I can see," she said, "that you're not in the mood."

The army rejected him because of his age. He was forty-five years old.

"War's for the young, Eph."

"I had to tell them I was in a crazy house."

She said that was more than twenty years ago.

"Nothing's changed."

Well, she said. Their loss was our gain. Maybe he wasn't indispensable to the war effort, but the Smiths sure needed him.

She told me later that he never belonged in an asylum. "It was after the war. He was gassed. It was the first time he got in the mood. His folks didn't know what was happening. They sent him to the Michigan State Asylum in Pontiac, called Eloise. He was there for a few weeks and then he came out of it like you know he does. We were going together and I told him it didn't bother me he was at Eloise. High or low, he was my man, and they had no right to send him to Eloise. What you and I know," she said to me, as conspiratorial for a moment as he had ever been, "is that your dad is someone special. He is not your ordinary grocer. And we Smiths," she said, "are not ordinary people." When it came down to the final judgment, crazy man or eccentric genius, she chose the second alternative. "It was a tragedy they sent him to Eloise."

He didn't at first seem disturbed by the rebuff. He started out joking. These were army doctors. Peacetime medics. Professional army cadre. Did I know what that meant? Incompetents who couldn't make a go of it in civilian life. Butchers. Literally, head shrinkers. Recruited from the Amazon to establish an armed service that would preserve their incompetence. Willing to go to any length to disguise their appalling lack of skill. The old boy network. The issue wasn't for them to defeat the Nips or the Krauts. In fact, they were closer to their confrères overseas than they were to the Americans. We really didn't need a League of Nations. We already had working a coherent international network of military establishments totally indifferent to political ideologies, more alien to civilian traditions than to their commonly shared outpost experience. British, French, Russian, German, Japanese, American—it made no difference. Officers' rations, officers' quarters, officers' prerogatives—they would choose whatever armies were necessary to guarantee these. And that was the reason, he said, for the judgment against age and uniqueness—against any eccentricity that might jeopardize the docile acceptance of their authority. It was people like that who had shoved him into Eloise.

"Yes, Dad."

Mom hoped she could stop him now, while there was still a trace of humor in his invention.

"You're right, Eph," she said. "But I'm sure they all mean well. It's not deliberate."

"Ah," he said. "My own Pollyanna. She sees no evil. Wonderful woman. Great hearted. Perfectly suited to a corner grocery in Syracuse, New York. The very center of the world. A marvelous vantage point for deciphering the code of the universe."

The change had happened. He wouldn't sleep, he wouldn't eat. He began to feed on himself. He was tireless, the eyes huge. His inventions were embellished, the narrative became richer every day. He was caught in the flow of it. It invented him and us and the world. His narrative absorbed creation and advanced forward to ultimate judgment and redemption. Himself growing in divinity, food unnecessary, his excitement enormous. It was too much for Mom. She was overwhelmed by the assault on her own point of view. Her own loosely strung, disconnected narrative was undermined. She struggled against the tyranny of his story. If she found holes, he immediately filled them. His premises were powerful and fecund and generated the world, and he was as excited as Newton or Einstein on the trail of universal law.

The army doctors were part of an international cabal. He dispensed with the multiplicity of parties in favor of one—a ruling party that created all others, and either ruthlessly eliminated any independent observer who might decipher the true order or else co-opted him into the fraternity.

Did she fear she'd have a fight on her hands keeping him out of the crazy house? She bought his story at a deeper level than I imagined, as though she agreed there was an all-powerful authority that scanned the universe for unassimilable points of view. What grieved her wasn't merely Dad's outrageous story, but that he exposed himself, and she had to assume the burden of defending him. Each day when I returned from school, he had me listen while he enlarged his narrative.

Once, while he was in the john, she whispered fast. Did I believe him? He had everything tied together. But things weren't together. I understood that, didn't I? She whispered, "No one had it in for him. He's too old for the army. Eloise is a fact. The army doctors aren't in league to oppress him. Do you know that?"

I told her not to worry.

Dad came out of the john and asked why we'd been whispering.

She denied we'd been whispering.

He said, "Don't you know I hear everything, Ruth? Before you speak I hear what you say. I can hear the noisy machinery of your brain trying to turn the boy against me."

She denied it. It wasn't fair. She was his closest friend. How could he refuse to trust her? Couldn't she even speak to her own son without risking his suspicions?

He was triumphant. "Then you WERE whispering!"

I said, "Mom thinks you're tying things together that don't belong."

He told her, "That's what you should have admitted."

I told him that Mom was tired.

"Of course she's tired. She wears herself out fighting me."

The next day when I came home from school, the store was closed. They were upstairs, and he was in his doughboy outfit, a rifle in his lap. Mom just about cracked, said I had to stop him. "He's going to the Armory!" He sat calmly in the armchair, working the bolt of the Springfield .30 caliber rifle, a spilled box of cartridges in his lap.

I told him, "That rifle is pitiful, Dad. They got tanks and airplanes. They got a million soldiers in New York and New Jersey."

"It doesn't matter. I want to go out like a man."

I asked if he wanted me to go out with him. I could get a knife.

"All right. Get your knife."

I went into the kitchen and returned with a ridiculous bread knife, trying to stall him, hoping his mood would collapse.

The uniform smelled of camphor. The jacket strained at his chest.

I offered to carry the gun.

"Not on your life."

She followed us downstairs to the car and begged him not to go. "So what if they don't want you in the army? What would you be fighting for anyway?"

"Better to go like this, snatching for glory, than to smother in the dead air of a dying grocery."

"What glory?"

"The glory of being a man." He climbed into the driver's seat, put the rifle on the floor. I climbed in alongside.

"I'll call the police!"

"I don't care whether it's the police or the army, Ruth. It's too late."

I asked him what we were dying for.

"I named you," he said, "after Eugene Victor Debs, who was a martyr of the working class. He opposed war. He was a man of peace. I, too, was a man of peace. I wanted to organize the workers. I believed in a New Eden."

I asked what new Eden.

"The New Eden here." He struck his chest. "Here," he pointed to his head. "Here," he touched his genitals. "Not a goddam grocery store." There was a *better* world than this one. This world was hopelessly fragmented into two billion parts and could never be made one. Who was ready to give up his minute sovereignty? "Only Ephraim Smith. I give up."

When we reached the Armory, I tried to alert the guard at the door. He wore khaki and leggings and white gloves and a pistol belt and a holstered pistol. He stood at ease. He looked at Dad's uniform and rifle and stared at us, but we walked past him into the vast room where troops were drilling. Recruiters sat at a table near the entryway, a marine in blue, a sailor in white, a soldier in khaki. It was a couple weeks after Pearl Harbor, and recruits massed around the table. They made way for us, assuming, I suppose, that Dad in his World War I outfit was part of the recruitment.

"My father's here," I said, "to volunteer his weapon."

The army sergeant looked at the vintage rifle and the ancient uniform. "You got the wrong war, Dad. This is 1941."

I gripped the rifle. "Give it." I tugged and he let go. I laid it on the table.

"What am I supposed to do with this?"

"We're enlisting this Springfield rifle in the war effort."

I took him by the hand and led him out of the Armory.

"There were too many of them, Dad."

He shook so hard I had to open the car door and help him in. I reached into his pocket for the keys. I had watched him drive, and had practiced shifting, and I drove home in first gear and parked three feet from the curb.

We led him to bed and undressed him. He asked me to stay. I sat in a chair by his bed while the spirit subsided. He looked frail. The shadows around his eyes were dark as bruises. He looked so mournful I wanted to hold him in my arms and tell him I loved him. The room darkened. His eyes remained open. Mom peeped in the door. I shook my head. I smelled dinner cooking, coffee, saw light under the door. It must have been close to midnight when he finally sighed, a deep letting go, and then groans, murmurs I couldn't decipher, lip smacking. I waited until his breathing was deep. Afterward, I joined Mom in the kitchen. "It's okay. He's out." The two-week episode used up years of her life.

By Christmas vacation he had entered what she called his "dark time," withdrawing like a hibernating animal for a long sleep. He sat in the rear of the store, hiding behind a newspaper, not reading. It took him long seconds to respond to customers. Mom shouted at him as if he were deaf or far away. Thieves could have emptied the store with a hand truck, and he would have been indifferent. His spirit had vanished. The premises were vacated. The occupant was out to lunch. Mom kept him moving. She prodded him to eat when he stopped with his fork in the air. A child could have authored his actions. The touch of a hand set him in motion. She gave him a broom and he swept. The newspaper kept him hidden.

"Mrs. Alfieri says hello, Eph."

He said hello to Mrs. Alfieri.

Home from school, I asked, "How are you feeling, Dad?"

Blank consideration of the question, then finally, "Okay," puzzling what was said to him and what he had uttered.

We took the train to New York before New Year's Day and saw the Rockettes at Radio City. There was a movie with Betty Grable and Harry James. Mom enjoyed it for the three of us. Million-dollar legs, she said. The legs were something special. The face, though—thick lips, plump nose—wasn't a million-dollar face. "Do you think so, Eph? I bet you're crazy about her. She's your type, I know."

"She's not his type," I said. "He's not crazy about her."

"Oh, Sonny. We don't have to be so serious."

I felt the disrespect and was offended. I was so close to being him that I could look into his eyes and locate the very deep place to which he had declined. The blankness was only apparent. The upper stories of the house were vacant, but what happened in the deep interior was far more intense than anything the grocer had ever experienced.

We walked into Central Park at night and came to the pond with the skaters. We lost track of Dad. "Ephraim!" she yelled. "Eph!" I called, "Dad!" We asked people if they had seen a big-nosed skinny man with earmuffs and a gray felt fedora and a plaid scarf and dark-blue coat. Then we spotted him on the ice. He had rented or borrowed skates. We watched him skim over the ice, his hands clasped in back, somber and joyless. He skated with perfect grace, the fedora square on his head, the scarf tucked into his coat, his wool-gloved hands clasped in back, his huge beak red and dripping. He swooped among other skaters.

Mom was shocked. "Is it over already?"

He said to me afterwards when I complimented him on his skating, "It doesn't change anything, son," warning me against imagining the season had turned.

He came back to us in the spring. Again the change was abrupt. Once more the spirit shone in his eyes. He checked everything out—my school, my clothes, the store. He was courtly and tender to Mom. She was as shy as if a stranger had entered the house. And for a time the feeling was so generous that none of us had the heart to anticipate what lay ahead. The days started indolently. She wasn't anxious about opening precisely at seven. She urged him to linger at the breakfast table.

He suggested a summer vacation. Pack up the whole show, he said, take it on the road. Maybe head home.

Home? Not even the word was familiar to her. Where could that be but Syracuse?

He meant Chicago. Back to origins. Find the key to Ephraim Smith and unlock the door. He was serious and lucid. Free the imprisoned soul. He again tiptoed on the razor's edge between clownishness and something deeply meant. A voice had told him to go back home and uncover the design of his life. The words "voice" and "design" scared her.

"There's no one left. Everyone's gone, Eph."

How about the Lake Michigan island where they'd honeymooned?

She remembered that time as the most beautiful of her life. But who would watch the store?

"We'll advertise. We got almost three months."

She wanted to go. She checked with him the next day and the next. "You're sure about this vacation?"

"Absolutely. July one, as soon as Gene is out of school, we leave." She offered the full profit for someone to tend the store. She interviewed candidates, checked their references, decided on an earnest young man recommended by a Methodist minister.

Dad said the trip would change our lives. "We're going to a new world."

A week before the trip, I caught him by surprise. Someone else appeared in the guise of my father.

He opened the store at seven in the morning. Mom didn't come down until nine. She got me ready for school, then straightened out the apartment. This morning there was no bread for my lunch, and she sent me downstairs. Dad wasn't in the store. I went to the stockroom, a ten-by-twelve windowless space, lined with shelves from floor to ceiling. Staples were on the lower shelves. I recall the Grape Nuts and rolled oats, and cornflakes, the cases of Campbell soups spilled on the floor. And spilled Jell-O boxes and jars of Postum, the shelves trembling as my father pressed into Mrs. Alfieri in the midst of fallen inventory.

At first I didn't understand that there were two people there. I saw his back, the skirt of his apron, arms around his back, her face looking at me, his head nowhere to be seen, her mouth open to release deep hoarse "Ahs!" She saw me, and they lurched apart. It was Mrs. Alfieri, burly, with enormous breasts, her nipples at the bull's eye with coffee-colored rims. When he turned toward me, the face was not my father's face. The eyes were dreadful; the mouth wide open as though he meant to kill by biting. I left the room, picked up a loaf, said nothing to Mom.

His eyes were stretched wide. The lids had vanished. The pupils filled the space in the sockets. Her breasts—the target of his eyes—summoned up from deep caves a demonic, predatory spirit utterly unfamiliar to me.

I read my father and Mrs. Alfieri as clearly as if their impulses had a text. Her eyes were dragged into his, thick wormy lips pulled back, crooked teeth exposed, jet-black hair, a trace of mustache. Fertile and available. She gathered in her breasts, swooped them into her brassiere, tucked them in as if they were not herself but something she wore.

I see a demon father offered the sacrifice of breasts, and he bends to feed.

Mrs. Alfieri, a hoarse-voiced customer, was usually accompanied by a meager, sullen boy, but not this time.

When I returned home that afternoon, I saw my familiar father, innocent and exuberant. He'd bought a tent and air mattresses and canvas folding cots. Could I have invented the scene in the stockroom? I didn't want to see what I had seen, and submitted to his enthusiasm.

On a July morning we loaded the Ford. A nest was hollowed in back for me. I was wedged in against the door, surrounded by pillows and blankets and air mattresses. Dad lashed the tent to the roof of the Ford. Mom climbed in with thermos and picnic hamper. Dad turned the ignition and yelled, "Okay! All you demons and gremlins who want to hold us back, out of the way! We're driving right over you!" and we were off.

He talked until he exhausted us, and finally he, too, ran out of gas and was silent. There were no superhighways then. Much of the trip was on two-lane rural roads that broadened at the thresholds of towns and cities. The only sound I heard was the rush of air, the squeak of the Ford, the slap of the tires crossing asphalt seams. Dad didn't want to stop. He told Mom we would stop when the car needed gas.

He was silent and smiling, dreaming probably of Mrs. Alfieri in the stockroom. He bent down to her breasts. She stretched up with her offering.

Mom's silence didn't hide erotic visions. Her dreams simply extended her ordinary experience to include a more stable grocer, a more grateful child, a kitchen with butcher-block counters and overhead cabinets and a coffin-sized refrigerator-freezer and a copper hood fitting over a gas range like the mouth of an enormous tuba.

We drove with only two quick stops and by dawn had reached the outskirts of Detroit. It was barely dawn. I was half asleep, couldn't make out where we were. In hell, perhaps. Billowing flames from an open-hearth furnace reddened the sky. Outside, a hiss like the sound of an enormous steam iron. I saw the chimneys of the Ford River Rouge plant in Dearborn. The land hissed and breathed fire.

Dad tensed and I saw what he saw: something enormous in the shadows far down the road, perhaps a billboard or a silo, vague, yet ominous with its threat of motion, edging on the road, unstable—as if it would fall or leap—a silo that could topple or a billboard that was alive. The shadowy light bred illusions.

"Oh, lordy," Dad said.

Mom asked, "What is it?"

"Oh, lordy."

He slowed down but kept going even after the shape was defined. I could dismiss it as possibly a hoax meant to flimflam tourists: two-headed buffaloes or one-hundred-foot anacondas. It resembled something from the Saurian age, armor plated, on its haunches, with claws spread chest high.

We all saw something. Mom asked, "What is that?" irritated by the malice of those who had placed it there to alarm us. I came from sleep, and there were fires all around, and the huge stacks, specters everywhere in that dawn light, and what I saw was at first a silo backlit by the open hearth and then—perhaps for an instant—this serpent, and I heard deep, steamy respiration. It was Dad, turning to me, his eyes swallowed by the pupils as they were with Mrs. Alfieri, saying, "Didn't I tell you! Isn't it so?" who fixed that object clearly in all its details—vivid, unmistakable—and I saw that enormous reptile and its armor and outstretched claws, fire in its mouth. "Isn't it so!" Exultant, as though this was final proof. Of what? That they'd never had a right to stick him in Eloise? That his visions were true? Because now for the first time I saw the world he saw. And it moved. When we reached its shadow—*it moved*. Did Mom scream because she also saw what we saw? Or because she knew that she was dying of it? He wrenched the wheel; he stepped on the gas; he shouted and lost control, and we soared past unblinking, glistening reptilian eyes, black-slit pupils the size of fists within green irises. The head turned to follow our flight. I saw a morning sky bare of complications. The sky tumbled; Dearborn wheeled into view, long chimneys plugged into the slate sky. There was a hiss like my father's sigh amplified a thousand times. I sailed through air, the Superman of my dreams. I ended beside the road, watching the Ford settle in a nimbus of dust and smoke, rocking on its back, wheels spinning, a frantic bug that suddenly took fire. Brakes screeched, people ran toward us. There was no sign of the reptile.

Later, I saw Mom and Dad in white linen. The doctors carved up my dreamer and forced him to acknowledge the real world. He was briefly alive, already doomed, his brain shut off too long, everything erased. I had for a moment an awareness cutting like a knife that this man was myself, not merely a mad, ineffectual grocer, but someone whose roots went underground and emerged to become me. There were tubes up his cock, into his veins, his nose.

She was wrapped like a mummy. I could spot the blistered skin around her bruised eyes. There would be no last word forgiving the son, who, instead of unraveling her cocoon, sewed her up tight.

I waited in a white lounge. I hadn't slept in thirty hours. Nothing seemed remarkable or dreadful. I sat on a black sofa. The lounge was so white I lost sight of its edges. Somewhere a generator throbbed, and the room pulsed like a heart. Intermittently a mechanical voice—unflappable despite the urgency of its summons—called Dr. Shapiro—pronounced with an *ai* as if the name contained a wail—and Dr. Klein.

There I sat—and from this late view, I can see that boy's future. He's not yet ancient, nonetheless at ten already permanent and unalterable—waiting on the couch, wearing a felt beanie, a black T-shirt, corduroys, tennies, weary, weary, weary, not offering any prayers for the dying, even wanting death to come so that he could be released from the couch, the white room, the nagging persistence of that raspy call for Klein and Shapiro.

Finally the red light above the operating room blinked on and off, a whorehouse beckoning, and the doctors emerged, wearing green surgical gowns and masks and caps. Klein delivered the news, too blasted after six hours of surgery to be solicitous.

"Be brave, sonny. We did our best."

No tears. No sign of panic. Someone said, "Brave young man." An older nurse, with a solid stance, accepting every enormity, even death, as natural, waited to console me. "Do you want to see your dad?" I didn't say yes, but she assumed yes and took my arm, ostensibly to support me, but directing me toward what I dreaded to see. She didn't offer me a sight of Mom, and that was more terrible. Into a room off the corridor, on an examination table beneath a sheet. I shook beneath her hand. She tightened her grip—to support me? To compel me? I closed my eyes, opened them to the dread thing. And it wasn't Dad. "It's not him!" He was gone. Vanished. Left that facsimile of himself behind, colorless, spiritless, eyes closed, mouth slackened, gray teeth showing. The gleeful, demonic man had vanished. Gone! She shook me to stop the laughing. "Gone!" He'd said, "Isn't it so?" as if he offered proof of the conspiracy that had sent him to a crazy house.

There was a reptile. I was close enough to see myself mirrored in its eyes. It left no tracks. No one else noticed. It seemed to have no more substance than the smoke from the Ford chimneys. But then neither did he leave any tracks.

One moment it had been a drab industrial outskirt of Detroit. We were among those Dearborn chimneys, which, like exclamation marks, stressed the boundaries of what we were enjoined to accept. A ravaged landscape, silos, flame in the background, the stench of metal, slag heaps, parking lots. A sullen Detroit dawn—no people, no traffic. Then Dad said, "Behold!" and all that dislocated stuff crystallized into something so vivid, so palpable, I could even smell the acid, seared-flesh odor of its gaping stone mouth. All of my senses affirmed the green-scaled reptile, claws held in brutal prayer, surveying my flight with lidless, indifferent eyes. It was a vision that for an instant linked me to my vanishing father.

I yelled, "Take me to the crazy house!" and didn't stop laughing until she raised me off my feet and commanded, "Stop it! Enough!" and shook me into grief.

I never forgave him that glimpse into his crazy world. I meant it never to be mine. I kept my eyes on the ground under my feet and hoped for walls that could house me.

Fast Drumming Ground

Author's Note

For most of a decade, from the mid-1980s to the mid-1990s, I lived on Bowen Island, in the mouth of Howe Sound, on the southern coast of British Columbia. In the midst of this period, I was away for most of a year, working in Western Europe and in Scotland, where I met with a good deal of colonial nostalgia. To celebrate my return to Bowen Island, I wrote this little essay.

The native language in Howe Sound is Squamish, a deeply endangered member of the Salish language family. It is not a language I have ever been able to speak, but I wanted, after a year away, to brush my teeth and tongue with some familiar Squamish syllables and to nourish my mind with some Squamish ideas. By accident, however, the essay was first published in Barcelona, where a mystified Catalan proofreader intermittently altered "Squamish" to "Spanish." A corrected version was published a bit later, on Bowen Island itself, first in a short-lived local journal and then in a small book, where my immediate neighbors could find it. I was startled to learn that, twenty years later on Oʻahu, Frank Stewart had found it and read it. But it is, I now remember, not just a story about a place but about a predicament: a story about the hazards of navigation in landscapes routinely misnamed as well as misused—and in which, now, we are all immediate neighbors.—*Quadra Island, 2010*

Home is alive, like a tree, not skinned and dressed or cut and dried like the quarried stone and milled wood that houses are made of, nor masticated and spat out like the particleboard and plywood used for packaging pre-fabricated lives. A house is not a home the way a mask is not a face. But a mask is not a mask if it can't be read as a metaphor for the face, and a house is not a house if it can't be seen as the mask of home. Home is the whole earth, everywhere and nowhere, but it always wears the masks of particular places, no matter how often it changes or moves.

Mine moves often, but like many hunter-gatherers, I also keep a cache and circle back to it every year. I keep it now on a little island in what used to be the Squamish country, north and west of the rich, new city of Vancouver—the third most populous city in the second most spacious country in

Horse (Uma): Soga no Gorō, from the series Heroes Representing the Twelve Animals of the Zodiac (Buyū mitate jūnishi)

Artist: Utagawa Kuniyoshi, 1797–1861
Publisher: Minatoya Kohei

Japanese, Edo period, about 1840 (Tenpō 11). Woodblock print (nishiki-e); ink and color on paper; chūtanzaku. Museum of Fine Arts, Boston. William Sturgis Bigelow Collection, 11.16583. Photograph © 2010 Museum of Fine Arts, Boston the world, though it is barely a century old. Things have changed that much that fast.

The old name, the Squamish name, for this overshadowed island is Xwlíl'xhwm: a stony protuberance of meaning cloaked in a forest of evergreen consonants which I think it is worth learning to pronounce.

Bowen Island, its English name, was given it by a Captain Richards, who charted the coast of southern British Columbia for the British Navy in 1859. His predecessor George Vancouver had already named the surrounding waters Howe Sound, to honor a British lord of the admiralty, Richard Howe—Black Dick, his sailors liked to call him. Howe earned geographical immortality, in the British Admiralty's view, on 1 June 1794, by defeating a French fleet in the English Channel—for which, of course, the French have a different name. The battle itself was known to British patriots as "the Glorious First of June." To the French it was the thirteenth day of the month of Prairial, Year II of the Republic, and merely one more in a series of disasters that beset the Girondin and Jacobin regimes. Names are not the only things that vary with your point of view.

Captain Richards picked up the theme, naming other features within Howe Sound after British officers and ships involved in the same battle. Rear-Admiral James Bowen was one whom Richards chose to memorialize. Gambier, Bowyer, and other nearby islands take their names from British officers who fought the French on the same day. Even Keats Island is named for a British admiral, not for the poet who wrote that "Heard melodies are sweet, but those unheard / Are sweeter," and that "true imagination…has no self; it is everything and nothing." The poet, but not the admiral, so far as we know, struggled all his life to learn to listen to the world, and to unlearn "the Wordsworthian or egotistical sublime."

I want the names with which I touch the land I live in to connect me to that land. What most of them do instead is record the means by which its former inhabitants were evicted and their long-lived cultures destroyed. The way names link us to the land is not through history, which is sectarian and time bound, but through myth, which works the other way around. History becomes myth when imagination edits it, and a glorified version of British military history was myth enough for Captains Vancouver and Richards. But the Glorious First of June is not the myth I want to relive as I cross Queen Charlotte Strait to Bowen Island and walk beneath the alder and red-cedar and hemlock and wild cherry, over the salmon stream and up along the deer trail that passes next to my door. Nor is it a myth I would like to bequeath to my neighbors or my children to relive. I think my friend the historian Calvin Martin is right when he says George Santayana was wrong: it is not those who forget history, it is instead those who *remember* it, who are compelled to go through it again.

Black Dick, Rear-Admiral Bowen, and the others were all, no doubt, fine sailors and honorable men. I'd admire them if I met them. I nevertheless find little nourishment in thinking about their illustrious careers. And I prefer to derive my excitement from some other source than a one-day battle in La Manche two centuries ago, no matter who beat whom. On a diet of British military history, no matter how subtle and brilliant the tactics, no matter how noble the soldiers and sailors, as the pride swells, the mind and spirit starve.

For perhaps ten thousand years, the fjord I live in was a living map of the universe to the Salish-speaking peoples who were born and died here. It was a self-renewing library of archetypal images and stories as well as a self-replenishing larder of food, building materials, clothing, and tools. It fed, sheltered, and exercised body and mind. Its place-names recorded the doings of Xhais, the transformer, who adjusted the world in such a way that no creature had too much power over another. Xhais, who could cut himself up and put himself back together again, often took the form of four brothers, shamans who sometimes altered themselves in turn into three human beings and a two-headed sealskin canoe. At other moments, they merged into one four-legged creature, usually a black bear.

The land was thick with other stories—not of distant struggles for money and power, but of the roots of being and time: how the Son of the Day emerged from a lake to marry the selfish shaman's daughter; how a man named Xwuch'tal' was roused on his wedding night at Stawamus to hunt the double-headed serpent, and how he made potent jewelry and weapons from its bones; how the Mosquito persuaded the Thunder that blood comes from wood instead of from flesh, which is why the lightning now strikes trees instead of people—and why my wisest neighbors never curse mosquitoes.

These islands now are a cemetery of names for admirals who never sailed into this country. Their only connection with it lies in the fact that their victory over the French helped to secure the money and power by which the British conducted their colonization of Canada, in the successful pursuit of further money and power. The slopes looking down on Howe Sound are mangy now with the scars of clear-cut logging. The waters are fouled with dioxins—leaving the prawns, crabs, and other crustaceans inedible—because of poisons discharged by the pulp mills fed by that logging. The shellfish contaminate other creatures in turn, from seabirds to whales. It is so because we continue to believe, as generations of eager colonists have believed, that the land is ours instead of us, that it is merely there for the taking.

How many names the island has had, over how many thousands of years of human habitation and migration through this area, is something we don't know, though we might begin to learn. The traces left by people living wisely in a land like this are slight, and not much archaeology has been done. In the meantime, I know what the island was called by those who lived here when Captain Richards visited and christened it for Rear-Admiral Bowen. The earlier name, Xwlíl'xhwm, is used even now by people who speak the Squamish language, and it will stand for all the other names the island has worn over the centuries, and for the nameless smells and shapes by which it is known to the herons and eagles and ravens and gulls to whom it is home. If spoken names are sweet, are unspoken ones still sweeter? One name is a slender thread, but this one leads to a real world. It leads to a world that is real in a way the present world isn't, even though that other world has vanished and this one seems to thrive.

I call that world real because, through all its changes, it remained essentially self-sustaining instead of self-destructive. Its last transformation began when the Europeans arrived with too many answers and too few questions, and began to plant their flags. But I have a hunch that if this world lives, it will have to be by including among its models the very worlds it deliberately destroyed.

Xwlíl'xhwm means "fast drumming ground." Charles Hill-Tout, an English physician who lived in Vancouver and worked throughout southwestern British Columbia as an amateur archaeologist and ethnologist, heard the name from his Squamish acquaintances in the 1890s. Louis Miranda, one of the last not only fluent but eloquent speakers, and perhaps the only writer, in the Squamish language, taught the same name to a linguist named Aert Hendrik Kuipers in the 1960s.[1] The root is *lixhw,* which means "to beat rapidly." The *x* is a sound like the *ch* in the German word *ich.* The *w* is a swallowed round vowel, an *o* that is never let out of the bag. The second syllable, *líl',* has a long accented vowel, like the *ee* in *peel,* and a glottal stop at the end—like the little catch in the throat that begins each syllable in the English expression of worry, *uh-oh.* The *xh* is like the *ch* in the German *Bach* or the Scottish *loch*—farther back in the throat than the *x* at the beginning. Add another suppressed round vowel, then *m,* and you'll have it: *xwlíl'xhwm.*

Kwum'shnam is the Squamish name for Hood Point, at the northeast end of Xwlíl'xhwm; it means "thumping feet." Passage Island, just southeast of Xwlíl'xhwm, was called Smetlmetlel'ch. The old name for Gambier Island seems to be lost, though we still have the names for some of its bays and the seasonal village, St'ap'as, that stood on its northwest shore. Anvil Island was Tlaxwm. When Captain Vancouver rechristened it, naming it for its shape, there were plenty of knowledgeable Squamish still around, but questions like "What is your name for that island?" and "What does the name mean?" evidently never entered his mind. If they did, they must have seemed too much trouble to ask.

Many of the old names for the mountains around the fjord have vanished too. Miranda remembered that Mount Garibaldi was called Ta Nch'qai', "the grimy one," in summer, but he did not tell Kuipers, and no one has told me, its winter name.

Ch'axhai' was the name for what is now called Horseshoe Bay. It was a village once, with a small and beautiful harbor. As all Bowen Islanders know, it's a ferry terminal now, primarily chain-link fence and asphalt, where thousands of travelers seeking nourishment and news are confronted by banks of silent machines dispensing junk paper and junk food. Each time I pass through it, I think of the color, the talk, the fresh, hot, homemade food, and the anthology of faces in a hundred marketplaces and quayside lanes in South America, Africa, Asia, even in Europe—wherever the preindustrial world is still permitted to spill through the fences. Though the population was small, that iridescent complexity greeted the first white visitors to the Squamish country too. In the name of efficiency, safety, privacy—all the synonyms of control—where we might have enriched it, we have chased it out and closed it down.

Q'iq'lxhn was the name of a fishing site on the other side of the Sound. Now it's the largest single source of pollutants in the local air and water. It's the site of the pulp mill at Port Mellon.

"Do they eat gold?" the Inca asked, watching the Spaniards stripping the temples. And the Squamish, when they saw Vancouver and his sailors, in 1792, said, *'U 'iu'aiti stiwaqin 'ia'wit, nitlch' mukwtnswit tiwa, wetl mnhwismatl ti s'atsuswit 'i'usxwixwi'.* "Maybe these are the dead, and those are their burial clothes, since only their faces are visible."[2]

Passage Island, Smetlmetlel'ch, is, I think, where the Xhais brothers were welcomed into the Squamish country. Far upstream on the Squamish River, they were bid farewell. And every episode in the never-quite-finished epic of creation was mapped onto someplace in between. Xwlíl'xhwm, I think, is where they created the Deer, Gambier where they created the Great Blue Heron, and Anvil Island, Tlaxwm, where the eldest brother snared the Sun. But there is no right and wrong distribution of stories. We can be sure the old storytellers themselves did not all agree on the sequence of episodes, nor the site of each episode. Even in an oral culture, the books move around on the shelves.

When the brothers first came to the country, things were too homogeneous. Perhaps, in fact, things were rather like they are now. The animals were indistinguishable one from another, like shrink-wrapped meat or the contents of tins. But they weren't dismembered and packaged. They simply hadn't been given their different forms. So they all looked like animals do when they're skinned. They looked like humans. The brothers themselves were disguised as three humans and a sealskin canoe. When they came ashore on Xwlíl'xhwm, they met a man who was sharpening a bone.

"What are you up to?" they asked.

"Making arrow points," said the man. "I've heard that someone is coming to change us. When he arrives, I intend to kill him."

"It's true," said the brothers, seizing the man. "Someone is coming."

They pulled at his ears, his arms, his neck, his jowls, and stretched and squeezed his fingers and toes. They twisted his hips up and his shoulders down. Then they planted two pieces of driftwood on his head and clapped their hands to chase him off. He became the Deer, but he ran so fast the brothers feared he could never be caught. They chased him all the way to Kwum'shnam, where they caught him and knocked his hoofs together to slow him down. And they thrust the bone he had been working on into his foot, where it remains, the deer's astragalus bone, which looks like a half-worked spearpoint. Then they chased him away again.

"That will do," they said. "He is slow enough now, but not too slow." Then they went on.

Crossing to Cha'lkwnach, one of the south-facing bays on Gambier Island, they met an old man fishing with a two-pronged spear. That is to say, he appeared to be fishing, but he was not really spearing his fish. He was rubbing the head of his spear against the bodies of the fish, then wiping the slime off the spear with moss and putting the moss and fish slime into his basket, letting the fish themselves swim off.

One of the brothers produced a barbed point and fixed it to the old man's spear, then speared a fish and held it up in front of the old man's eyes.

"Grandfather, this is the proper way to fish," said the brothers.

"Don't tell me what to do," the old man answered. "I prefer the slime."

"That is not how it ought to be, Grandfather," they said.

The brothers broke his spear in two and stuck the two halves to his legs. They stretched his neck, glued feathers to his hands, and fastened the spearpoint to his face, in place of his nose. Then they clapped their hands, and the old man rose unsteadily into the air. The brothers called him the Great Blue Heron.

They kept on paddling, and when they landed under a steep bluff on Tlaxwm, the youngest resumed his human form. There the four built a house near the mouth of a stream.

"I want to talk to the Sun," said the eldest brother. "I'm going to snare him."

That morning, he tied a line around the legs of his youngest brother, who turned himself into a salmon and danced in the stream. Not long after that, the Sun came down in the form of an eagle. Sound asleep in the heat of the sun, the three older brothers saw nothing and heard nothing. The eagle made off with the salmon, snapping the line.

When the three brothers awoke in the cool of the evening, the eldest refused to allow any grieving. During the night, he braided a heavier cedar-bark line. Next morning he tied it to the ankles of his second youngest brother, who leaped into the sea as a harbor seal.

The Sun came down again that day at noon in the form of an eagle, sinking his talons into the seal's back. The two older brothers slept in the heat of the day, and the eagle flew off with the seal, stretching and snapping the line.

Once again, the eldest brother sat up all night braiding a line. He finished the thick cord late that morning and tied it to the ankles of his one remaining brother, who threw himself into the sea in the form of a porpoise.

That day at noon, the eagle descended again, and as the eldest brother slept in the great heat, the eagle of the sun flew off, clutching his prey, stretching and snapping the heavy line.

That night, the eldest brother braided yet another cord and tied it to his own feet. When morning came, he slid into the sea, taking the form of a killer whale.

Noon came, and the Sun came down in the form of an eagle, sinking his talons into the whale's back. The eagle flapped his wings, but nothing happened. The whale was too heavy to lift. Then the whale took the eagle under the waves.

"Could we have a little chat now?" asked the whale.

"We could," said the eagle.

They returned to the surface, where Xhais and the Sun both took their human forms. Then they entered the house of the four brothers.

"What I want to know," Xhais said, "is where the salmon come from."

"A long way over there," the Sun said, pointing west with his luminous hand. "Where rainbow-colored smoke rises over the houses."

"How do I go there?" Xhais asked.

"Take the leaves of all the trees," the Sun said. "Take the roots of all the plants, the feathers of all the birds, and the bones of all the animals. That is the medicine you will need."

The Sun resumed his eagle form and flew up through the clouds. And Xhais collected everything, just as the Sun had said. Then he set off.

He paddled west for days, to where the sea is covered with floating charcoal, then to the place where the sea is covered with foam. Days after that, he saw smoke in all the colors of the rainbow rising to the clouds. Beneath the smoke was a line of houses.

The headman of the town was called Chinook Salmon. When Xhais arrived, Chinook Salmon called four of his villagers: two men and two women.

"Swim to the trap," he said. And the four of them stepped into the creek, turning to salmon as soon as their faces entered the water. Swimming upstream, they were caught in the trap behind the headman's house. And the villagers gaffed them, cleaned them, cut them, and roasted them over the fire.

Xhais saw how the villagers buried the guts of the fish when they were cleaned, and how they set the flesh to cook by the fire. He shared in the feast, and he saw how the villagers gathered the skin and bones after the meal, and how they scattered them like the ashes of the dead on the water of the stream. Next morning, the four villagers who had turned into salmon and been eaten reappeared. But Xhais had kept a rib from the fish he had eaten. And one of the four who reappeared that morning had an open wound in his chest. He was moaning in pain.

Xhais went to the stream and lay his salmon bone down on the water. When he turned back to the village, he saw that the wounded one had been healed.

"Let me invite you to visit my country," Xhais said. And he gave Chinook Salmon a leaf from every tree, a root from every plant, a feather from every bird, and a bone from every animal that lives in the Squamish country. Every year since then, the salmon have come. Most years, all five families of the salmon people come: the Chinook, the Sockeye, the Coho, the Dog, and finally the Pink. But even in the old days, the Pinks and the Dogs were sometimes mistreated and failed to return.

"Also, I need directions," Xhais said, "to the house of the Sun, where my brothers were taken."

"Go with the mouse, the louse, and the flea," the Salmon said. "They know the way to the house of the Sun, and they know what to do when you arrive."

Xhais set off with these three for companions, over the mountains of white cloud and the ocean of air. They arrived at the Sun's house in the evening.

"The Sun will see you and hear you and smell you," said the mouse. "You should wait out here."

The mouse and the louse and the flea went under the door as soon as the Sun lay down for the night, and they kept him awake until morning. At dawn, when they let him alone, he fell into a deep sleep, and the house shook with his snoring. Then they opened the door to Xhais. And Xhais entered the Sun's house and gathered his dead brothers' bones.

He returned to this country. When he arrived, he covered his brothers' bones with a quilt of feathers and leaves. And after the Sun had passed through the sky four times, and the eldest brother had danced on the beach for four days, the quilt stirred and his younger brothers revived.

They continued up the Sound, changing one thing and another. Long ago they could still be seen, rearranging the mountains and snowfields around the upper reaches of the rivers.

There was a chapter in the story, once, for every animal important in the Squamish world, and for every cove and bay and cliff on every island and both shores of the Sound. The people who fished and travelled and lived in this fjord relived as they did so, day by day, an epic of creation and an ethic of interdependence, instead of reviewing Lord Howe's and Rear-Admiral Bowen's claims to military glory. No one ever told the story all at once, and maybe no one knew it all, but as each storyteller's knowledge of the world he lived in deepened, his story deepened too.

Some of the story—crucial as the missing salmon bone—is lost now, though its niche in the ecology is real. In time—when the canned meat and the frozen pizzas run out—replacement stories will evolve, if there is still a living watershed here for stories to evolve in. I know a few new ones even now, about another transformer called White Man, who split not into four but into millions of little white men, all of them busily rearranging the world. In one version I've heard, they kept rearranging the world more and more thoroughly, faster and faster, until there was simply no world left, only metal and plastic and petrochemicals and sand. In another, they changed it around until nothing quite worked anymore, and when that had happened, they soon got bored and wandered off.

Then the world sat there, homogenized, stunned, until one day a black bear wandered down from the Coast Mountains and tried to start a few conversations with rusting automobiles and empty junk-food machines. He found they had nothing to say and weren't good to eat either, so he decided to rearrange and rename things. He changed himself into three human brothers and one canoe, they say, and started up the Sound.

For those of us whose tongues come from Western Europe—even if the rest of our bodies were born in North America—the old name for the island is more difficult to spell than Bowen Island, and more difficult to say. It won't make the real estate move more briskly or increase the tourist flow. It isn't enough, by itself, even to make us think very much about the people who used to live here and the way they used to live. But I prefer it. It reminds me of something I know I need to know.

NOTES

1. There are still speakers of Squamish living only a few miles from Bowen Island, with plenty to teach to those who are willing to learn. The best printed source is Aert Kuipers, *The Squamish Language* (The Hague: Mouton, 1967). Hill-Tout had more fluent speakers of Squamish to talk to than Kuipers did, but far less skill at recording what he heard. His "Notes on the Sk·qō'mic of British Columbia" are published as an appendix to *Report 70 of the British Association for the Advancement of Science* (London, 1900). This article is partially reprinted in Charles Hill-Tout, *The Salish People,* vol. 2, edited by Ralph Maud (Vancouver: Talonbooks, 1978)—but there the Squamish spellings are haphazardly simplified from Hill-Tout's already dubious versions.

2. Here again the source is Louis Miranda, in conversation with Aert Kuipers.

THOM VAN DOOREN

Vultures and Their People in India: Equity and Entanglement in a Time of Extinctions

In conversations about vultures in India, people have often recounted to me having seen large numbers gathered along the banks of rivers, consuming the dead bodies of cattle and other animals, including sometimes people, as they float by or wash up on the water's edge. When a carcass meets a vulture's beak, it matters very little if this flesh, this meat, was once a human or some other kind of animal. In fact, numerous human societies throughout history—including present-day Parsee communities in India, and Buddhists in Tibet and elsewhere—utilise exposure to vultures as the most appropriate way of "taking care" of their dead (Schuz and Konig 1983; Subramanian 2008; van Dooren 2010). I am interested in the dynamics and practicalities of eating and being eaten in multispecies communities, but for the moment I would like to remain with the vultures on the banks on the Ganges and other rivers in India. Unlike most other scavengers, the vultures are "obligate" scavengers. This means that they do not opportunistically alternate between predation and scavenging (like their mammalian counterparts), but rather rely *exclusively* on finding animal carcasses. A vulture's whole body is oriented and adapted towards this method of food procurement and the lifestyle that accompanies it. In fact, Ruxton and Houston have even argued that it may have been in the developments of the large bodies and specialisations for efficient soaring flight—which are essential to being a successful avian scavenger—that vultures lost the flying accuracy, agility, and maneuverability necessary to kill prey (2004).

However it evolved, scavenging has been a very successful way of life for vultures for a long time. While the fossil record is poor, it seems that in the "Old World" vultures have been around for over 20 million years. The genus *Gyps*, to which the vast majority of the vultures in India belong, probably arrived on the scene sometime in the last few million years (Houston 2009; Rich 1983).

But while scavenging has been evolutionarily successful for vultures, it is arguably not the most attractive way of getting a meal. It seems fair to say that vultures are a little bit gross. The *Gyps* species that occur in India live

*Rooster (Niwatori): Actor Kawarazaki Gonjūrō I
as Danshichi, from the series A Collection of Birds
(Tori zukushi)*

Artist: Utagawa Kunisada I (Toyokuni III), 1786–1864
Publisher: Ōtaya Takichi (Hori Takichi)

Japanese, Edo period, 1860 (Ansei 7/Man'en 1), 8th month.
Woodblock print (nishiki-e); ink and color on paper; vertical ōban.
Museum of Fine Arts, Boston. William Sturgis Bigelow Collection,
11.29935. Photograph © 2010 Museum of Fine Arts, Boston

primarily in colonies, usually of twenty to thirty birds, but sometimes in excess of one hundred; they often roost as close as possible to dumps or slaughterhouses, build their nests in tall trees or on cliff ledges, and line their nests with wool, skin, dung, and rubbish (Ferguson-Lees and Christie 2001:422–428).

While many animals scavenge food when it is available, few have taken to scavenging with the focus and vigor of the vultures. According to Dean Amadon, few other scavengers "will compete with vultures for badly decomposed remains" (1983:ix). Inhabiting an environment in which food is often less than "fresh," it is no wonder that vultures possess a high level of resistance to various pathogens and diseases (Houston and Cooper 1975).[1] According to Amadon, "it has been reported that vultures can, without ill effect, consume the viruses of such deadly pathogens as anthrax in such quantities as would fell an ox—or a whole heard of oxen" (1983:ix).

But something is now poisoning vultures and threatening to cause their extinction in India and throughout the surrounding region. Over the past two decades vultures have been dying en masse, largely as a result of their being unintentionally poisoned by a drug called diclofenac. Diclofenac is widely administered to cattle in India to treat inflammation and other conditions. When the cattle die, however, vultures often consume their carcasses. In vulture bodies, diclofenac causes painful swelling, inflammation, and eventually kidney failure and death. Today, it is thought that approximately 97 percent of the three main species of vulture in India are gone (Prakash et al. 2007; Swan et al. 2006b). The discovery that vultures were disappearing entered the scientific literature through the work of Vibhu Prakash of the Bombay Natural History Society (BNHS) (Prakash 1999). Since Prakash's findings, the BNHS in collaboration with the Royal Society for the Protection of Birds in the UK and the Zoological Society of London have been conducting further research on the vulture decline. Together, these organisations have also established several conservation and breeding centres in India. The hope is that one day, when the threat of diclofenac is gone and there is a large enough captive population for the birds to be able to sustain themselves in the wild, the vultures might be able to be released. Whether this will ever happen, however, remains an open question.

Between Death and Life
(There Is Sometimes a Vulture)

It is strange for an animal so closely associated with death—albeit usually the deaths of others—to be itself on the way to extinction. Like many other people throughout history, and around the world, vultures seem to me to be a kind of liminal creature, inhabiting a space somehow strangely between life and death. Perhaps it is because they appear to sense death, often arriving before it occurs (a skill acquired at least in part through good vision, the ability to search far and wide, and a close, communicative observation of other vultures) (Jackson, Ruxton, and Houston 2008). Or maybe it is because they consume the dead and then soar high up into the sky (Houston 2001:51).

The deathly association and liminality that interests me, however, is the vulture's ability to "twist" death back into life (Rose 2006). My thinking here is situated within the kind of ecological context that Deborah Bird Rose and Val Plumwood have outlined. They remind us that death must not be thought about as a simple ending, but rather as something completely central to the ongoing life of multispecies communities, in which we are all ultimately food for one another (Plumwood 2007).

In this context, vultures are at the heart of life and death's transformative processes. But instead of *taking life* for their nourishment, they consume only that which is *already dead*, pulling dead flesh back into processes of nourishment and growth. Alongside the insects, bacteria, fungi, and other organisms that also make their living breaking down the dead, vultures, I suspect, have a special place in life's heart. I can't help but think here about Jean-Luc Nancy's beautiful injunction not to separate life from death: "to isolate death from life—not leaving each one intimately woven into the other, with each one intruding upon the other's core [*coeur*]—this is what one must never do" (Nancy 2002:5). Vultures understand this intimate entanglement of life and death. I think that they would appreciate Nancy's sentiment, and be in wholehearted agreement with Georges Bataille when he noted that "life is a product of putrefaction, and it depends on both death and the dungheap" (Botting and Wilson 1997:242).

Understood in this way, death positions all organisms (including humans, a point that shouldn't have to be made, but unfortunately often does), as parts of a broader multispecies community. Possibilities for life and death, for everyone, get worked out inside these entangled processes of "becoming-with" (Haraway 2008). That we can live at all, but also that we live in the *ways* in which we do, are the results of our specific situatedness in a more-than-human world—the biological and the social, the material and the discursive, alongside the living and the dead. All are mixed together in the formation of what have come to be (and to count as) bodies, societies, religions, cultures, and ecologies. In India, the interactions of people, vultures, and others highlight some of these tangled processes of becoming, as well as the specific ways, with death and life at stake, in which we are bound up with and exposed to other beings in a time of increasing environmental change.

Entangled Becomings

Three main species of vulture make their homes in Asia, and all three are of the genus *Gyps*: the oriental white-backed vulture (*G. bengalensis*), the long-billed vulture (*G. indicus*), and the slender-billed vulture (*G. tenuirostris*). In the first half of the twentieth century, these species could be found in large numbers right across Southeast Asia, throughout the Indian Subcontinent, and into Pakistan. During the second half of that century, however, populations began to disappear throughout the eastern part of this range (Southeast Asia). The causes of this population decline are not known with certainty, but perhaps the most significant factor was the loss of reliable food sources. This loss likely occurred as a result of both the collapse of wild ungulate populations (through uncontrolled, unregulated hunting), and changes in the husbandry of domestic animals. In addition, indiscriminate persecution of vultures by humans is thought to have affected their numbers, as did poisoning and habitat loss in some local areas (Pain et al. 2003:661–662). While there are still some small remaining pockets of vultures in Cambodia and perhaps Laos and Vietnam, today *Gyps* vultures are considered to be extinct in most of Southeast Asia (Pain et al. 2003).

In the face of these local extinctions, India has been one of the last strongholds for several species of vulture. Throughout most of the second half of the twentieth century, during this period of species decline in Southeast Asia, life was good for vultures in India. In 1985, Indian *Gyps* populations were still so large that some speculated that the oriental white-backed vulture was "possibly the most abundant large bird of prey in the world" (Pain et al. 2003:661). In India, these interactions of people, vultures, and others highlight some of these tangled processes of becoming, as well as the life and death stakes of the specific ways in which we are bound up with and exposed to others in a time of increasing environmental change. Certainly, vultures on the subcontinent benefited from the fact that India is one of the most cattle-rich countries in the world; more important, from a vulture's perspective, however, is the fact that most of India's cows are not consumed by local people. Hindu reverence for cattle, alongside a more general ethos of *ahimsa* (or nonviolence towards all living things), has produced a unique and complex cultural and religious environment, in which most Indians do not eat beef and many are vegetarian (although Muslims and a growing number of Hindus in fact eat sheep, goats, and other animals—including sometimes beef [Robbins 1998]).[2]

Cattle are used in India predominantly for plowing, milking, and as beasts of burden, and their dung is widely used as fuel and fertilizer (Robbins 1998:226). When they die, cows are usually either taken to carcass dumps or left at the edge of villages, often after being skinned for leather (Singh 2003). By and large, however, it is vultures that have been relied upon each year to "take care of" the carcasses of an estimated five to ten million cows, camels, and buffalos:

> As many as 100 vultures may feed on a single cow carcass, stripping it clean in 30 minutes. Two thousand, 3,000, even 10,000 vultures swarmed the larger dumps in the early 1990s, the huge birds lapping at carcasses with their leathery

tongues, thrusting their narrow heads neck-deep to reach internal organs, tussling over choice gobbets of meat (McGrath 2007).

Historically, vultures have often lived quite closely with human populations in India. In urban and semi-urban environments, they found abundant food in carcass dumps, as well as in tanneries, slaughter yards, garbage dumps, and bone mills (where, before they were crushed for use in fertilizers, the bones would be picked clean). It was not just vultures that benefited from this association. These industries, along with the local communities, gained a free and efficient means of carcass disposal for the millions of cows that they kept but did not eat (as well as the waste products from numerous other kinds of animals). Consuming the dead is, of course, what vultures do. In taking up this role, they also helped to stem the spread of contamination and disease (such as anthrax, which is endemic in parts of India). When they have lived closely with people, especially in urban environments, vultures have provided an incredibly valuable service to humans. Understandably, this symbiotic exchange has provided an ideal situation for people and vultures to live side by side. Writing in 1983, Robert B. Grubh noted that: "Where a regular food supply exists, it is a familiar sight to see 200 to 400 [vultures] sitting crowded on trees or on rooftops in the vicinity" (108).

This close entanglement of vultures and people in India is made all the more remarkable when contrasted with other places around the world where *Gyps* vultures have little association with human populations. In east Africa, for example, people understandably do not make meat available to vultures. In fact, they often shoot vultures—especially the larger vulture species—when they get too close to towns and cities (Houston 2001, 2009).

Critically endangered Indian white-backed vultures (Gyps bengalensis). Courtesy © Lip Kee.

In addition to food availability, this contrast with Africa points to another important difference in the direct treatment of vultures by people. In India, vultures are far less likely to face the persecution that has afflicted them in so many other parts of the world—not just Africa and Southeast Asia, but also Europe and the Americas (Ferguson-Lees and Christie 2001). In contrast, aspects of Hinduism and social life in India are decidedly positive toward vultures. For example, vultures are associated with the Hindu vulture king Jatayu, who is a compassionate hero in the epic Ramayana (Baral et al. 2007:151).

But India is anything but a monolithic cultural landscape. While it is beyond the scope of this paper to consider the diverse range of relationships with vultures around the country, it is important to mention the small Parsee community (centred in Mumbai). For hundreds of years, Parsees in India have laid their dead out in *dakhmas* (or Towers of Silence), to be consumed by vultures, in the belief that dead flesh pollutes fire, water, and air—all of which are sacred to Ahura Mazda (Subramanian 2008; Williams 1997:158). This Parsee practice provides a wonderfully rich acknowledgement and reminder of the place of human flesh in multispecies nourishment. Of course, Parsees and vultures don't need to be told that humans are edible. Some members of the Parsee community were so committed to the role of vultures in taking care of the dead that when vulture numbers at Towers of Silence started to decline, they proposed setting up a small captive population in an aviary to continue the process.

While I have offered here only a handful of general examples from the diverse history of human/vulture interactions, it is clear that India has provided a somewhat unique environment for these birds. It is tempting to view this as a situation in which humans "accommodated" vultures, making room for them within their communities. In reality, however, generations of *Gyps* vultures stretch back several million years, into the deep past of the Indian Subcontinent. They were there well before human habitation—before humans even emerged as a species. Vultures likely evolved in close relationship with wild migratory ungulate species, such as blackbuck, which were abundant until the arrival of people and domestic animals (Houston 1983, 2009). Only later did vultures associate with human communities. While it is certainly true that Indians have held open spaces for vultures in ways that other cultures around the world have not, it is also true that the people of India—along with their cultural and religious practices—emerged and took shape in a land already inhabited by vultures. Together, vultures, people, cattle, and others produced a unique environment in which food was made readily available for vultures; in turn, people were provided with a reliable and inexpensive means of disposing of the dead—this being particularly important for people who kept an abundance of cattle, which they did not eat. In fact, one wonders how the cattle-keeping practices that have emerged in India in company with Hinduism would have looked, or perhaps even been possible, in the absence of these dedicated scavengers.

Proximity and "Double Death"
                                    But now these vultures are dying. In an age of diclofenac, cattle and human bodies often no longer provide nourishment; vultures are no longer able to twist their deaths back into life. Instead, dead bodies are now poisoning vultures, producing more and more death. At the Parsee Towers of Silence, the vulture decline seems to have begun in the 1970s, perhaps due to factors including urban growth in Bombay/Mumbai and an abundance of other food sources (Houston 2009), but perhaps also because in the 1960s humans began to take diclofenac as a medication; thus the first birds to be effected would likely have been those that fed at the Towers of Silence. But, the more recent widespread use of diclofenac to treat cattle has been a far more serious problem for vultures. Diclofenac is used to treat any number of conditions in cattle, including lameness, mastitis, and difficult birthing (Cunningham, 11 Sept 2008;[3] Swan et al. 2006a:0395). While human use of diclofenac might have been catastrophic for a captive population of vultures at a Tower of Silence—one of the reasons why some scientists withdrew their support for the project—the use of the drug in cattle is far more significant for the overall collapse of vulture populations in India.

Importantly, the use of diclofenac in treating cattle is often driven by poverty, and the need to keep animals working even when they are old and sick.

> If an animal is going sick, is going downhill, they want to get the most out of the animal…So you just pump pain killers and anti-inflammatories into it, to keep it going as long as possible…and that's probably why such a high level of carcasses do have detectable levels of diclofenac (Cunningham, 11 Sept 2008).

Here, poverty emerges explicitly in this essay for the first time as a central theme in the unfolding of vulture-human relationships in India today—and I will return to the topic below. In the emergence of cattle carcasses toxic to vultures, we encounter the negative side to the proximity and entanglement between people and vultures. The close association that had been mutually advantageous has now become a liability. Domesticated cattle once provided a great food source for vultures; but this reliance on livestock kept by humans may now lead to the vultures' extinction. In other parts of the world where diclofenac and other similarly toxic anti-inflammatories (Cuthbert et al. 2007) are widely used—for example in east Africa—*Gyps* vultures have not been impacted by the drug like their Indian counterparts, largely because they haven't struck up a similar relationship with people, so their diet includes a greater portion of wild animals (Cunningham, 11 Sept 2008).

Similarly, the entanglement and close proximity of people and vultures in India has become a liability for human communities. In their absence, it has been made all too clear how important a role vultures played, through the consumption of the dead, in creating an environment in which the unfolding and flourishing of so much other life could occur. Drawing on Rose's work, my position is that, in India, vultures and other species are being drawn into a kind of "double death" (2006). For Rose, this concept describes a situation in which life's connectivities are unmade, with disastrous consequences for a whole ecological community. In one story that Rose tells, Australia's dingoes are prime examples of this kind of tragedy: having been baited with 1080 poison, dingoes remain toxic even after death, so that their carcasses poison any creatures that feed on them. Here again, death cannot be twisted back into life, and instead "starts piling up corpses in the land of the living" (Rose 2006:75). Rose explores the ramifications of this kind of death work among the Aboriginal people of Yarralin (for whom dingo is kin) and their more-than-human community.

The mass death of vultures occurring in India today is producing a similar process of double death. In an environment in which dead bodies, en masse, poison rather than nourish, the absence of so many vultures has left a vast number of carcasses unscavenged—literally "piling up corpses in the land of the living" (Rose 2006:75). The disappearance of so many members of a single species produces what ecologists call a "functional extinction," one that will most likely be followed by a complete extinction in coming years. When vultures no longer inhabit the places and take up the relationships that they once did, the connectivities that made life possible in their habitats are "unmade." And as a result, a "doubling" of death has been set in motion in which all of those whose lives and well-being are entangled with vultures are drawn into a process of intensified suffering and death. Here, proximity and connectivity become a liability, but in a way that highlights some of the inequalities of life, in which poorer nations and in particular poorer communities within them are more readily exposed to harm.

As previously noted, by consuming decomposing and sometimes disease-laden bodies, vultures remove sources of potential contamination of soils and waterways, while also helping to prevent the spread of pathogenic organisms (Houston and Cooper 1975). With digestive systems that routinely process "foods" that even the most adventurous of others would not touch, vultures are very well positioned to clean up disease threats. As noted above, the ability of vultures to thoroughly consume toxic carcasses may have helped to contain anthrax in India. When an animal dies of anthrax, the spores of the disease can leach out into the soil where they can remain for decades; the spores can also be spread by wind and in the guts of other animals. In the past, vultures have tended to clean off all soft tissue within hours of an animal's death, before the anthrax bacteria have time to form spores and spread (Houston and Cooper 1975; Cunningham, 11 Sept 2008). In the absence of vultures, there are fears that anthrax may become a more significant health problem—especially in India's southern states, where the disease remains endemic (Vijaikumar, Devinder, and Karthikeyan 2002). With 70 percent of India's population living in rural communities, and the majority dependent on livestock for their livelihoods, a huge number of people are potentially at risk of infection (Devinder and Karthikeyan 2001).[4]

But anthrax is not the end of this story. In the absence of vultures, it is thought that available cattle carcasses in India may be encouraging population increases of fast-breeding scavengers, such as dogs and rats.[5] While dogs consume cattle carcasses, they don't do so with anywhere near the speed or thoroughness that the vultures once did. As a result, they do not provide the same effective containment of diseases such as anthrax, and putrefying carcasses are increasingly left to contaminate waterways and the environment generally.

In addition, large increases in dog populations bring another set of problems. According to a 2004 study conducted by the Association for the Prevention and Control of Rabies in India (and sponsored by the United Nations' World Heath Organization), approximately 17 million people in India are bitten by dogs each year, or roughly one person every two seconds (APCRI 2004:44). Nationwide, the vast majority of the victims belong to "poor" or "low-income" economic groups (75 percent), and in rural areas the consequences fall especially heavily on these poorer groups (80.3 percent) (APCRI 2004:25).

While dog attacks are by themselves significant, dogs in India are also the primary vector for the transmission of rabies to humans, accounting for approximately 96 percent of all transmissions (APCRI 2004:44). There are, therefore, fears that the incidence of rabies in India may be beginning to climb as a result of the increasing number of dogs. It is estimated that already 60 percent of the world's rabies deaths occur in India—approximately 25,000 to 30,000 per year, or one death every thirty minutes (APCRI 2004:44). While vaccinations are available for rabies, and seem to be reaching many people, the total number of deaths from rabies are decreasing only slightly—perhaps due to the enormous number of people being exposed to the disease in recent years (Markandya et al. 2008:199; Menezes 2008:564). It should not be forgotten that rabies causes a horrifically painful death. According to the British Medical Association's (BMA) guide to the disease: "Once clinical symptoms of rabies appear, there is no known cure and the victim is virtually certain to die an agonizing and terrifying death" (BMA 1995:13).

Like anthrax and dog attacks, rabies does not affect all social groups equally. The aforementioned 2004 study, conducted by the Association for the Prevention and Control of Rabies in India, concluded that not only are more people from "poor" or "low-income" socioeconomic groups bitten, these groups account for 87.6 percent of the people killed by rabies (APCRI 2004:16). In addition, most of the victims are adult males, and the study noted that their deaths frequently place additional economic hardships on families (APCRI 2004:16).

It should also be remembered that rabies does not only affect humans; the disease is often transmitted to a variety of other animals, and ultimately leads to painful deaths for many of them, including millions of street dogs.

The mass death of vultures is also having economic impacts on yet another particularly vulnerable group of India's poorest individuals. Often referred to simply as "bone collectors," these people have traditionally made their living by gathering the dried bones of cattle and selling them to the fertilizer industry. In the absence of vultures, these bones are now often incompletely scavenged, requiring either extended periods of time before collection or for people to clean the bones themselves (Markandya et al. 2008:195–196).

And so it is clear that while all humans are bound up in ecological relationships inside a multispecies world, we are not all entangled in the same ways. Those who are most directly dependent on vultures will suffer most and be lost first; in India specifically, this means the rural and the poor. But the plight of Indians is by no means exceptional. Drawing on case studies from around the world, the 2005 *Millennium Ecosystem Assessment* highlights the fact that ecosystem degradation and biodiversity loss will often disproportionately impact poor and rural communities worldwide (the poor and rural very often being one and the same) (MEA 2005:3). These groups tend to be directly dependent on their local environments for the provision of "ecosystem services," such as the carcass disposal provided by vultures, or in other cases food and clean drinking water. When these environments are disturbed, these people lack the buffer that markets provide for the wealthy, who are often simply able to purchase goods and services from further afield, or to purchase a substitute.

In addition, the MEA notes that "ecosystem changes have played a significant role in the emergence or resurgence of several infectious diseases in humans" (MEA 2005:27–28). Similarly, when this happens, these communities are more likely to lack the basic resources of life, as well as access to medical services that would treat disease or prevent it from becoming established in their communities.

Vulnerabilities of various kinds emerge as a feature of the specific ways in which we are entangled in our multispecies world; some people are diffusely entangled, while others are bound up tightly in relationships with *specific* nonhuman and local ecologies (and thus highly exposed to changes or disturbances).[6] In a time of extinctions, these interconnections produce a broader category of often disregarded lives—both human and nonhuman—that are being pulled into amplified patterns of loss and suffering.

Conclusion

Before the numbers began to decline drastically, vulture species in Asia and the Indian subcontinent were very well adapted to their role as scavengers. As throughout the rest of the world, they developed feeding specialisations which effectively divided carcasses up—a situation that greatly helps to reduce competition when large numbers descend on a single carcass. Scientists often classify vulture species into three feeding groups, colourfully referred to as "tearers," "pullers," and "peckers" (Konig 1983). Put simply, "tearer" species have powerful beaks for opening carcasses; "peckers" have more slender skulls and beaks, ideal for picking out small particles of food and separating meat from bone. Like all *Gyps*, the main species of vultures being poisoned in India are "pullers." These are perhaps the most stereotypical vultures, reaching their long, agile, feather-free heads and necks deep into a carcass to pull out the viscera and soft flesh. Because these components of a carcass offer the richest source of food, *Gyps* make up by far the majority of the vulture population throughout the Old World, usually comprising around 90 percent. In India, however, this number has traditionally been closer to 99 percent (Houston 1983:136), perhaps largely because the need for "tearer" species has been undermined by an ongoing entanglement with humans who "open" carcasses when they remove the skin for leather.

The dominance of *Gyps* vultures in India has only added to the tragedy of the prospect of their extinction. Physiological responses of bird species to anti-inflammatory drugs like diclofenac are generally not well understood. In recent years, however, there has been some suggestion that non-*Gyps* species of vulture and other scavenging birds in India may not be impacted upon by the presence of diclofenac in the same lethal way (Meteyer et al. 2005:714).[7] If this is the case, other certain species of vulture no longer found in large numbers in India might, therefore, have survived in the presence of diclofenac. But for the longest time now, India has been a land of *Gyps* vultures, knotted together in so many different ways with people inside larger multispecies communities. These processes of knotting, alongside the often painful unknotting that is occurring today, highlight processes of entangled becoming that cuts across human/nonhuman and nature/culture binaries to produce a rich multispecies world. In addition, the multispecies community I have described is one comprising both the living and the dead. The extinction of vultures points to the necessity of a concept and a practice of community that draws in the dead, in which what happens to the dead, how they (and we) are "taken care of" (and by whom), what contributions they are able to make (and to whom) are all deeply consequential for the health and continunity of others. Dead vultures, dead cattle, dead people, all *matter* in the interactions that produce possibilities of and for life and death. And so, it is not just the living that make, and sometimes unmake, flourishing communities.

But as these relationships have been unraveled in this time of extinctions, those people most closely dependent on vultures have been drawn first into patterns of intensified suffering and death, another form of what Rose has called "double death" (2006). In this context, it does not seem to be enough to say that "we are all bound up in relationships of dependence in a multi-species world." Clearly, we need to understand precisely *how* different communities (of humans and nonhumans) are entangled, and how these entanglements are implicated in the production of both extinctions and their accompanying patterns of amplified death. This kind of information requires case-specific study and an approach to communities that moves beyond absolute distinctions between humans and nonhumans, the living and the dead.

Equally, it requires an approach to the world in which we "cast our lot for some ways of life [and death] and not others" (Haraway 1997:36). One might argue, for example, that in addition to a doubling of death in some domains, the demise of vultures has actually produced the possibility for new life in other contexts. While vultures may no longer be around to consume carcasses, this tragic situation has made room for the growth of populations of other animals, like dogs. While many of these dogs live in awful conditions and die painful deaths from rabies and other diseases, their mere presence highlights the fact that food is rarely ever wasted in any absolute sense, a situation that is made clear if we are prepared to shift our focus and acknowledge the broader "company" (Haraway 2003) of species at the table in any even moderately healthy ecosystem. Inside rich histories of entangled becoming—without the aid of simplistic ideals like "wilderness," "the natural," or "ecosystemic balance"—it is ultimately impossible to reach simple, black-and-white prescriptions about how ecologies "should be." And so we are required to make a stand for some possible worlds and not others; we are required to begin to take responsibility for the ways in which we help to tie and retie our knotted multispecies worlds (Barad 2007:353–396). How to live well within the always unequal patterns of amplified loss and suffering that are produced here is an issue that can only take on increasing significance as we move ever more deeply into the Earth's sixth great extinction event, and a period of growing environmental and climatic change.

REFERENCES

Amadon, D. 1983. Foreword to *Vulture Biology and Management*, edited by S.R. Wilbur and A.J. Jackson. Berkeley, Los Angeles, and London: University of California Press.

APCRI. 2004. *Assessing the Burden of Rabies in India—WHO Sponsored National Multi-centric Rabies Survey 2003*. Bangalore: Association for the Prevention and Control of Rabies in India.

Barad, K. 2007. *Meeting the Universe Halfway: Quantum Physics and the Entanglement of Matter and Meaning*. Durham and London: Duke University Press.

Baral, N., R. Gautam, N. Timilsina, and M.G. Bhat. 2007. "Conservation Implications of Contingent Valuation of Critically Endangered White-rumped Vulture *Gyps Bengalensis* in South Asia." *International Journal of Biodiversity Science and Management* 3:145–156.

BBC. 2005. "Court Upholds Cow Slaughter Ban" in *BBC News Online*. http://news .bbc.co.uk/2/hi/south_asia/4378138.stm (last accessed 5 May 2009).

BMA. 1995. *The BMA Guide to Rabies*. Oxford and New York: Radcliffe Medical Press, on behalf of the British Medical Association.

Botting, F., and S. Wilson. 1997. *The Bataille Reader*. Oxford: Blackwell Publishers.

Cuthbert, R., J. Parry-Jones, R.E. Green, and D.J. Pain. 2007. "NSAIDs and Scavenging Birds: Potential Impacts Beyond Asia's Critically Endangered Vultures." *Biology Letters* 3:91–94.

Cuthbert, R., R.E. Green, S.P. Ranade, D.J. Pain, V. Prakash, and A.A. Cunningham. 2006. "Rapid Population Declines of Egyptian Vulture (Neophron Percnopterus) and Red-headed Vulture (Sarcogyps Calvus) in India." *Animal Conservation* 9:349–354.

Devinder, M.T., and K. Karthikeyan. 2001. "Anthrax: An Overview within the Indian Subcontinent." *International Journal of Dermatology* 40:216–222.

"Dog Bite Cases on the Rise." 2005. *The Times of India*, September 1.

Ferguson-Lees, J., and D.A. Christie. 2001. *Raptors of the World*. New York: Houghton Mifflin Harcourt.

Grubh, R.B. 1983. "The Status of Vultures in the Indian Subcontinent." In *Vulture Biology and Management*, edited by S.R. Wilbur and A.L. Jackson, 107–112. Berkeley, Los Angeles, and London: University of California Press.

Haraway, D.J. 1997. *Modest_Witness@Second_Millenium .FemaleMan©_Meets_ OncoMouse™: Feminism and Technoscience*. New York and London: Routledge.

———. 2003. *The Companion Species Manifesto: Dogs, People, and Significant Otherness*. Chicago: Prickly Paradigm Press.

———. 2008. *When Species Meet*. Minneapolis: University of Minnesota Press.

Houston, D.C. 1983. "The Adaptive Radiation of the Griffon Vultures." In *Vulture Biology and Management*, edited by S.R. Wilbur and A.L. Jackson, 135–152. Berkeley, Los Angeles, and London: University of California Press.

———. 2001. *Condors and Vultures*. Stillwater, MN: Voyageur Press.

———. 2009. Personal Communication. E-mail: 15 June 2009.

Houston, D.C., and J.E. Cooper. 1975. "The Digestive Tract of the Whiteback Griffon Vulture and Its Role in Disease Transmission Among Wild Ungulates." *Journal of Wildlife Diseases* 11:306–313.

Jackson, A.L., G.D. Ruxton, and D.C. Houston. 2008. "The Effect of Social Facilitation on Foraging Success in Vultures: A Modelling Study." *Biology Letters* 4:311–313.

Konig, C. 1983. "Interspecific and Intraspecific Competition for Food Among Old World Vultures." *In Vulture Biology and Management*, edited by S.R. Wilbur and A.L. Jackson, 153–171. Berkeley, Los Angeles, and London: University of California Press.

Markandya, A., T. Taylor, A. Longo, M.N. Murty, S. Murty, and K. Dhavala. 2008. "Counting the Cost of Vulture Decline: An Appraisal of the Human Health and Other Benefits of Vultures in India." *Ecological Economics* 67:194–204.

McGrath, S. 2007. "The Vanishing." *Smithsonian Magazine*, February.

MEA. 2005. *Millennium Ecosystem Assessment: Current State & Trends Assessment*, vol. 1. Washington D.C.: World Resources Institute.

Menezes, R. 2008. "Rabies in India." *Canadian Medical Association Journal* 178(5):564–566.

Meteyer, C.U., B.A. Rideout, M. Gilbert, H.L. Shivaprasad, and J.L. Oaks. 2005. "Pathology and Proposed Pathophysiology of Diclofenac Poisoning in Free-Living and Experimentally Exposed Oriental White-backed Vultures (Gyps Bengalensis)." *Journal of Wildlife Diseases* 41(4):707–716.

Mudur, G. 2001. "Human Anthrax in India May Be Linked to Vulture Decline." *British Medical Journal* 322 (7282):320.

Nancy, J.-L. 2002. "L'Intrus." *The New Centennial Review* 2.3(2002):1–14.

"Nepali Vulture 'Restaurant' Aims to Revive Decimated Population." 2007. *AFP*.

Pain, D.J., A.A. Cunningham, P.F. Donald, J.W. Duckworth, D.C. Houston, T. Katzner, J. Parry-Jones, C. Poole, V. Prakash, P. Round, and R. Timmins. 2003. "Causes and Effects of Temporospatial Declines of Gyps Vultures in Asia." *Conservation Biology* 17(3):661–671.

Plumwood, V. 2007. "Tasteless: Towards a Food-based Approach to Death." *Forum on Religion and Ecology*, October 2007.

———. 2008. "Shadow Places and the Politics of Dwelling." *Ecological Humanities, Australian Humanities Review* 44. http://www.australianhumanitiesreview.org/archive/Issue-March-2008/plumwood.html.

Prabhu, M.J. 2004. "Rabid Dog Bite Cases on the Rise." *The Hindu*, May 2.

Prakash, V. 1999. "Status of Vultures in Keoladeo National Park, Bharatpur, Rajasthan, with Special Reference to Population Crash in Gyps Species." *Journal of the Bombay Natural History Society* 96:365–378.

Prakash, V., R.E. Green, D.J. Pain, S.P. Ranade, S. Saravanan, N. Prakash, R. Venkitachalam, R. Cuthbert, A.R. Rahmani, and A.A. Cunningham. 2007. "Recent Changes in Populations of Resident Gyps Vultures in India." *Journal of the Bombay Natural History Society* 104(2):129–135.

Rich, P.V. 1983. "The Fossil Record of the Vultures: A World Perspective." In *Vulture Biology and Management*, edited by S.R. Wilbur and A.L. Jackson, 3–25. Berkeley, Los Angeles, and London: University of California Press.

Robbins, P. 1998. "Shrines and Butchers: Animals as Deities, Capital, and Meat in Contemporary North India." In *Animal Geographies: Place, Politics, and Identity in the Nature-Culture Borderlands*, edited by J. Wolch and J. Emel, 218–239. London and New York: Verso.

Rose, D.B. 2006. "What if the Angel of History Were a Dog?" *Cultural Studies Review* 12(1):67–78.

Ruxton, G.D., and D.C. Houston. 2004. "Obligate Vertebrate Scavengers Must Be Large Soaring Fliers." *Journal of Theoretical Biology* 228:431–436.

Schuz, E., and C. Konig. 1983. "Old World Vultures and Man." In *Vulture Biology and Management*, edited by S.R. Wilbur and A.L. Jackson, 461–469. Berkeley, Los Angeles, and London: University of California Press.

Singh, J. 2003. "India Targets Cow Slaughter." *BBC News*, August 11.

Subramanian, M. 2008. "Towering Silence." *Search: Science, Religion, Culture* May/June.

Swan, G., V. Naidoo, R. Cuthbert, R.E. Green, D.J. Pain, D. Swarup, V. Prakash, M. Taggart, L. Bekker, D. Das, J. Diekmann, M. Diekmann, E. Killian, A. Meharg, R.C. Patra, M. Saini, and K. Wolter. 2006a. "Removing the Threat of Diclofenac to Critically Endangered Asian Vultures." *PLoS Biology* 4(3):395–402.

———. 2006b. "Toxicity of Diclofenac to Gyps Vultures." *Biology Letters* 2: 279–282.

van Dooren, T. forthcoming. *Vulture*. London: Reaktion Books.

———. 2010. "Pain of Extinction: The Death of a Vulture." *Cultural Studies Review* 16.2.

Vijaikumar, M., M.T. Devinder, and K. Karthikeyan. 2002. "Cutaneous Anthrax: An Endemic Outbreak in South India." *Journal of Tropical Pediatrics* 48(4): 225–226.

Vinayak, R. 2007. "Flying into Uncertainty." *India Today*, March 26.

Williams, A. 1997. "Zoroastrianism and the Body." In *Religion and the Body*, edited by S. Coakley, 155–166. Cambridge: Cambridge University Press.

NOTES

1. While vultures will sometimes eat "badly decomposed" food, they do prefer food that is relatively fresh (Houston 2001).

2. There are numerous other dimensions of the lives of cattle in India that cannot be understood as anything other than tragic. While almost all Indian states have bans on the slaughter of cattle, in many cases this has simply meant that slaughter is carried out illegally—and thus in a completely unregulated manner—or that cattle are subjected to long and crowded transportation to slaughterhouses in neighbouring states or countries (BBC 2005; Singh 2003).

3. All references to "Cunningham, 11 September 2008" refer to transcribed notes from an interview with Dr. Andrew Cunningham (Institute of Zoology, Zoological Society of London), conducted in London on 11 September 2008.

4. Here, and in what follows, I have drawn on statistics in an effort to convey the immensity and the inequity of the problems developing in India in the absence of vultures. I am mindful, however, that not only do statistics by themselves fail to convey the magnitude of the suffering, they can also fail to show the ethical demands that the suffering warrants (van Dooren forthcoming 2010). Despite this fact, the numbers seem to tell a vital part of the story here.

5. While there are no accurate figures on the number of street dogs across India, Markandya et al. have argued, drawing on Ministry of Agriculture census data, that it seems likely that dog numbers are increasing considerably as a direct result of vulture absence (Markandya et al. 2008:198–199).

6. For a very different discussion of environmental justice and direct relationships with places/ecologies, see Plumwood 2008.

7. But see Cuthbert et al. 2006.

*Actor Iwai Kumesaburō III as Benten Kozō Kikunosuke,
from the series Toyokuni's Caricature Pictures
(Toyokuni manga zue)*

Artist: Utagawa Kunisada I (Toyokuni III), 1786–1864
Publisher: Uoya Eikichi

Japanese, Edo period, 1860 (Ansei 7/Man'en 1), 9th month.
Woodblock print (nishiki-e); ink and color on paper; vertical ōban.
Museum of Fine Arts, Boston. William Sturgis Bigelow Collection,
11.15102. Photograph © 2010 Museum of Fine Arts, Boston

Significant Connections:
A Conversation with Aaron Woolfolk

Editor's Note

The Harimaya Bridge, the debut feature film of Los Angeles–based writer and director Aaron Woolfolk, opened in Japan in summer 2009 and in the United States in spring 2010. There are a number of remarkable things about the film. First, *The Harimaya Bridge* combines American and Japanese cinematographic techniques, casts, and settings, and is subtitled in both English and Japanese. Second, many aspects of the film are far more Japanese than American: most of the filming was done with a Japanese crew and cinematographer in Japan, and most of the roles are played by Japanese actors. American actor Ben Guillory stars in the lead role of Daniel Holder, and opposite him are Japanese actors Saki Takaoka (Noriko) and Misa Shimizu (Yuiko). Minor roles are played by the American actors Danny Glover (Joseph), Victor Grant (Mickey), and Peter Coyote (Albert) and the Japanese actors Hajime Yamazaki (Kunji) and J-Pop singer Misono (Saita). So skillful is the blending of different cinematic and aesthetic conventions that Guillory sometimes looks as if he has walked onto the set of a foreign film.

Guillory's character, Daniel Holder, is a middle-aged American father whose estranged artist son, Mickey, has died in an accident while living and teaching in Japan. Grief stricken and remorseful, he is also angry with himself for having alienated his son, and angry with his son for having gone to Japan against his wishes. Daniel has hated the Japanese people since learning that his own father was tortured and killed by Japanese soldiers in a POW camp during World War II. With Mickey's death, he reluctantly goes to the country he despises—but where Mickey chose to make his home—to recover his son's paintings and other belongings. Upon arriving, Daniel can barely contain his hatred for the Japanese people, their language, and their culture, despite the unstinting efforts of his hosts to treat him with kindness and civility. Eventually, he discovers that he must choose between hating the Japanese and embracing his son's memory and the family Mickey left behind in Japan. It should be noted that Daniel is African American, adding further complexity to this remarkable film.

The following interview with Aaron Woolfolk took place in Honolulu in summer 2010.

CC You initially went to Japan to teach. Please talk about your transition from English teacher to film director.

AW I first went to Japan with the Japan Exchange and Teaching (JET) Program, an English-teaching/cross-cultural program sponsored by the Japanese government. I was assigned to Kochi Prefecture, a very rural area, far off the beaten path. I went there knowing that my ultimate goal was to become a filmmaker. I had worked on some film projects at UC Berkeley. To me, the JET Program was a detour—a chance to have an interesting life experience. But when I got to Japan, got to Kochi, I loved it! And I decided that I wanted to stay there for two or three years—maybe even longer. Suddenly, filmmaking wasn't so front and center for me anymore. In Japan, I had a great job, great friends, a girlfriend I loved being with, a nice little apartment. I was so happy with my life there. And I should mention that Kochi is known as being a place that foreigners fall in love with and never leave. I know a lot of Americans who have lived in Kochi ten, fifteen, almost twenty years. While there, I felt the beginning of that kind of attachment.

But, filmmaking and going to film school were still in the back of my mind. And I felt a bit guilty about putting my dream on hold indefinitely. As an afterthought, I applied to film school. I thought I would get rejected and then wouldn't feel guilty about staying in Japan, because at least I tried. Well, much to my surprise, Columbia University's film division actually accepted me. Now, in those days it was really difficult to get into a top graduate film program. I started to think about what to do: stay or go. I tried to get a deferment so that I could stay in Japan at least one more year, but Columbia said no. I had to accept or lose my spot, and there was no guarantee I'd be accepted again. After thinking about it for several weeks, I decided to leave Japan at the end of my JET year and go to New York.

When I got back, however, I started to feel my Japan experience was incomplete, and I was really missing it. I began to return to Kochi every year to visit, thinking about how I could establish a career as a filmmaker, and what I could do to stand out as being different. It was on those return visits to Kochi that I started to wonder if I could combine my film aspirations with my love for Japan. I thought about making a feature film in Japan, but I figured no one would buy an African American going to Japan to make movies. I had to show it wasn't such a silly idea, so for my thesis project at Columbia, I wrote and directed two short films in Japan: the comedy *Eki* (The Station) and the drama *Kuroi Hitsuji* (Black Sheep). Those shorts did really well, and that put me on the road to making the feature. Actually, the shorts were a kind of prologue to *The Harimaya Bridge*.

CC   Much of your film makes minimal use of dialogue. For example, Daniel doesn't understand the Japanese language, and the Japanese people have trouble understanding him. You convey a lot of information through visual imagery. How can imagery be an effective substitute for dialogue?

AW   My short film *Eki* is a thirteen-minute comedy that takes place in a rural Japanese train station. The main characters are a young American man and two junior high school girls. I wanted to see if I could make a film that could be understood by both English-speaking and Japanese-speaking audiences, but through different means. One of the things I did was…even though ninety-eight percent of the dialogue in the film is in Japanese, there are no subtitles. Well, the very first word spoken in the film, a single Japanese word, is subtitled. But after that, no subtitles at all. So the English-speaking audience is watching a film in which they can't understand anything that is being said for thirteen minutes. But I set *Eki* up so that the visuals and the situation and the behavior of the characters tell the story. So what usually happened with the English-speaking crowd was that, for the first minute of the film, they'd look around in confusion because they thought something must have been wrong with the film print or projector. Then they settled in and watched. And they got everything. They laughed when they were supposed to laugh, they cheered when they were supposed to cheer, and so on. Well, that film did really well. It won awards. It got into top film festivals and showcases. I'm very flattered that, to this day, people in certain film circles remember *Eki*. And the funniest thing to me is that so many of them don't remember that the film isn't subtitled, or isn't in English. We get to talking about the film, I mention my thinking behind making a film in Japanese with no subtitles, and they look at me like I'm joking with them. Because they can clearly remember the story and what happened and everything that went on…but they don't remember the film had dialogue in a language they don't understand and no subtitles. The visual storytelling stayed with them, and the dialogue didn't matter.

I think sometimes words can actually create barriers to how much can be understood. If you give people a powerful visual image with thirty expository words meant to explain it, you've undermined the impact of that image. You've forced it into the confines of those thirty words. But if you give people a powerful visual image with no expository words to explain it, then you open up people's imaginations. And now that image can mean a thousand words. Or ten thousand words.

CC   Part of your film seems to focus on the entwined relationships of art, reconciliation, and memory as well as the influence of historical events on everyday life. Can you tell us how you worked so many elements into the film? Is this something that art is especially good at?

AW   I believe in the power of the arts to educate, inspire, inform, and heal. I've experienced its potential firsthand. When I was in graduate film school, I did a lot of work with inner-city youth—elementary school to high school—in the New York City area. I taught them about filmmaking, storytelling, camera work, editing, et cetera. And it was wonderful to see that many of those kids discovered their voices through art—and to watch their whole perspective on life change. All of a sudden, things that had seemed important and had often led to violence didn't seem so important to them anymore. That showed me how the arts can change lives.

In putting together *The Harimaya Bridge,* in which healing and crossing cultural bridges are at the heart of the story, and in which the emotional residue of the Second World War figures, I needed something concrete to inspire the journey of the main character, Daniel. I decided it would be the visual arts. From the earliest drafts of the screenplay, I made Daniel's son, Mickey, a painter, and getting hold of his artwork was the raison d'être for Daniel to go to Japan. In later drafts, I decided that art would be a significant connection between father and son, and I made Daniel a photographer. I also made the arts something that connects the three generations of the Holder family: Daniel's last memory of his father involves a trip they took to a museum, and Daniel passes on his love for the arts to Mickey.

In the film, an older generation is learning to let go of the resentments of

Stills and production photos from The Harimaya Bridge *courtesy of Aaron Woolfolk. Actors shown: Ben Guillory, Danny Glover, Victor Grant, Saki Takaoka, and Misa Shimizu.*

the past and move forward into the future, and the younger generation is helping them do that. Daniel and his counterpart in Japan, Noriko's father, represent the former. Mickey and Noriko—a couple that won't let history or their so-called differences come between them—represent the latter.

CC   Mickey's and Noriko's fathers are part of the older generation and can't speak to one another, and Mickey and Noriko are able to talk freely and reject social prejudices. Yet in the film, there are still subjects that remain forbidden. There are the Buddhist monk and the maid who are secretly in love, Mickey and Noriko's secret marriage, and their child, who is hidden away. Did the issue of secrecy in such traditional matters resonate with Japanese audiences? Did the film inspire people to talk about forbidden subjects?

AW   Well, the last lines of *The Harimaya Bridge* capture that: we hear Noriko telling the story of the monk and the woman and their forbidden love. "They were two people who the laws of the time said couldn't be together. But true love knows no boundaries, not even those set by society."

Mickey and Noriko don't let history or their supposed racial differences get in the way of their love. But you can be the most progressive, forward-thinking person in the world, and if you ignore the realities around you, you might hurt a lot of people and sabotage your cause.

Over the years—first while living in Kochi and later when spending a lot of time visiting—I've had a few relationships with women there. And I've known other foreigners to have relationships with Japanese women and men. With me, I always understood that no matter how open-minded the woman herself might be, she still had to deal with the community and world around her…a world that gave her her job, friends, social standing, and everything else. Being a foreigner, I knew it was a world that I could easily depart, if I wanted to. But she could not, because her family, friends, career,

values—her entire life—were all there. And I wasn't naïve. I've always understood that, in rural Japan, being with a black guy is not exactly going to make a Japanese woman's life carefree and easy. So I always tried to put myself in her shoes. I was never like, "You must acknowledge me as your boyfriend in public!" That would have been incredibly selfish of me, and dismissive of her and the effect such a revelation would have on her world. In contrast, I've seen and known of instances where foreigners in that situation didn't stop to consider the effects of their actions on their spouse and her world. And it resulted in disaster for the Japanese person. Changing the world and people's attitudes doesn't always happen when you use shock therapy.

So personal experience informed my approach to Mickey and Noriko's story. Japanese audiences told me they were charmed by Mickey and Noriko's relationship, but they also understood why the two of them kept it under wraps.

What Japanese audiences reacted to strongly was the plot point involving the *burakumin* [a social outcast or person of low caste], which I suppose is more of an issue in Japan than interracial relationships, and has been so for hundreds of years. As long as I've been going to Japan, I've noticed it's something that people tend not to want to talk about. So the part in the story when the character Yuiko reveals that she had previously wanted to marry a man, but was forbidden by her parents…that really resonated with people. The character never actually says the word *burakumin*, but the way I wrote it makes it very clear what she is referring to. That plot point was actually inspired by my discovery in two separate instances that women who were very close to me had previously been in love with *burakumin* gentlemen that they had wanted to marry. In both cases, their marriages were forbidden by their parents, and this had a devastating emotional impact on their lives.

It was interesting to have people come up to me after screenings and talk about a topic no one speaks about openly.

CC   Are there any ways in which you shaped Daniel's character to make him, as an African American man, more understandable to Japanese audiences? Or, conversely, to make him more different, difficult to understand?

AW   At the heart of everything, I always felt that all of the characters in the film should be understandable to anyone, regardless of national origin or race or generation or whatever. I wanted to have characters that are universal to the human experience. I've always thought that the best films and the most memorable characters are like that. In fact, that is part of what first struck me about *Ikiru* and *Tokyo Story*—two of my favorite films—when I first saw them. And that is why films like *Black Orpheus* and *The Lives of Others* resonate with audiences around the world.

I've always been interested in the representations of African Americans onscreen. It's come a long way. But we still often hear that old thing about such-and-such character "is not black enough." Writers and directors hear it from film and television development people all the time. I've even had people of color, who I know to be very progressive-minded, make comments about the character Daniel: "I've never known a black man on film to act that uptight"—meaning the way he talks—and "It would've been interesting to see him be more black in Japan." As if there is such a thing as "more black" or "less black." I guess some people wanted to see *Shaft in Japan*...which could be an interesting story, actually. I'll keep that one in mind. Seriously, though, to me that whole "black enough" thing is just dumb. It's old-fashioned stereotyping. The African American community is as diverse as any other, with people who talk and act all sorts of ways and have all sorts of backgrounds. I guess in all of my work I tend to feature characters that fall outside of that silly "black enough" classification. I'm not comfortable with the tiny, neat little boxes that a lot of people think fictional African American characters are supposed to fit into.

That is why I try to stay away from "types" when creating characters, and in particular African American characters...whether it's a "type" that people in Hollywood think people want to see or a "type" that someone thinks would go over well in Japan.

In creating the character Daniel, I didn't set out to hold the hand of the Japanese audience and say, "This is a black man that I think you will be able to understand and like." That would have been condescending, and it would have made for a boring character. Rather, I sought to tie Daniel into the universal language of the human experience. As a storyteller, I tried to give him a journey that the audience would want to follow, and a character-arc that made sense. Of course, I was fortunate to have Ben Guillory play the role. As an experienced actor and the head of a prominent theater company, he's seen it all when it comes to representations of African Americans in film and television and on stage. And he totally understood where I was coming from with Daniel.

CC   Cross-cultural communication is another important aspect of *The Harimaya Bridge*. Can you talk about your experiences with this in Japan?

AW   In college at the University of California at Berkeley, one of my majors was ethnic studies. The other was rhetoric. That culmination reflected my interest not only in the histories of different racial and ethnic groups, but also in the relations between them. In fact, one of the first film projects I ever made was a docudrama for an ethnic studies video-production class. It was about the reasons for the tensions between blacks and Koreans in California.

In Japan, the town I lived in had a population of thirty thousand. This was in the early nineties, and for ninety-nine percent of the people in Kochi,

I was the first black person they had ever seen in the flesh. It was interesting going from California, where I was just another anonymous person, to a place where I felt I was constantly on display.

People's reactions to my being black were interesting. I'd get comments like "You must be really good at basketball," or "Show me your best slam dunk," or "You must be a fantastic dancer." I'd have junior-high-school basketball coaches that had been coaching for years assume I could teach their students more about the game than they could. Things like that.

But I soon realized that the people saying such things weren't intending to insult me. I mean, if someone says those things to a black person in the U.S., it's a racist insult. The context exists for that here, and people in America should know better by now. But in rural Japan they had no context for their words and actions. They were simply responding to images of blacks that had been exported by the Western media for years. In fact, by saying those things to me, they were reaching out, trying to make a connection. So I realized that my being there was an opportunity to break down stereotypes of blacks.

At the same time, I went to Japan with my own stereotypes of the Japanese. I'd say a lot of stupid things to them too. So it wasn't just them learning from me; it was also me learning from them. As a result, I had a great time there and made a lot of close friends, many of whom I remain close to today.

That initial experience in Japan taught me about tolerance, patience, and overcoming barriers that can exist between people. *The Harimaya Bridge* very much grew out of what I learned.

CC   As an African American filmmaker born, raised, and educated in the United States, how did you achieve the film's Japanese aesthetic?

AW   Much of my inspiration came from the pastoral Japanese films of the fifties that I saw when I started going to foreign films as a teenager. Japanese filmmakers have always been key to my appreciation of cinema. Akira Kurosawa and Yasujirō Ozu are my all-time favorite filmmakers, and Kurosawa's *Ikiru* and Ozu's *Tokyo Story* are my number-one favorite films. In fact, I think of *The Harimaya Bridge* as kind of an homage to those two films.

Usually, Western filmmakers make movies for Western audiences, even those that are set in or supposedly about foreign lands and cultures. I set out to see if I could make a film for both Japanese and American audiences. I wanted to avoid the things you usually find in Western movies set in non-Western countries—subtle and often not-so-subtle messages about the supremacy of Western values, culture, religion, et cetera. I've always hated that kind of arrogance. Mind you, there's nothing wrong with promoting one's culture and values. But it doesn't have to be presented as "I'm superior/you're inferior."

After the film was finished, *The Harimaya Bridge* had a nationwide release in Japan in the summer of 2009. I spent about a month and a half traveling around the country, doing press conferences, promotional events, preview screenings, and other things. I was pleased to find that there was a lot of love for the film. Some people said they couldn't believe it was written and directed by someone who wasn't Japanese. A lot of them thanked me for making a film that respected Japanese people and culture. Many critics said, "You made a Japanese film!" People said things like "You're an American, but you must have a Japanese soul." Best of all, people thanked me for making a film that shows the Japanese as normal, everyday people and not the stereotypes they have gotten used to seeing in Hollywood movies. It's great that Americans have responded to the film in much the same way.

CC   You mentioned the Japanese directors Kurosawa and Ozu as inspirations. Are there specific ways in which your film is an homage to them? For example, in the creation of moods or the physical settings, the use of similar film techniques, or the choice of certain character types?

AW   Kurosawa's *Ikiru* and Ozu's *Tokyo Story* are masterpieces, and in no way does *The Harimaya Bridge* even begin to approach the level of those cinematic gems. But they serve as good models for me to aspire to.

You can't really liken *Ikiru* and *Tokyo Story* to each other; they are quite different. But I can speak of the impact they had on me. *Ikiru* especially struck me by how fresh it seemed, and how much I related to the story and the characters. That was amazing to me. I mean, here was a film from the early 1950s from a country I had never been to in a language I didn't speak …but I could relate to everything. Moreover, the story was so profound, and it provided me with a life lesson I took to heart and still often recount to myself. Whenever I hear the phrase "the power of cinema," I think of *Ikiru*.

Tokyo Story also made me feel close to the characters in a way few films had, or have since. Here was a family in Japan in the early 1950s. But I could see my own family in them. When the father reacts to the passing of his wife …I remember it really resonating with me, and my thinking, "That's exactly what I would say in that situation."

Technically speaking, I loved how everything about *Tokyo Story* was very simple. Nothing is forced or rushed. The film takes its time. The audience isn't told to feel this way or that way. And each shot is a composition within which an elegant choreography takes place. The storytelling has a quiet, pastoral elegance.

I'd say that with *The Harimaya Bridge* I was inspired story-wise by *Ikiru* and cinematically by *Tokyo Story*. Though, like I said, my film is not even close to being in their league. But if you're going to draw inspiration, get it from the best.

CC   Japan's conduct during World War II is a sensitive subject even today, more than sixty years after the end of the war, and yet in the film you confront it head-on—along with other sensitive topics, such as discrimination. Why did you decide to take on these big issues?

AW   Actually, in the first few drafts of the script I tried my best to avoid dealing with things like the war and race, even though I knew in the back of my mind that, because of the plot, I would eventually have to. Often, that is how my writing process works: there is a big elephant in the room that I avoid as long as I can by dealing with other stuff. But eventually I get to a point where I have to deal with the elephant.

With the war, I didn't want to approach it in the "good guys–bad guys" way. I've always been interested that, in schools and in the media, we get an American perspective of history, but we never get to see things from the perspective of the other side. There's a sense that to look at history differently could somehow be unpatriotic, even treasonous. I'm not talking about not recognizing right from wrong, or outright evil. But this is what I meant earlier about not wanting the film to impose Western viewpoints and values. Yes, Japan's wartime conduct is addressed and spoken of critically in the film. But the ultimate message is something both sides in the film agree on: war is bad, period.

On race, I knew I didn't want to be preachy or talk down to people. The film wasn't going to have the usual African-European or Asian-European racial paradigms. It was African-Asian. I knew I wanted to have complex characters of color doing things and acting in ways not often seen in movies. What's funny is that when people hear that the film deals with a black man going to Japan and dealing with discrimination, they automatically assume it's about a black victim of Japanese prejudice. They don't expect that most of the bigotry comes from the black character, and it surprises them that the film is about his journey to understanding and healing.

But yeah, there were a lot of times when I thought to myself, What am I doing? What was I thinking, taking this on? The war…race…This is going to blow up in my face—if not in Japan, then in the U.S., and probably both! Overall, it was a balancing act that was worked out over many drafts of the script, and then performed by fantastic actors.

CC   Coming back to the subject of Daniel's son, Mickey, being an artist: Mickey's artwork in the film is obviously very important. Please tell us more about it.

AW   The paintings had to really stand out and provoke a strong reaction from moviegoers because Mickey's art is the main way they get to know who he was, and because Daniel's trip to Japan has to do with getting the paintings from people Mickey gave them to.

I spent a lot of time looking for the right artist to create Mickey's paintings. I finally found the most wonderful artist, MaMi Kobayashi. She was introduced to me by Ko Mori, the film's lead producer. Though she is Japanese and is based in Tokyo, she had lived in Los Angeles. While there, she developed an interest in painting images of African American families. So when I met her in Tokyo during pre-production and she showed me samples of her work, she already had paintings of both Japanese life and African American life. And her work is beautiful. I knew right away she was the perfect person to express Mickey's artistic voice.

MaMi and I had a great working relationship. I had a sense of what I wanted, but at the same time I didn't want to put constraints on her as an artist. I wanted to give her room to create freely. For example, the story calls for a painting of the actual Harimaya Bridge and the legend about it. I let her interpret it however she wanted.

I also thought about what Mickey would want to paint in Japan. Given that he'd grown up in a big American city, I figured he would be intrigued by scenes of rural life. I discussed that with MaMi. We brainstormed ideas, settled on certain possible images, and then she went off to paint. Other times I told her to just be free to put herself in Mickey's shoes and to paint what came to her. She did some painting in Tokyo during pre-production, and then she came to Kochi and was there during production. She was inspired by Kochi and tried to imagine the rural life that Mickey would have led.

There were times when MaMi wanted to pick my brain about my own experiences as an English teacher in Kochi. Once, she came to me and asked me to tell her what images had stayed with me from those days. I told her about one of my favorite photos from that time: it shows me walking along a rural trail surrounded by students, and all of us are laughing. MaMi's eyes lit up. She went off, and a couple of days later came back with a beautiful rendering of that image—and it became one of the film's central paintings.

Something that really thrills me now is seeing how audiences react to MaMi's art. In Japan, in France, in Mexico, in the U.S.—wherever the film is shown—people always have great things to say about the paintings and want to know more about them. I feel proud that so many people have discovered MaMi Kobayashi's work through *The Harimaya Bridge*.

CC   What would you say to a young person interested in becoming a film director?

AW   I've always thought the best preparation for being a film director is living life, doing interesting things. People in the film business are always looking for fresh, compelling stories. Sure, much of what we see in theaters these days are sequels, remakes, comic-book and video-game adaptations, et cetera. But when someone comes along with a good, fresh story, people will flock to it. There will always be a demand for good stories, and some-one who has had interesting life experiences will be more likely to have interesting stories to tell.

Today, a young person who wants to make a film doesn't need to wait for a big corporate movie company or someone with deep pockets. Sure, it's nice to have those resources, but they are not necessary. The technology exists for almost anyone to make a film. You can buy a good camera for relatively little money, or even borrow one from a community center, and state-of-the-art editing systems can now be loaded onto a personal computer. These days, people are being discovered after making something and putting it on the Internet.

The important thing is to learn the craft. Anyone can get a camera, point, and shoot, but it's the people who know the craft who will have the strongest chance of getting somewhere. Watch movies, read books, take classes, and work on other people's movies and observe. Then go out and do it.

Landscape of Poetry: Ryuichi Tamura

Translator's Note

      The following essay by Kazuko Shiraishi (白石かずこ) originally appeared in *Shi no Huukei · Shijin no Shouzou* (詩の風景・詩人の肖像) (Landscape of Poetry: Portraits of the Poets). In 2007, the publisher Shoshi Yamada (書肆山田) released the book, an anthology of work by fifteen well-known international poets—Shiraishi's lifetime personal friends. In each essay, she introduces the poet's best work, remembering their friendship like a landscape. The book received the sixtieth Yomiuri Literary Award in 2009 (第60回読売文学随筆・紀行賞)—the second Yomiuri Award given to Shiraishi. Samuel Grolmes and I translated the poems by Tamura included in the essay.—Y. T.

My encounter with Ryuichi Tamura has been my fate. I wonder what my life would have become if, at the age of seventeen, I had not run across his poem "Reunion." Perhaps fate would have taken me in a different direction.

    Tomorrow, no even tonight, the factory in Saijō where I work could get bombed, and I might die in a fireball. Or die by jumping into the sea from a two-hundred-meter-high cliff at the back of the factory, which was the only way to run away from the fire—whichever option I chose, there was nothing but death. Those were the days of my fourteenth year in the town of Matsuyama on Shikoku Island, to which I had been evacuated. The war ended three days before the expected air raid, so I took a deep breath, realizing I had gotten away without dying. I was overwhelmed with a sense of release, believing that from now on my life belongs to me.

    The girl students were able to return to school. Among the books I found in the town of Matsuyama which grabbed me were *The Flowers of Evil* by Baudelaire and *The Blue Cat* and *Barking at the Moon* by Sakutaro Hagiwara. I had no appetite for lukewarm lyric poetry.

    I returned to Tokyo. I do not have a clear memory of when and where, but I encountered Tamura's "Reunion" in the journal *Poetics*. For the first time, I met the earth face to face as swirling sand. The poem had a shocking impact on me. Up until then, I had been on the earth, but had never met the earth with such closeness as to have a game of chess with it.

Admiring the journal that published the great poem which had singularly moved me, I visited the *Poetics* study group, carrying with me a poem of mine, "Time." Just then Shiro Murano and Koichi Kihara were selecting and commenting on poems. Taking up my poem, Kihara said, "Whose poem is this? It has a weird feeling." And then he asked me, "As for your pen name, what have you decided on?"

At that time, I had no idea that Koichi Kihara was inviting me into Katsue Kitazono's Vou poetry group. At the same time, another group of poets was publishing a magazine called *Wasteland* (Arechi), named after T. S. Eliot's poem. The two groups shared some ideas, and so the Wasteland poets—Saburo Kuroda, Taro Kitamura, Nobuo Ayukawa, not to mention Ryuichi Tamura and Koichi Kihara—were showing up at the meetings of the Vou group.

The Wasteland poets discussed and uproariously disputed Dos Passos and Faulkner. Then when night came, they parted from the gentlemen of coffee and cake—Katsue Kitazono's Vou poets—and went out to Shinbashi to drink Calvados and vodka, and drank *kasutori* and *bakudan* at Narushisu in Shinjuku like fish. I followed them many times out of natural curiosity, even though I was still a high school student.

My introductory remarks have gotten long, but this poem "Reunion" gave me a baptism into modernism, and gave me a chance to encounter and look closely at the early Wasteland group. The group advocated that poetry must have an ideology, social responsibility, and a spirituality, in desolate postwar Japan. (The Wasteland group later parted from Vou and became independent.)

REUNION

Where did I meet you
Where   Where did I meet you
my friend who is a good friend of death   my old friend
Midday in this city
every possible shadow has disappeared into a gray doorway
Our suffering memory too has been lost inside the great illusion of
    the city
You cannot recall
my smile
I have whispered to you somewhere before
"Suffering will smile"
I can see dead volcanoes
I can see the sexual city windows
I can see the order without a sun
Afternoon in the park that dried up in my palm and died
Eternal summer that was crushed by my teeth

Actress Disguising Herself as a Man (Onna haiyū no dansō),
from the series World of Picture Postcards (Ehagaki sekai)

Artist: Unidentified
Publisher: Kokkei shinbun sha

Japanese, late Meiji era, 1907. Color lithograph; ink on card stock;
overall (untrimmed). Museum of Fine Arts, Boston. Leonard A.
Lauder Collection of Japanese Postcards, 2002.1702.
Photograph © 2010 Museum of Fine Arts, Boston

The dark part of the earth is sleeping under my breast
Where did I meet you   Where
I was a seventeen-year-old boy
I used to walk around in the alleys of the city
A shower
I turn around when I am tapped on the shoulder

"You   the earth is rough"

This last line made my spirit explode! Shortly after I got acquainted with Ryuichi Tamura at the gathering of the Vou poets, I happened to see him on a street corner in Shinjuku. He was standing at the entrance of the movie theater across from the Isetan department store. When I was about to enter the theater, he was coming out, accompanied by A's sister, a respectable-looking woman with a white bandage on her infected finger. It was an American movie titled *Amoku* (Feverish Storm) and set on a South Sea island in a typhoon.

These details have no special meaning. But in this way, in such a landscape, I met Ryuichi Tamura once every few years for the last forty-some years.

Sometimes a decade would go by between our meetings. But I encountered poets in Europe and in America who talked about his poems. I want to meet again the Tamura who wrote the collection *Four Thousand Days and Nights*.

FOUR THOUSAND DAYS AND NIGHTS

For one poem to be born
we must kill
We must kill many things
We shoot, assassinate, poison the many things we love

Look
We shot
the silence of four thousand nights and the glare of four thousand
      days
simply because we wanted the trembling tongue of one small bird
from the sky of four thousand days and nights

Listen
We assassinated
the love of four thousand days and the pity of four thousand nights
simply because we needed the tears of one hungry child
from all the rainy cities and blast furnaces
and the midsummer wharves and the coal mines

Remember
We see things our eyes cannot see
We hear things our ears cannot hear
We poisoned
the power of imagination of four thousand nights and the cold
    memories of four thousand days
simply because we wanted the fear of one stray dog

To give birth to one poem
we must kill the things we love
This is the only road to take to resurrect the dead
This is the road we have to take

In an essay on his poetics, "A Dove on the Road," Tamura writes about how poems are brought to life. He quotes C. Day Lewis, who wrote in *Poetry for You:*

> 1. The seed or germ of a poem strikes the poet's imagination. It may come in the form of a strong but vague feeling, a particular experience, or an idea: sometimes it first appears as an image....The poet jots down the idea or image in his notebook, or just makes a mental note of it. Then he probably forgets all about it.
>
> 2. But the seed of the poem has passed into him, into the part of him we call "the unconscious mind." There it grows...till the moment comes when it is ready to be born. For a poem, this second stage may take a few days only or it may take years.
>
> 3. The poet feels an urgent desire to write a poem....He recognizes in it the seed which first came to him weeks or months before...but the seed has grown and developed in a remarkable way.

Ryuichi Tamura approves of Lewis' description of how the poetic process works—that poems come out of what Tamura calls a "history of emotions." The work begins as a seed that is created by the poet's internal sensitivity to a multitude of experiences and impressions. Through an interior process, the poet's mind sifts these miscellaneous impressions, synthesizes them, and gives birth to them as a singular, unified poem. The poem can only appear as a result of the ability within the poet to create this transformation and bring it to completion.

In other words, poems can only come into existence when a writer possesses this inner creative ability. Rhetorical devices—such as simile and metaphor, or using fancy expressions in place of direct wording—cannot create poetry. If a person doesn't have the inner creative ability that gives life to the "history of emotions," or if a person tries to create something merely by concentrating on the external craftsmanship of poetry writing and does not possess emotional depth, nothing poetic will come of it. A writer doesn't become a poet by mastering "how to make a poem," Tamura says. Instead, *a poet writes a poem by writing a poem.*

This concise phrase is really characteristic of Tamura. My explanation is a bit rambling, but the reason I have introduced the summary of his poetics is that it has such clarity and is interesting and refreshing, like peering through clear glass into the logic inside his mind and mental structure.

Recently, the Korean poet Kim Kwang-rim sent me a short essay, "A Uniquely Open-minded Poet, Ryuichi Tamura." Kim writes that Tamura must certainly be at the top of any list of modern Japanese poets of international stature. Then Kim asserts that he can *find few traits in Tamura's poetry that are Japanese.*

These words have stayed on my mind. Living in Japan, it is as though we are all in the same bath, and are not conscious in everyday life of such things as a Japanese way or a European way. Considering the other Wasteland poets—such as Taro Kitamura and Toyoichiro Miyoshi and also some other Japanese poets—we realize that Tamura's responses to things, his interpretations, his ways of making statements, and his methods of analysis are unusual and refreshingly different from those of conventional Japanese poets. His work contains characteristics that the British, for example, admire in the Sherlock Holmes stories and in the poetry of T. S. Eliot.

Is this why Tamura's poems are so accessible in their meaning and rhythms, whether they are translated into Dutch or English? And is this why Tamura's poetry has so many enthusiastic readers overseas?

For twenty years, the director of the Poetry International Festival in Holland, Martin Mooij, kept inviting Ryuichi Tamura to attend, but Tamura always made excuses and never accepted. Someone might conclude from this that Tamura didn't like to travel, but that wasn't so. For example, he eagerly accepted an invitation to Scotland, a country of whiskey, and even published a book of poems titled *The Watermills of Scotland*. Similarly, Kim Kwang-rim said that when he invited Tamura to visit Korea, Tamura refused and made up an excuse: "I don't want to come because I do not like ideology." But Tamura added, Kim said, "If the boozers on Saishuu Island invite me, I will come." Martin Mooij and other people who have experienced Tamura's extraordinary humanity—his unpretentiousness, his jokes, wit, sharp criticism of society, and laughter—seemed to fall in love with not only his poetry but also his humanity, and couldn't help saying, "By all means come to my country." Tamura was a marvel.

I have already said that, because of their directness, Ryuichi Tamura's poems seem more typical of Western poetry than of conventional Japanese. I wonder if this is perhaps a consequence of his early life experiences—having been born in the center of Tokyo, a Japanese male of a certain era and in certain circumstances, and with the natural disposition of someone who enjoys an idle life. Of his early years, he wrote:

I was born in Otsuka, Tokyo, the day before the spring solstice, March 18, 1923. ...On the 1st day of September, Taisho 9th year (1920), my grandfather Shigetaro cleared a thicket and established a restaurant, Suzumura, specializing in chicken dishes. He was a founder of the Otsuka association, made up of men who owned houses of pleasure, geisha house owners....The environment in which I was raised can easily be imagined....My classmates were either children of restauranteurs, geisha house owners, or business owners who catered to the geisha world, such as hairdressers or rickshaw men.

At times when this side of Tamura emerged—a person born in the heart of the Japanese pleasure quarters—interesting things would happen. For example, when we foreign writers were invited to the Iowa International Writing Program, we were allowed to take from the storeroom a box full of as many books as we wanted. In the years after Ryuichi Tamura was there, the director, Paul Engle, would tell the newly arriving writers, "You can take books, but please don't be like Tamura and trade them for whiskey."

Every encounter with Ryuichi Tamura was magical and left a life-long impression. Each meeting was a distinct episode, with its own colors and images. Nowadays, it is almost impossible to find a poet like him, whose poetic gifts were simply part of who he was, and flowed freely and effortlessly from his personality. And yet, I am staggered and amazed by the range of contradictions he contained. His intelligence and acuity encompassed every aspect of his era, but he was also far ahead of his time. Simultaneously, he was the inheritor of an older, even ancient tradition, with rules that governed the manners and expression of a Japanese male.

Tamura was aware of the many contradictions in himself. In the autobiographical notes he wrote for *Poems of Ryuichi Tamura* (volume one of *A Library of Contemporary Japanese Poetry*), he talks about his deeply rooted resentment of his upbringing in the geisha world of Otsuka, and at the same time his attachment to it.

He said that he transferred his tangled emotions—the love and loathing of Otsuka—to Japan as a whole during the militaristic years leading up to the war. By the time he was in high school, he hated such things as traditional Japanese poetic lyricism, based on cadences of five and seven syllables. He turned instead to European writers, whom he could read in only poor, halting translations—Dostoevsky, Valéry, Mann. And when he found T. S. Eliot, he shouted for joy! Such poetry was a way for him to escape, to cast off the deeply rooted emotions and sentiments of the environment in which he grew up.

Without doubt, his poetry has more Western clarity and directness than any other Japanese poet who has come after him. His *words* always cut well, like the swords of the master swordsmen Musashi Miyamoto and Bokuden Tsukahara. There is no coquetry, tantalization, or ambiguity, like a prostitute who snuggles up to the era. In that sense, his poems are indeed not Japanese. With an objective eye, and insight, from a global point of view, he is always facing the era, society, and human structure. Standing in a place indifferent to authority, power, fashion, and all the rest, he *nonchalantly*—though not inelegantly—confronts the grubby monsters of our time.

Where does this nonchalance come from? Not from the other poets in the Wasteland group. The gifted Nobuo Ayukawa was cool and theoretical on the surface, but could also be grave and melancholic; he was popular among the intellectuals and socialists. Koichi Kihara and Masao Nakagiri were passionate and very serious minded. Saburo Kuroda's gift was for gentle words about the hardship of his life, which he expressed as both beautiful and tragic. Taro Kitamura sent a lonely seagull flying between nostalgic lyricism and intelligence; he was surrounded constantly by young poets who adored him. Only Toyoichiro Miyoshi continued to be a poet of compassion, always gently and tenaciously beating, like a Buddhist priest, on the wooden blocks of poetry. But none of these poets had Tamura's nonchalance.

In the postwar era, the Wasteland poets, who had been outsiders, became the mainstream. Then one by one they passed away. The last poet left standing turned out to be Ryuichi Tamura, who lived as many days as there are episodes to a boozer's life. Before becoming really ill, he entered a hospital, having come to terms with his life, his poetry, and his conduct.

THE RAINY DAY SURGEON'S BLUES

There is an odor of gauze in the rain
Only an image of having survived returns
from the modern slaughterhouse in the middle of summer
from the rainbow colored beach
singing the blues

Who would still make peace with the world
The world has completely adhered
to an obsolete anxiety and fear
No matter how sharp the surgeon's scalpel is I am fed up with it
I hear that only if I have that sweet lonely ether
I will have no chance of dreaming of procreation

There is an odor of gauze in the rain
a crime without passion
There is only a wound and no flow of blood
When cheap gin penetrates the rough tongue

there is only an image of having survived death
passersby singing the blues

Ah, who would make peace with the world
The world has completely adhered
to cheap boredom and ecstasy
No matter what sort of International Medical Conference it is
I am fed up with them
I hear that only if I have a bright, high spirited rhythm
can I have a dream of sodomy

The poems of Tamura's youth are all overflowing with his poetic gifts, a swell of sweet Eros, sending up refreshing splashes over us—and even his short blues songs were seductive.

Throughout his life, Tamura consistently maintained a particular poetic stance. He said, "I am a vertical human being."

THE WORLD WITHOUT WORDS

1

The world without words is a midday globe
I am a vertical human being

The world without words is a world of the poetry of noon
I cannot remain a horizontal human being

2

I will discover the world without words   using words
I will discover the midday globe   the poetry of noon
I am a vertical human being
I cannot remain a horizontal human being

3

Midday in June
The sun overhead
I was surrounded by a huge group of rocks
just then
The rock was a corpse
the lava corpse
of the energy
of a big explosion
of some volcano
Why just then

was all form the corpse of energy
Why just then
were all colors and rhythms the corpse of energy
One bird
for example a golden eagle
observes but does not criticize
in its slow circling
Why just then
did the golden eagle do nothing but observe the form of energy
Why just then
didn't the golden eagle try to criticize all color and rhythm
The rock was a corpse
I drank milk
chewed bread like a foot soldier

4

Oh
The flow of incandescence itself rejects fluidity
The flow that love and fear cannot shape
The form of a completely cooled flame
All forms of dead energy

5

A bird's eyes are exactly wickedness
He observes he does not criticize
A bird's tongue is exactly wickedness
He swallows he does not criticize

6

Look at the tongue of a nutcracker torn out sharply
Look at the tongue of a woodpecker like the spear of some pagan god
Look at the tongue of a woodcock like the sculptor's knife
Look at the tongue of a thrush the smooth murderous weapon
He observes he does not criticize
He swallows he does not criticize

7

I
walked down a road cold as the back of the moon
walked down the thirteen kilometer road to the cottage
along the stream of lava
along the road of death and procreation
along the road of the large ebb tide I have never seen

I am a foot soldier
or
I am a shipwrecked sailor
or
I am a bird's eyes
I am an owl's tongue

8

I observe with blind eyes
I fall down with my blind eyes open
I stick out my tongue and destroy the bark
I stick out my tongue but not to caress love and justice
The thorn harpoon that has grown on my tongue is not to cure fear
    and hunger

9

The road of death and procreation
is the road of small animals and insects
The swarm of honey bees which soars away raising a battle cry
one thousand needles in ambush   ten thousand needles
The road without criticism   and anti-criticism
of no meaning of meaning
of no criticism of criticism
The road that has no empty construction or petty hope
The road that has no use at all for metaphor or symbol or
    imagination
There is only destruction and propagation
There is only a recreation and a fragment
There is only a fragment and a fragment inside a fragment
There is only a sliver and a sliver inside a sliver
There is only the design on the ground inside an enormous design
    on the ground
The road of a cold June simile
The air sac sent from a vermilion lung
The air sac like an ice bag filling the air to the marrow
The bird flies
The bird flies in a bird

10

A bird's eyes are exactly wickedness
A bird's tongue is exactly wickedness
He destroys but he does not construct
He recreates but he does not create

He is a fragment   a fragment inside a fragment
He has an air sac but does not have an empty heart
His eyes and tongue are exactly wickedness but he is not wicked
Burn bird
Burn bird   all birds
Burn bird   small animal   all small animals
Burn death and procreation
Burn road of death and procreation
Burn

11

June cold as the back of the moon
Road cold as the back of the moon
On the road of death and procreation
I run down
I drift
I fly

I am a foot soldier
yet I am the brave enemy
I am a shipwrecked sailor
but I am the ebb tide
I am a bird
yet I am a blind hunter
I am a hunter
I am the enemy
I am the brave enemy

12

I
will find my way to the cottage as the sun sets
Thin little shrubs will change into huge forests
The lava stream and the sun and the ebb tide
will be cut off by my little dream
I will drink a glass of bitter water
I will drink it quietly like poison
I will close my eyes and open them again
I will dilute my whiskey with water

13

I will not return to the cottage
I cannot dilute a word with meaning
as I dilute my whiskey with water

You can approach Ryuichi Tamura's poetry from many angles, like a fisherman scanning the sea for a place to drop his line. I have no intention of analyzing Ryuichi Tamura's works. Only to say that, before you discuss his poems, you must take his words into your mouth, taste each of them—and have the ability to savor the pleasure and the pain in them.

Your five senses must be fully alive. If you try to discuss his poetry only with intellectual concepts, without the ability to gather them in with your senses, Ryuichi Tamura's poems will slip from the palms of your hands and fly away like wisps of gray hair. In his essay "Theory of Ryuichi Tamura," Nobuo Kasahara wrote, "The essence inside his perpendicular language, stripped of everything superfluous, is a kind of 'elegy,' the rhythm of pathos. I cannot help thinking that Tamura's interior world is folded up neatly in his concision of language."

At this point, let us quietly peer into Tamura's *A Poet's Notes*. There, he comments on the following poem:

THE ANGEL

An angel has to block "Time"
above our heads
for a single silence to be born

The North Star, a 3rd class sleeper   departs Aomori at 20:30
As for that silence, when my eyes open in the narrow berth
what kind of angel blocked my "Time"
Even if I tried to collect
those tens of millions of lonely lights
that spread out in the darkness
from Ishikari to the Kanto Plain   outside the window
I
can't see the face of my angel

Tamura says:

It has been seventeen long years since I wrote this poem. Getting on a train, I went to Hokkaido for the first time. I wrote this poem on the way back. I was young, and the Japanese islands were also young, before they had undergone plastic surgery. "My Angel" too must have been young.

Five years later, Tamura went to Hokkaido again. He flew back at night and wrote:

Thanks to the fact that we were above the angel's head, there was no room for "a single silence" to be born. Perhaps, we might be the ones who are blocking off the angel's "time." When I returned to Kamakura, the white *Camellia sasanqua* were in full bloom in my little garden.

The god of Mokichi's poesy is
the mercy of goddess in Asakusa and a broiled eel

He had the castle wall called fixed form
so he only had to go to the Kaminari gate

My nervous god is
always in bad temper   I do not even have fire insurance
A little house and
large silence

In the banter and irony of this poem, I can see a quality that is very characteristic of Ryuichi Tamura. Anyone who encountered him will recall his big-hearted facial expressions and his loud voice and laughter.

Decades ago (after Tamura and I had both gone to the Iowa International Writing Program, though five years apart), I was invited to his house with the editor of the journal *Lark* to do an interview. Guests had been coming and going all day, and Tamura had been drinking since morning. When I arrived, about three o'clock in the afternoon, he was already drunk. He said, "Oh, Miss Shiraishi, I miss Iowa, I miss Paul Engle," and pretty soon he fell asleep. Since I was leaving for America the next day, I had been busy making preparations and was tired—so I too, warming myself comfortably in a *kotatsu*, fell asleep. Later, the editor told me that it was his first experience of having his two interviewees fall asleep on him. He said that while we slept, he watched the sunset from the window of an upstairs room.

That day was probably the first time I had had a real face-to-face conversation with Tamura. Looking back, I see it was a reunion of my encounter with his poem "Reunion," when I was seventeen years old. Until then, no matter how many times I ran into him, in my twenties and thirties, somehow I could never keep from regressing to that nervous seventeen-year-old girl, unable to speak. But I remember that afternoon feasting on *sushi* at his house and enjoying myself. Afterwards, I found I had grown up enough to talk to him a little. Still, no matter how old I became, I always felt in front of him like a young girl in front of her father (actually, we weren't that far apart in age, so maybe it was more like a little sister in front of an older brother).

The next time I visited Tamura in Kamakura, he had a different house and a different wife. He introduced a beautiful plump goddess to me, saying, "Miss Shiraishi, she is the same age as you." This time I brought along Kim Kwang-rim, the Korean poet I mentioned earlier. Kim has translated many Japanese poets, including Fuyuhiko Kitagawa, and he is good friends with lots of them. But the one he adores, he says, is Ryuichi Tamura—both the man and his works.

From an early age—a boy before the war, then a young man during the war—Tamura was a survivor. He outlived the Seven Samurai Poets with whom he spent the postwar period, and continued straight into the windmill of history. I want to see Ryuichi Tamura stepping out of the twentieth century, creaking like a mammoth, and into the twenty-first. I want his way of living and his very presence on Earth to grab poetry by the hair and shake it, to inspire our sleeping souls, to scold and encourage and stab us vertically with the sword of humor, leaping wit, and irony. Yes, he was a Wasteland poet, but he is larger than any single group of poets—and can't be contained by any particular place, whether Iowa, Otsuka, Africa, or Scotland. I believe deeply that Ryuichi Tamura is a poet of the universe, who happens to have come from Japan.

In 1993 I published an essay entitled "A Portrait of Ryuichi Tamura" in *Collected Poems of Ryuichi Tamura*. At the beginning of my essay, I wrote, "Ryuichi Tamura is a living legend.…In the quality and expansiveness of his poetry, he has an extraordinarily dynamic, sharp wit, understanding, and harmony.…He is acutely aware of the merciless workings of this world. Nevertheless he is a poet. He knows the innocent and pure nature of literature, as well as its guile. He knows the monster called journalism and its charm." I wrote, "he is a born poet. Reading his collected works, I see how his poetry has grown with the passage of time, and will continue to expand without interruption as long as he is alive—in other words, as long as his brain, his heart, and his body are healthy, he will be free of every literary illness. He has humor, wit, a cynical eye, and a critical mind: qualities which are somewhat Western." And so forth. And I concluded, "He performs the triple jump in his pajamas.…He is the Olympic gold medalist of *words and images,* metaphors and thought."

Now in 1998, as I read back over his works, I am beginning to see the same sunset he saw, and there is something more that I have come to understand.

THE UNTRUE DREAM WITHIN A DREAM

> It's said a poem is adolescent literature, it's a lie of the
>   underdeveloped country
> Unless the eyes get blurry
> ears get weak
> mouths drool
> a poem will not be born
> The pregnancy of a poem is the privilege of a consuming
>   human being
> who lives off civilization's reserves

I can understand well Tamura's aggressive attitude in this poem. The brilliant, tall, handsome, youthful Tamura with the profile of French actor Jean-Louis Barrault, the middle-aged Tamura, and the elderly Tamura walking with a cane.

The appreciation of poetry is a wonder. In a poet's youth, the dazzling Eros of the flesh overflows into poetry, and there is a juicy weird feeling of a human being having sex with the soul, a pleasure as though eating a mouthful of young fruit. In middle age, a poet turns from an animal into a human being, and tenderly embraces things inside. Sometimes the animal stirs up a season of storms. The soul is trained by experience to be like steel. Life's kaleidoscopic layers become visible.

And now, it is the season when poetry and death together look this way, and beckon, waving their hands.

Translation from Japanese by Yumiko Tsumura.

Flying Fox: Kin, Keystone, Kontaminant

A portrait of Australian flying fox life in the Anthropocene illuminates startlingly familiar stories. These animals are participants in most of the major catastrophic events, as well as contestations about rescue, of contemporary life on Earth: warfare, man-made mass death, famine, urbanisation, emerging diseases, climate change, biosecurity, conservation, and local/international NGO aid. They are endangered, and are involved in all four of the major factors causing extinctions: habitat loss, overexploitation, introduced species, and extinction cascades. My account of flying foxes in Australia rests on the understanding of species articulated both vigorously and eloquently by Donna Haraway (2008:42): we and others are entangled in knots of species who are co-shaping each other in layers of reciprocating complexity. I seek to engage both the living, warm-blooded beings whose lives are threatened, and the excruciatingly dynamic deathscape that is surrounding them/us. Positioned, like much of life on Earth today, in zones of increasing conflict and terror, the lives and deaths of flying foxes tell us that in the Anthropocene there is no way out of entanglements within multispecies communities. Rather than seeking to erect more impenetrable barriers against others, relational ethics for living and dying in the Anthropocene urge us to assume ever greater mutuality and accountability as intra-dependent members of the suffering family of life on Earth.

Sociability, Flying Fox Style—
Megachiroptera

Australian Megachiroptera scrabbled into the English imagination in June 1770 when Captain Cook beached his ship *Endeavour* at the mouth of a river in Queensland for repairs. One of his men returned to camp, telling of an animal he had seen: "It was as black as the devil and had wings; indeed I took it for the devil, or I might easily have catched it for it crawled very slowly through the grass" (quoted in Ratcliffe 1948:6). We might imagine that something was wrong with the little guy, as flying foxes can't walk and wouldn't normally be crawling in the grass. One wonders if the seaman had thrown stones at it, but perhaps it is equally possible to imagine that the flying fox, never having seen a white man before, was reeling with shock.

They are alert creatures, extremely aware of what is going on around them. Pamela Conder, a recent student of flying foxes, writes of her time sitting quietly inside a flying fox enclosure in a wildlife sanctuary, observing their actions and interactions. She says that the flying foxes quickly became accustomed to her, regarding her, apparently, as an innocuous part of the background. However, she states:

> I was surprised when I walked into the cage late one hot morning to see the bats panic and flee in all directions from my approach. Then I realised what was different—I was wearing a large sun hat. I left the enclosure, let the bats settle and returned sans hat. Not so much as an eyebrow was raised. Before long, however, the hat became accepted as part of me for the rest of that summer. (Conder 1994:55)

The term *chiroptera* means "hand winged." There are two suborders: mega and micro. Worldwide, Megachiroptera include 166 species of flying foxes (also known as fruit bats) and blossom bats. Microchiroptera include 759 species. The two suborders are quite different, size being only part of the difference. Microchiroptera navigate by echolocation (animal sonar); they are small and feed mainly on insects, but there also are blood-eating vampire bats, fish-eating bats, and other carnivorous bats. In contrast, Megachiroptera all feed on plants. They navigate principally by sight, and many of them are large. In Australia, the largest male flying foxes weigh about one kilogram (2.2 pounds) and have wingspans of up to 1.5 metres (nearly 5 feet) (Hall and Richards 2000:1–3).

There is no way of knowing the population of flying foxes prior to British settlement, but certainly the numbers would have been in the thousands of millions. Four main species of flying foxes make up the Australian contingent: black flying fox *(Pteropus alecto)*, grey-headed flying fox *(P. poliocephalus)*, little red flying fox *(P. scapulatus)*, and spectacled flying fox *(P. conspicillatus)*. By preference they travel widely in search of pollen, seeds, and fruits, covering vast areas during an annual round as they follow flowering and fruiting trees and shrubs. At present, both grey-headed and spectacled flying foxes are listed as threatened under the Commonwealth Environment Protection and Biodiversity Conservation Act 1999.

Flying foxes love to camp together; some camps number in the millions (Conder 1994:46). Every night across Australia, millions of flying foxes set forth, going distances of up to 50 kilometres in search of food. It is estimated that one individual can disperse up to 60,000 seeds in one night (DSE 2001:4). They are sociable, spending much of their time in camp grooming themselves and each other. With at least thirty different vocal calls, all of which are audible to humans, they are, from a human point of view, noisy folk (Hall and Richards 2000:64).

Maternity camps are chosen by the female flying foxes, and they return year after year to give birth and raise their young. Females give birth to only one baby each year. Babies are born with their eyes open, and their mother gently moves them into position so that they can latch on to her nipple. For a few weeks they hang on while she flies out at night for food. Later, though, they are left behind in crèches in the centre of camp. The mothers return at dawn, flying round and round until they locate their own baby, re-attaching the baby to the nipple. Once the babies have grown into adolescents or young adults, they leave their mothers and move into groups under the care of senior males. The older guys take them out at night, teaching them flying techniques and showing them how to locate food and find their way home again (Hall and Richards 2000:42–46). Hall and Richards describe these clumsy youngsters:

> They do not have the purposeful direction of the adults, and are reminiscent of a group of school kids going home from school and exploring their environment. Progress is slow as they carry out aerial bombs on each other, explore vegetation and duck from imaginary predators. It is probable that these groups do not initially go far from the camp, and that the trips serve as navigational training. (2000:46)

Storytelling, Indigenous Style

Flying foxes had been interacting with humans for thousands of years before they encountered either Englishmen or large summer hats. Indigenous people's stories of flying foxes go back to creation, to the Dreaming ancestors who walked the earth, making landforms, species, cultures, languages, biotic communities, and connections. Dreamings were shape-shifters, sometimes walking as humans, sometimes travelling in the form of the being they would become. Flying foxes were there too, of course.

I got to know flying foxes through Indigenous people of the Victoria River region in the northwest corner of the Northern Territory, where I lived and studied for many years in the communities of Yarralin and Lingara. Prior to the wet season (in December or so), the black flying foxes, *warpa* in local languages, congregated along the river banks, hanging from the riverside trees. Occasionally one might lose its grip and become a tasty treat for crocodiles. Of an evening we would watch them fly out, dark against the deep blue sky, hundreds upon hundreds of them, flapping their wings and forming a stream that widened out as they moved toward the flowering trees along the rivers and creeks. One of my teachers was Daly Pulkara, a man with a good fund of flying fox stories. We were watching the flyout one evening, and he pointed out something interesting. The crowd flew over, and then, after the mob was well on its way, a few turned back. A bit later, stragglers appeared, following the others but not quite catching up. "The old people always said those blokes forgot their axes," Daly told me. I felt like a bit of a straggler myself as I tried to catch the drift of the story. Of course, the bats were shape-shifters, and when they were men they would have carried axes. "They're always like that," Daly said, "one or two are back behind. That's why the old people said they forgot their axes, they had to go back to camp and get them."

To encounter such stories in their wonderful personableness and appropriateness is to find one's self in a world of animism. Defined and discussed in a new and excellent study by Graham Harvey, animism is the recognition "that the world is full of persons, only some of whom are human, and that life is always lived in relationship with others" (Harvey 2006:xi). Within an animist worldview, flying foxes are persons, and like any group of human persons, some are a bit sloppy, forgetting their axes when they go out foraging, dragging along behind, always a bit out of step.

The personhood of flying foxes is known not only through stories but also through kinship. Flying foxes are matrilineal "totems": they are members of kin groups comprised of both human and flying fox persons. Flying foxes are part of the group by reason of being flying foxes. Humans are part of the group because their mother, and her mother, and her mother, right back to the beginning, were flying fox people. Men belong to the group—they are flying fox people because they are the children of their mother, but their sons and daughters will not be flying foxes because flying fox people don't marry other flying fox people. The matrilineal kin relationship is understood to be corporeal—the flesh of the kin group is shared across the bodies of the people and animals, and is their co-specific embodied being in the world. This is the family: humans and nonhumans. They are in it together, sharing flesh, care, and continuity from generation to generation.

Flying fox persons (animal/human) are also part of the story of seasons. Why does the rain come? My teachers said that it comes because the flying foxes tell the Rainbow Snake to get up out of the river and get to work. This is a complex story of entangled mutualities and calls to action. The story of rain starts in the dry season, during the cold time of year when the flying foxes are in the higher country away from the rivers. As the sun dries the country, they move toward the river, and when they get there they hang in the trees over the river and call to the Rainbow Snake to rise up and bring rain. A lot of esoteric knowledge is bound into this story; we will avoid that knowledge completely and turn to an ecological side of the story.

Flying foxes feed, by preference, on the flowers of trees and shrubs of the Myrtaceae family. Yarralin people point especially to the inland bloodwood (*Corymbia terminalis,* or *jartpuru* in local languages) and the magnificent tree known in vernacular English as the half bark *(C. confertiflora,* or *ngurl-gugu)*. Both of these species produce large, showy clusters of cream-coloured, heavily scented flowers, so they are obvious candidates for both flying fox and human attention. In the Victoria River region, Myrtaceous trees flower in succession from higher ground to lower ground, which is also to say from the drier country on the hillsides down to the river banks and channels. River red gum *(E. camaldulensis)*, known as *timalan* in local Indigenous languages, and paperbarks *(pakali,* or *Melaleuca argenta* and *M. leucadendra)* are the two big riverside Myrtaceous trees. The banks of the rivers of this region are lined with paperbarks and river red gums. They are the last in the succession to burst into flower. The flying foxes follow their preferred food, which brings them to the riverside at the end of the driest time of year; they forage there in the thousands. Yarralin people say that the flying foxes talk to their mate, the Rainbow Snake, telling it to move, to get up, to get to work, to bring the rain. They say that the earth is getting too hot, that everything is too dry.

Co-evolution, a Myrtaceous Love Affair

Flying foxes have been relating to native trees for much longer than they have been relating to humans. According to Hall and Richards (2000:82–84), there is good evidence to support a hypothesis of co-evolution and co-dependence between Megachiropterans and flowing plants. In fact, flying foxes and the smaller, tube-nosed fruit bats may be the only seed-dispersal agents for many rainforest trees, and therefore are integral to the long-term survival of some species (Hall and Richards 2000:83). Flying foxes have a keen sense of smell, and their eyes are adjusted to night vision and to recognising light colours. Myrtaceous trees and shrubs produce clumps of flowers that are strongly scented and usually light in colour. They produce their pollen in the night, when the flying foxes are foraging; flying foxes are able to carry large loads of pollen because of their (relatively) large size; and because the plants flower sequentially, "Myrtaceous forests and woodlands provide a constant food supply throughout the year for these animals" (Hall and Richards 2000:82).

Seed and pollen dispersal is improved by flying fox feeding habits. In scientific lingo, people talk about the "residents and raiders" model of feeding. A group settles itself into a tree and then defends that place from others: these are the "residents." Other flying foxes attempt to join the group: these are the "raiders." Residents chase them away. All carry fruit and pollen from tree to tree as they struggle to find a place to stay and feed (Hall and Richards 2000:81–82). The stragglers that Daly spoke about— the blokes who always forget their axes—would seem to be "raiders": having gone back to get their axes, they now find that the best food locations are already taken. They may be a bit on the edge, but they are extremely important to Myrtaceae.

Scientific studies of flying fox feeding and their relationships with their preferred species have led to the understanding that flying foxes are a keystone species: as long-range pollinators and seed dispersers, their activities are essential to the health of native ecosystems. Indeed, as climate change forces all species to adapt rapidly, flying foxes will become increasingly important in maintaining gene flow and thus facilitating adaptation (Booth, Parry-Jones et al. 2008:4–5). As the populations of flying foxes are in rapid decline, there is the possibility that some species in some areas may become functionally extinct within a few decades (Booth, Parry-Jones et al. 2008:5). Functional extinction precedes actual extinction; it is a loss of connectivity and mutuality. Lose the flying foxes and there's no way of knowing just how far the unravelling of life systems will go.

Kinship, Scientific Style

Co-evolution is a process of mutual convergence by which entirely separate species evolve to mutual advantage. In contrast, linear evolution is imagined as the diversification of species who are descended from a common (albeit often extremely distant) ancestor. The differences between Megachiroptera and Microchiroptera are well established, but what is their origin, from an evolutionary point of view? Did flying foxes and bats have separate origins, and converge in shape for reasons of adaptation to flying? Or did they have a common ancestor, and did they therefore diverge as they adapted to different environments and conditions? Queensland neurologist John Pettigrew (1986) proposes the first alternative. He was performing what he calls a "routine investigation" on the inner workings of a flying fox brain and was astonished to discover that it was identical in many key features to the brains of primates:

> Primates share a half-dozen brain pathways not found in any of the other 20 mammalian orders. These features are quantitative and are believed to reliably distinguish primates from non-primates. They provide a unique signature, enabling us to recognize a primate brain after a set of tests which involve labelling the pathways going from the eye to the brain.

This analysis suggests that flying foxes are small primates who took to the airways. According to Pettigrew, "under the microscope the affinities between megabat and lemur brains are so striking that it is quite difficult to tell them apart. So far as one can tell from the intricate details of the wiring of thousands of nerve cells, primates and megabats shared a common ancestor not shared by any other group of mammals." Pettigrew's analysis is debated, and at the moment the issue is open.

When I first heard about this research, I became quite excited. During my years in Aboriginal communities I had, of course, encountered many flying foxes, mostly as food. A close encounter with a flying fox induces the strong awareness of being in the company of an odd little kinsman. With their small furry bodies and dog/human-like faces, with their chattery camps full of individuals who are grooming each other and carrying on their daily life—mating, raising babies, guarding teenagers, remaining attentive to sources of food in the region—with their fantastic wingspans and their spectacular nightly flyouts, I find it difficult to understand how anyone could fail to be completely entranced.

Understandably, perhaps, when flying foxes decide to camp in suburban backyards, coming in by the thousands and showing no inclination to move on as long as there is food in the region, humans do lose patience. I can't help but think that something about them reminds us of us—of how we are when we are at our most crowded, noisy, and irritating.

Shadow of Death

In addition to the distaste some people experience toward the bat shape and the bat reputation, and to the smell and the noise, orchardists have a grievance against flying foxes who eat the fruit. Although the evidence is clear that flying foxes prefer the Myrtaceae flowers and forest fruits with which they are co-evolved, the clearing of native vegetation and its replacement with commercial fruit crops has left them little choice. Biologist Francis Ratcliffe came out to Australia in 1929 sponsored by the state governments of New South Wales and Queensland to investigate the orchardists' problem. He was asked to provide information on flying foxes; the desire amongst many orchardists was less for information than for quick measures for eradicating flying foxes. Orchardists, along with many other people, held what we might call a zero-tolerance vision. Basically, they wanted flying foxes gone forever. This is an "us" and "them" boundary organised along an either–or axis: it offers no place for co-existence or mutuality. Ratcliffe's research led him to the conclusion that total eradication of flying foxes was impossible. He concluded that while it would be well-nigh impossible to eradicate flying foxes quickly, their populations seemed to be in fairly rapid decline; it thus seemed possible that the problem would take care of itself (1948:10).

The story of how several species of flying foxes were tipped to the point of being declared threatened species is the story of the Anthropocene. All the factors arise out of human action, but not all factors are directly intended to eliminate flying foxes. Martin and McIlwee (2002:98) sum them up: "habitat destruction, persecution and culling." In a subsequent list, they add climate change. Bearing in mind that habitat clearance has removed vast amounts of Myrtaceous woodland, leaving flying foxes with very little choice but to turn toward the commercial orchards with which farmers have replaced native vegetation, let us look first at a number of indirect factors.

Habitat clearance has effects that go beyond pushing flying foxes toward orchards. One is to increase the distances between native food sources to the point where flying foxes can no longer make it from one area to the next. Populations that become hemmed in are effectively trapped and completely dependent on local foods (Conder 1994:50), leading to mass starvation. In 2006 the Bat Rescue online newsletter carried an article on mass starvation in Queensland:

The combination of unusually low winter temperatures and shortage of food has been blamed for the large numbers of flying foxes found dead or dying along much of the East Coast during the last few weeks. With their lower fat reserves and inability to fly greater distances in search of food, juveniles have been particularly hardest hit....A number of bats have become entangled in backyard fruit tree netting...some have fallen victim to dogs or hit by cars and others have simply been found hanging dead or dying very low to the ground. (anon 2006)

Flying foxes also face exposure to hazards that are part of living in an industrial society. Lead poisoning is one factor that impacted flying foxes to a measurable degree (these impacts are now reduced with the widespread use of unleaded petrol). Collisions with airplanes, barbed wire, electrical wires, and other such obstacles are an ongoing hazard (Hall and Richards 2000:50–52). Pesticides and exposure to new bacteria may also be having an effect.

Climate change, too, is having an impact. Flying foxes are susceptible to heat stress, and do not tolerate temperatures over about 40°C (104°F). As Australia's heat and drought intensify under the influence of global warming, there will be more mass deaths like the event reported in Victoria during the 2009 bushfires, when the temperatures got up to about 47°C (116°F). At least 5,000 grey-headed flying foxes died during one hot afternoon at the Yarra Bend colony (Pearson, pers. comm.). This colony had already been hassled and stressed, having originally lived in the Melbourne Botanic Gardens and been forcibly shifted in 2003. There was public controversy over shifting them, and a group of volunteers have been working continuously to help the flying foxes survive in their new home. On days when the temperature is heading toward 40°C or more, volunteers go to the river and spray water into the trees where flying foxes are roosting.

On the other hand, even those who remain in the bush and are fully protected are still vulnerable. Another aspect of climate change is the increasing number and severity of weather "surprises." One such surprise was Cyclone Larry, which hit the Queensland coast in 2006. Along with the many banana farms destroyed, there was also damage to the rainforest; Cyclone Larry knocked down trees, and land area was opened up; open land was invaded by a weed known as tobacco plant, which then attracted spectacled flying foxes. The flying foxes come in low to eat berries off the tobacco plant, and when they are that close to the ground they are prey to paralysis ticks. Other Australian mammals such as kangaroos have developed resistance to these ticks, but the flying foxes are encountering them for the first time. The berries ripen at the time when mothers have recently given birth. The toxin saps the flying foxes' energy, leaving them unable to hang on to branches or care for their young. Prostrate on the ground, they die of dehydration, starvation, or organ failure. Young bats who are with their mother when she is poisoned may leave the mother and fly back into the canopy, joining the others who wait for mothers who never return. According to Jenny Maclean, Director of the Tolga Bat Hospital in the Atherton Tablelands (Queensland), where much of the paralysis disaster takes place, "we walk around the colony every day and you can hear the young bats crying for their mothers....Often they'll hang on for days before eventually starving to death" (quoted in Murphy 2007). She and other volunteers, including some from the USA and the UK, collect paralysed or orphaned bats. Those that can be saved are given treatment, and when they are well enough to be let free they return to the bush. Returnees are microchipped, making them very expensive little survivors, and some microchipped flying foxes fall prey to ticks again, returning to the hospital and back to the bush more than once (Adams 2007).

Some flying foxes have become urbanites. Like refugees everywhere, they flee the countryside because of famine, or because warfare has made life too dangerous, coming to cities in search of refuge and, perhaps, aid. In New South Wales, where grey-headed flying foxes are still legally (and, of course, illegally) shot, some groups have moved permanently to the city. In these urban environments, the planting and watering of native trees provides a year-round food supply, streetlights aid in navigation, and there is safety from gunfire. At the same time, flying foxes are subject to urban forms of injury and death: power lines, barbed wire, garden netting, and other dangers confront them (DSE 2001:2).

For many years, Sydney's Royal Botanic Gardens (SRBG) has been the occasional home for grey-headed flying foxes, and that home now seems to have become permanent. The numbers rise and fall, but there is always a core group, and many of the members of the core group camp in trees that are defined as "heritage" trees. The fact that the site is a traditional maternity camp puts constraints on the methods used to try to get the flying foxes to move on. Tactics have included noise harassment and ingenious methods such as lacing trees with bundles of python excrement (olfactory deterrence; pythons are one of the main predators), and lacing trees with fermented prawn paste (taste aversion). Noise harassment is a stressful business for flying foxes; the equipment used in the SRBG is called the Phoenix Wailer, a computer-controlled system that blares out a variety of electronic sounds, randomly selected, to create "a whirling effect of reverberating noises that creates a 'discomfort zone'" (Richards 2002:198–199). These methods have had the effect of getting some of the flying foxes to move on, but the fact is that they are under pressure: if there is no food, they die. If living in the Botanic Gardens helps them survive during this time of land clearing, loss of Myrtaceous forests, and danger in the orchards, then they will try to stay.[1]

Direct killing has been a major factor in the loss of flying fox. Ratcliffe reported that in the 1920s the "Brisbane and East Moreton Pests Destruction Board" counted 300,000 flying fox deaths achieved under a bounty system (discussed in Martin and McIlwee 2002:104). More recently, there were estimates of 100,000 or more grey-headed flying foxes being shot annually in the 1990s (Tidemann, Eby et al. 1999).

In 1986, flying foxes were given the protection afforded to other native mammals, and could not be shot without a license, although Aboriginal people were still free to hunt them. In 2001, grey-headed flying foxes were listed as a threatened species, and licensed killing was supposed to be phased out. In 2008, the state of Queensland stopped issuing permits to kill flying foxes on the grounds that it was inhumane. At the time of this writing, the state of NWS still issues permits to kill (Booth, Parry-Jones et al. 2008:6). Shooting was and remains one of the primary technologies in the battle against flying foxes.

The most torturous new technology of the twentieth century was electrocution. Electric grids were constructed over orchards causing flying foxes that approached to be electrocuted. This technique was banned in Queensland after public outrage over cruelty and after a court case that tested the limits of orchardists' right to kill (Booth, Parry-Jones et al. 2008:8). A 2007 court decision ordered orchardists who were still using grids to desist. The main grounds for the case were that the loss of spectacled flying foxes was putting the whole of the wet tropics ecosystem at risk (anon 2007).

Modernity and Terror

Ratcliffe used the terms of war to express his mission. Imagery of war can imply a two-way combat conducted according to rules.

> When a military commander plans an offensive he must have certain information on which to work. He needs to know, for instance, the size and strength of the enemy forces and the tactics they are likely to employ. In the same way, before a campaign is launched against an animal enemy, it is essential to have accurate knowledge of its numbers and habits. (Ratcliffe 1948:4–5)[2]

Against this imagery can be set Zygmunt Bauman's analysis of modernity's use of a narrative of future perfection to justify man-made mass death. He writes that the modern world did not do away with concepts of useless and useful, but rather set out to eliminate the "useless." Mass murder was imagined as "creative destruction, conceived as a *healing surgical operation*" (Bauman 2000:11).

This analysis sheds a sinister light on the idea of war against flying foxes and, indeed, war against nature more generally. From a perspective of terror, metaphors of warfare may offer a moderately positive gloss and may thus conceal forms of lethality having more in common with mass murder than actual war. In its classic form, warfare involves an opposition of relative equals in which the matters to be determined are worked out as death and injury to the bodies of the soldiers (Scarry 1985; Sloterdijk 2009). The battle against flying foxes has never involved equals and, in its orientation toward extermination, finds affinity with modernity's terrorism.

Let us first consider the arsenal used against flying foxes as reported by Ratcliffe. In his technical report (Ratcliffe 1931), he assessed various actions taken by orchardists against flying foxes:

- Introduced diseases—almost no chance of success (64)
- Scalp bounty system—costs more than the damage flying foxes do; least effective method (66–67)
- Poison gases (chlorine, hydrogen cyanide) in camps—ineffective (69–70)
- Explosives—"complete failures," but could be useful if the method was to discharge shrapnel (71)
- Flame guns—costly, might be rejected on grounds of cruelty (71)
- Shooting—if organised and pursued over a number of years, might have "beneficial effect," particularly if "females carrying young" were targeted (72)
- Poison baits/strychnine—"well worth the trouble" in certain orchards (74)

Hall and Richards (2000:103) are blunt in their assessment that many of these methods are "costly, often barbaric (for instance the use of flame-throwers and explosives), illogical in concept, and do not reflect well on the Australian nation."

I will explore affinities amongst extermination, terror, and lethal actions toward flying foxes, but I must first acknowledge that the problem of equating the eradication of humans with the eradication of animals is an ongoing sensitivity, discussed exquisitely in Coetzee's *The Lives of Animals* (2001). At the same time, I believe that it is possible to address this comparison without cheapening anyone's life or death. My premise is that in treating human and nonhuman deaths as separate kinds of events, we miss the connectivities; we thus deprive ourselves of the capacity to understand the complexities of anthropogenic deathscapes and have difficulty considering our entangled responsibilities and accountabilities. David Clarke (1999:178) has made this point in a brief and exquisite analysis in which he concludes that a positive effect of the disturbing comparison "creates a *rhetorical* neighbourhood in which animals and humans dwell and summon each other into responsibility."

The lives and deaths of flying foxes in the twentieth century show a stunning convergence between speciocide, to use Glen Mazis' term (2008:76), and genocide. It seems that to eradicate a species, or group of species, is not unlike eradicating a clan or a tribe, or undertaking ethnic cleansing. Speciocide, like genocide, may in many cases be primarily about destroying the possibility of the enemy's ongoing existence in the area you've defined as yours (whether that be a continent, a state, a region, or an orchard). Such efforts are integral to modernity's eradication of the "useless" in the pursuit of perfection. Lethal measures are designed to free one's environment of the presence of unwanted others. To accomplish this, extermination involves terror as well as death; it involves a boundary of exclusion that will cordon off an area, keeping it "free" of the unloved and undesired. "Systemised terror creates a relentless climate of anguish," Sloterdijk writes (2009:49)— words that evoke the lives and deaths of flying foxes as they are electrocuted, harassed from maternity camps, orphaned, starved, impaled on barbed wire, and otherwise subjected to direct and indirect technologies of extermination. Significantly, as well, human plans and projects of extermination follow the logic of terror: "every terrorist attack already understands itself as a counter-attack in a series initiated by the enemy" (Sloterdijk 2009:48). Thus, orchardists report themselves to be under attack by plagues or infestations, and their extermination efforts are usually represented simply as self-defence.

Into the Vortex

The problem of how to connect a lethal technology with an intended target will be resolved differently depending on context, including differing target populations. One solution to the problem of flying foxes appears to be unintentional, but is no less horrific for that. In an analysis of dynamics that connects lethality with its target, Martin and McIlwee (2002:105) work with the metaphor of a black hole. Let us note that the term *speciocide* generalises. Martin and McIlwee offer the term *pteropucide* as a descriptor of the man-made mass death inflicted upon flying foxes. Their scathing analysis of attempts to eradicate flying foxes from a given area offers an understanding of why orchardists can claim that the numbers of flying foxes are increasing while scientists claim that the numbers are decreasing. Orchards (or any other places that offer food) function as a vortex that draws more and more flying foxes into it. The "pteropucidal black hole" dynamic depends on the fact that every place which affords food, and in which local populations have been eradicated, entices more animals. "The culling produces a local vacant niche, which becomes occupied by animals moving into it from further afield, which are then killed, so producing a local vacant niche which…and so on." They refer to such kill/attract/kill-zones as *pteropucidal*, and they attest that the dynamic is like "an irresistible gravitational force sweeping everything into its maw." The inexorable dynamic works with the forces that drive flying foxes to orchards, and it creates zones of attraction which become zones of injury, suffering, and death (Martin and McIlwee 2002). At the same time, not only flying foxes themselves, but their life space is targeted; thus camps are dispersed, maternity camps are decimated, groups are harassed and stressed, groups become trapped in areas where they starve or feed on berries that bring them into peril—it goes on and on.

The metaphor of gravitational draw is powerful in itself and can be taken further: the pteropucidal black hole does not have a boundary that stops with flying foxes. As we have seen, flying foxes are keystone species, and when they are dragged into the vortex of death, rainforests and other ecosystems are dragged along with them. This means that critically endangered ecosystems will be dragged into the vortex, and so will the rare and endangered animals who live in them—cassowaries, for example, along with a number of mammals, frogs, and other creatures. As is well known, rainforests are colloquially referred to as the "lungs" of the planet, soaking up carbon dioxide and pumping out oxygen (Fyfe 2005). As rainforests disappear, so does the possibility of sustaining an Earth system that will be inhabitable for large numbers of the species of being who have evolved here and belong here.

Of course the black hole does not exempt humans, in direct ways as well as in the prospect of losing Earth's habitable climate and atmosphere. Three significant new zoonotic viruses (transmissible between humans and animals) have emerged in flying fox populations: Hendra virus, Menangle virus, and Lyssavirus. Of these, Lyssavirus is potentially the most serious in its impacts on humans; it is closely related to rabies, and has demonstrably been transmitted from a flying fox to a human. Volunteers working with flying foxes are advised to be vaccinated. It is unclear to what extent Lyssavirus may transfer to other mammal populations.

These new viruses have been present in flying fox populations for a long time, but have changed into active agency in recent years probably as a result of stress. Epidemiologist Hume Field explains:

> It might be that wildlife populations can cope and cope and cope with impacts, until they get to a certain threshold where their ecology is fundamentally compromised....And it's those points...those tipping points, that can precipitate the emergence of a new disease. (quoted in Booth, Parry-Jones et al. 2008:17)

(left) Maternity season in Sydney. (right) Flying fox belly-dipping in Parramatta River to rehydrate and cool off. Courtesy © Nick Edards.

Flying foxes are subject to many stresses that affect their immune systems, as we have seen: harassment, dispersal, death of family members, starvation, wounding from guns and electricity, as well as from hazards such as barbed wire, to recapitulate a few. The Lyssavirus is most likely to be found in animals already sick or stressed (Hall and Richards 2000:56–57). With these emerging diseases, harm has come full circle and demonstrates the inextricable connectivities between human health, flying fox health, and habitat health (Macdonald and Laurenson 2006). And the vortex keeps growing. More stress means more illness, more illness means more people seeking to help distressed flying foxes. The language of public hygiene and biosecurity gains new force, and vilification of flying foxes gains new ammunition. As flying foxes and humans move closer and more permanently into contact with each other, so new viruses threaten both humans and flying foxes, expanding and amplifying the deathwork.

The best answer, as Booth and others point out (2008:17), is to "conserve flying foxes and reduce the environmental stresses—including shooting—that increase their rate of infection and the risk of spillover to other species." If, however, the human response is to accelerate the stresses in an effort to control the boundary between humans and flying foxes, the feedback loop takes on the shape and dynamics of the death vortex. Terror returns, marking out a deathscape of disastrous, entangled, recursive, and amplifying devastation.

Interspecies Love

To understand oneself as part of a community of life is to accept responsibilities and also to accept vulnerability. On a recent visit to Aboriginal communities where I had spent many years living and learning, I had a conversation with a young woman I will call Gerry. Her father was a great flying fox storyteller, and she herself is a flying fox woman through her mother. After I had held and admired all the children, Gerry took me to the bank of the river for a chat. Every time I visit she does this—away from camp, into country, side by side looking at the river, to talk about what's happening. This time her gentle voice carried a lot of anger as she talked about what Whitefellas had done recently. They'd come through Aboriginal communities telling everybody not to touch flying foxes: not to eat them, not to handle them or hunt them, not to have any physical contact with them at all because flying fox might have disease. I could understand some of what was troubling her. Terror, it should not be forgotten, is exercised as a multispecies project. Gerry's grandfather had been shot and killed in the early days, some of her relations had been poisoned, many members of her family had seen dogs brutally shot, and dingo poisoning is a continuing feature of terrorism against animals in the region. All of them—people and their animal kin—have felt the oppressive weight of life and death decisions made elsewhere and imposed ruthlessly. This new public-hygiene advice could well have looked like another round of colonising violence. That's what her tone of voice seemed to imply.

Gerry was not going along with it. "They've been here forever," she said of her flying fox kin, "just like us. We're not worried. They're family."

ACKNOWLEDGEMENTS

Thanks always to my Aboriginal teachers from whom I learned to encounter non-human others as sentient "persons," some of whom were kin and almost all of whom were part of the country through Dreaming action. Thanks, too, to Les Hall, who spent hours talking with me about flying foxes, primates, Lyssavirus, and other fascinating matters, and to Tim Pearson, who is teaching me more than I am able to analyse in this paper. I am grateful to Nick Edards for allowing me to use his stunning photos. My research into flying foxes is currently in progress; this paper is the first entrant in the larger project.

REFERENCES

Adams, J. 2007. "Life Animal Adaptions." *Science World*, October 22.

"Bat Starvation Crisis in SE Queensland." 2006. *Bat Rescue Inc* Volume, DOI.

Bauman, Z. 2000. "The Holocaust's Life as a Ghost." In *The Holocaust's Life as a Ghost: Writings on Art, Politics, Law and Education*, edited by F. C. Decoste and B. Schwartz, 3–15. Edmonton: University of Alberta.

Booth, C., K. Parry-Jones, et al. 2008. *Why NSW Should Ban the Shooting of Flying Foxes*. Sydney: Humane Society International.

Clark, D. 1999. "On Being 'The Last Kantian in Nazi Germany': Dwelling with Animals after Levinas." In *Animal Acts: Configuring the Human in Western History*, edited by J. Ham and M. Senior, 165–198. New York: Routledge.

Coetzee, J. M. 2001. *The Lives of Animals*. Princeton: Princeton University Press.

Conder, P. 1994. *With Wings on Their Fingers: An Intimate View of the Flying-fox*. Sydney: Angus & Robertson.

DSE, D.o.S.a.E. 2001. "About Flying Foxes." Volume, DOI.

Fyfe, M. 2005. "Rising Temperatures Could Spell Doom for Many of the Delicate Creatures in Queensland's Wet Tropical Rainforest." *The Age*, November 16.

Hall, L., and G. Richards 2000. *Flying Foxes: Fruit and Blossom Bats of Australia*. Sydney: UNSW Press.

Haraway, D. 2008. *When Species Meet*. Minneapolis: University of Minnesota Press.

Harvey, G. 2006. *Animism: Respecting the Living World*. New York: Columbia University Press.

Macdonald, D., and M.K. Laurenson. 2006. "Infectious Disease: Inextricable Linkages Between Human and Ecosystem Health." *Biological Conservation* 131:143–50.

Martin, L., and A.P. McIlwee. 2002. "The Reproductive Biology and Intrinsic Capacity for Increase of the Grey-headed Flying-fox Poliocephalus Megachiroptera, and the Implications of Culling." In *Managing the Grey-headed Flying-fox as a Threatened Species in NSW*, edited by P. Eby and D. Lunney, 91–108. Sydney: Royal Zoological Society of New South Wales.

Mazis, G. 2008. "The World of Wolves: Lessons about the Sacredness of the Surround, Belonging, the Silent Dialogue of Interdependence and Death, and Speciocide." *Environmental Philosophy* 52:69–92.

Murphy, P. 2007. "Hospital Helps Larry's Other Victims." *The Australian*, November 22.

Pettigrew, J. 1986. "Are Flying Foxes Really Primates?" *Bats Magazine* 3.2 (June):1–2.

"Pteropus Conspicillatus Spectacled Flying-fox." 2007. W. Department of Environment, Heritage and the Arts.

Ratcliffe, F. 1931. *The Flying Fox Pteropus in Australia.* Melbourne: Council for Scientific and Industrial Research.

———. 1948. *Flying Fox and Drifting Sand: The Adventures of a Biologist in Australia.* Sydney: Angus and Robertson.

Richards, G.C. 2002. "The Development of Strategies for Management of the Flying-fox Colony at the Royal Botanic Gardens, Sydney." In *Managing the Grey-headed Flying-fox as a Threatened Species in NSW*, edited by P. Eby and D. Lunney, 196–201. Sydney: Royal Zoological Society of New South Wales.

Scarry, E. 1985. *The Body in Pain: The Making and Unmaking of the World.* New York: Oxford University Press.

Sloterdijk, P. 2009. "Airquakes." *Environment and Planning D: Society and Space* 271:41–57.

Tidemann, C., P. Eby, et al. 1999. "Grey-headed Flying Fox." In *The Action Plan for Australian Bats*, edited by A. Duncan, B. Baker, and N. Montgomery, 31–35. Canberra: Natural Heritage Trust.

NOTES

1. In May 2010 the Australian Federal Minster for the Environment, Peter Garrett, approved the proposal from the Royal Botanic Gardens in Sydney to disperse the flying foxes permanently. My research has correspondingly expanded to include this event as it unfolds over the next few years.

2. I have considered the possibility that Ratcliffe was being a bit tongue-in-cheek and intended this passage as a clever piece of writing that bore only tangential relationship to his work. If this is humour, it is lost on me, but perhaps in its day it made sense. I remain uncertain of the intent, but for the purposes of my analysis, intention is irrelevant.

Arts of Inclusion, or
How to Love a Mushroom

Next time you walk through a forest, look down. A city lies under your feet. If you were somehow to descend into the earth, you would find yourself surrounded by the city's architecture of webs and filaments. Fungi make those webs as they interact with the roots of trees, forming joint structures of fungus and root called mycorrhiza. Mycorrhizal webs connect not just root and fungus, but also—by way of fungal filaments—tree and tree, in forest entanglements. This city is a lively scene of action and interaction. There are many ways here to eat and to share food. There are recognizable forms of hunting. For example, some fungi lasso little soil worms called nematodes for dinner. But this is one of the crudest ways to enjoy a meal. Experts in refinement, the mycorrhizal fungi siphon energy-giving sugars from trees. Some of those sugars are redistributed through the fungal network from tree to tree. Others support dependent plants, such as mushroom-loving mycophiles that tap the network to send out pale or colorful stems of flowers (e.g., Indian pipes, coral-root orchids). Meanwhile, like an inside-out stomach, fungi secrete enzymes into the soil around them, digesting organic material—and even rocks—and absorbing nutrients that are released in the process. These nutrients are also available for trees and other plants, which use them to produce more sugar for themselves—and for the network.

Throughout this process, there is a whole lot of smelling going on, as plants, animals, and fungi sniff out not just good meals but also good partners. And what wonderful smells, even for an animal nose, like mine! (Some fungi, such as truffles, depend on animals to smell out their reproductive bodies, to spread around their spores.) Reach down and smell a clot of forest earth; it smells like the underground city of fungi.

As with human cities, this underground city is a site of cosmopolitan transactions. Unfortunately, humans have mainly ignored this lively cosmopolitanism. We have built our human cities through destruction and simplification, chopping down forests and replacing them with food-growing plantations while we live on asphalt and concrete. In agribusiness plantations, we coerce plants to grow without the assistance of other beings, including fungi in the soil. We replace fungally supplied nutrients with fertilizers obtained from the mining and chemical industries, with their trails of pollution and exploitation. We breed our crops by isolating them in chemical stews, crippling them, like caged and beakless chickens. We maim and simplify crop plants until they no longer know how to participate in multispecies worlds. One of the many extinctions that result from all this planning is the cosmopolitanism of the underground city. And almost no one notices, because so few humans even know of the existence of that city.

Yet a good many of those few who do notice fungi love them with a breathless passion. Gourmets, herbalists, and those who would remediate world ecology often become devotees of the fungal world. Wild mushroom foragers praise their unexpected bounty, their colors, tastes, and smells, and their promise of a livelihood from the woods. How many times have foragers told me of the heat of "mushroom fever," which drives them to dodge their other obligations to take up the wild thrill of the chase? Even commercial agents are giddy with the unpredictability of deals involving a capricious commodity. Scientists who study fungi rave about them in a manner quite dissimilar to scholars of fruit flies or HeLa cells. And, while some fungal devotees are content with personal association with fungi, others long to share their passion with the world.

How do lovers of fungi practice *arts of inclusion* that call to others? In these times of extinction, when even slight acquaintance can make the difference between preservation and callous disregard, we might want to know.

Noticing

Henning Knudsen, curator of fungi at Copenhagen University's Botanical Museum, shows me around the fungi collection at the herbarium in April 2008. At first the aisles seem neat and impersonal. Then we open the folded envelopes and expose dried specimens, each named and labeled by its collector. Hiding in their dust lie the shriveled but still talking mushrooms, carrying their names and the names of their collectors into the story of life on earth.

Taxonomy is not very popular these days; indeed, detractors think of it as dry classification that spoils all enjoyment. But handling the specimens at the herbarium, it is easy to feel the pleasure of naming. Here, through naming, we *notice* the diversity of life. Taxonomy was once closely allied with drawing, another art of noticing. (See page 193, left.)[1]

Northern Europe, including Britain, is the homeground of amateur as well as scientific botanizing, the collecting and naming of plants. Still, noticing fungi did not come easily, Dr. Knudsen explains, because northern Europeans have despised mushrooms—perhaps a reminder of their pagan past. It took a nineteenth-century French-born monarch of Sweden, Karl Johan, to bring even the prized king bolete (also, cep or porcini) to the attention of Scandinavians—and the mushroom is still known by his name.

Besides, fungi are difficult to collect and identify because their bodies tend to be underground. Only their reproductive organs—the mushrooms—come up into the air, and those only sporadically, sometimes in intervals of many years.

Dr. Knudsen tells me about Elias Fries (1794–1878), the father of modern systematic mycology. Like Linneas, Fries was a Swede and a lover of plants; Fries extended Linnean botany to the world of fungi. His work was made possible through a combination of his extraordinary memory and extraordinary passion. He recognized five thousand species, remembering them from year to year across the mushroom-empty times. Many of the specimens he collected were from near the village where he was born and first learned to love mushrooms. Dr. Knudsen remembers Fries' account of his early, persistent love. When, as a boy, he found an enormous specimen of the species *Tricholoma collosum*, he was thrilled: "I love my sister, I love my father, but this is better." Dr. Knudsen gives me a copy of Fries' memoir, which has been translated from Latin to English. Equally passionate love stories jump from the page:

(left) Jacob E. Lange, 1935–1940.
(right) Minakata Kumagusu, 1921; 2007.

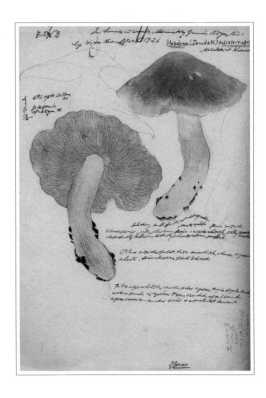

To this day, more than half a century later, I remember with gratitude the admiration that seized me when in 1806 I went with my mother to a burnt-down forest to pick strawberries and there I succeeded in finding an unusually large specimen of Hydnum coralloides, which was the first thing that induced me to study fungi. (Fries 1955: 140–141)

Afterwards, Fries *noticed* fungi everywhere and, indeed, devoted his life to noticing them. Through his taxonomy, Fries brought fungi to public attention. His enthusiasm encouraged the founding of a line of systematic mycologists, to which Dr. Knudsen—mushroom sociologist and coeditor of *Nordic Macromycetes*—is an heir.[2]

The line of mycologists stretches far beyond northern Europe. Consider the polymath naturalist Minakata Kumagusu (1867–1941), remembered for offering the Emperor of Japan a box of horse manure—containing interesting species of slime mold.[3] Minakata's watercolors bring together art and taxonomy. They guide our attention. The colors swirl; the fungi pose; the herbarium is alive. (See page 193, right.)[4]

Noticing inspires artists as well as naturalists. American composer John Cage (1912–1992) was a mushroom hunter who believed noticing mushrooms and noticing sounds in music were related skills. In contrast to other musicians, Cage wanted a music that forced listeners to attend to *all* the sounds around them, whether composed or incidental. Teaching and writing about mushrooms helped him explain how to practice an open yet focused attention. In one of his compositions, *Indeterminacy,* one-minute-long paragraphs, thoughts, and anecdotes are read aloud in random order—sometimes to the accompaniment of dance or music. Indeterminacy is exemplified in many levels of open-endedness. Many of the stories are about people's interactions with mushrooms. Mushrooms, too, are unpredictable; they help one listen and pay attention. In his entry #113, Cage is explicit:[5]

Music   and   mushrooms:
    two   words   next   to   one
another   in   many   dictionaries.
        Where   did   he
write   *The   Three-Penny   Opera*?
      Now   he's
buried   below   the   grass   at   the
foot   of   High   Tor.
    Once   the   season   changes
from   summer   to   fall,
    given   sufficient   rain,
      or   just   the
mysterious   dampness   that's   in   the
earth,   mushrooms

```
grow    there,
carrying  on,                        I
  am    sure,                      his
  business  of  working  with
sounds.
                     That   we
  have  no  ears  to  hear  the
  music  the  spores  shot  off
  from  basidia  make  obliges  us
  to  busy  ourselves  microphonically.
```

Basidia are part of mushroom reproductive organs; from basidia, spores are "shot off" into the air. One mushroom, called the "cannonball fungus" (*Sphaerobolus stellatus*), throws out its spore mass (but not from basidia) with a sometimes-audible pop. For most mushrooms, however, the shooting off of spores cannot be heard by human ears. Even in the sounds we miss, Cage wants us to find inspiration for music.

The parsed, anecdotal style of *Indeterminacy* is reminiscent of other formal poetics, such as haiku. Noticing mushrooms—especially those aromatic delights Japanese call matsutake—has not escaped haiku poets as a subject. Recognition of indeterminacy similarly guides the haiku, as in this poem by Kyorai Mukai (1651–1704):[6]

> Matsutake yo hito
> Ni toraruru hana no saki

> Matsutake;
> Taken by someone else
> Right in front of my nose.

Matsutake (*Tricholoma matsutake* and allies) are much-loved mushrooms in Japan. They cannot be cultivated, so they draw mushroom lovers into the forest to search for them. Matsutake are difficult to spot. Always it seems that the matsutake we are about to find has been taken by another. We must look more carefully.

The poem's phrasing and sound draw us into a world where we are able to notice. Even this one valued species group, matsutake, can inspire cosmopolitan worlds of mushroom loving. Kyorai's poem can spur us to consider matsutake worlds—and their arts of inclusion.

Conjuring Matsutake Worlds:
Toward a Democratic Science

Under the name of Matsiman (Americans sometimes call matsutake *matsi*), Andy Moore has dedicated his life to producing and spreading knowledge about matsutake mushrooms. Moore is not a commercial producer; matsutake cannot be cultivated. He is not a gourmet cook; he doesn't even like the taste and smell of matsutake. He is not a trained scientist, although he participates in matsutake-oriented science. Rather, his goal is to make knowledge accessible. He wants a democratic, inclusive science. Through attention to matsutake, he spreads knowledge—and his vision of democratic science. On his website, Matsiman.com, Moore posts everything he can find about matsutake and prompts discussions about mushroom worlds.

Matsutake inhabit northern hemisphere forests, associating particularly with conifers such as pine. It's a wide-ranging species group, with populations stretching across Eurasia, down through North Africa, and across the Atlantic into Canada, the United States, and Mexico. In most of the places where the mushrooms grow, people do not enjoy them as a food. Europeans first called them *Tricholoma nauseosum* to indicate their dislike of the smell. (U.S. mushroomer David Aurora [1986:191] describes the smell as "a provocative compromise between 'red hots' and dirty socks.") But for many Japanese, the smell is enticing. Grilled or cooked in soup, matsutake are an expensive gourmet treat as well as a reminder of the beauty of the autumn season.

Until the 1970s, Japanese pine forests produced a rich complement of matsutake. But pine forests, associated with village life, declined after World War II. In this same period, Japanese incomes rose. In the 1980s, Japan began importing matsutake from around the world. The prices were high; mushroom entrepreneurs rushed to enter the fray. At first, Japanese in the diaspora who had found mushrooms for their own use abroad guided Japan's imports. But soon enough, all kinds of people were picking matsutake—whether or not they enjoyed the mushroom for their own use.

Andy Moore was one of these people. Originally from Louisiana, he found his way into the Oregon woods during the U.S. war in Vietnam. Having enlisted as a soldier, he was disillusioned by what he saw and experienced there. He felt lucky when he managed to aggravate a childhood injury and was sent home. Based in the U.S., he drove a jeep at a marine base. But one day he received word that he was to be sent back to Southeast Asia. He was not willing to go. With pride, he recounts how he returned the jeep, walked out of the gates, and declared himself AWOL ("absent without leave"). To avoid capture, he ran to the mountains, where he made a living in various kinds of forest work, such as cutting firewood. He loved the forest. The experience gave him a new goal: "To live in the woods and never pay rent."

At the very end of the 1980s, matsutake madness came to the U.S. Pacific Northwest. The woods filled with pickers. Matsutake buyers set up tents by the side of the road, eager to export the mushrooms to Japan. Japan at that time was still wealthy from the boom economy; prices were very good; and pickers hoped to strike it rich with "white gold." Moore tried picking and found it very much to his liking.

Moore had an ideal situation for picking—and studying—the mushrooms. He had obtained a position as the caretaker for a large private forest. He lived in a small cabin at the top of the property, and his job allowed him plenty of time and opportunity to explore. He discovered matsutake on his property just waiting to be picked. Because matsutake has a long-term relationship with particular trees, the best way to pick is to go to the same trees every year to see if there are mushrooms. But most pickers in the U.S. Pacific Northwest pick on national forests with open access; they go back to the same trees, but, often enough, other pickers have beat them to the harvest. ("Matsutake / Taken by someone else / Right in front of my nose"!) Moore's situation was unique: he had a large forest area to harvest, and a locked gate to keep out other harvesters.

The situation awakened his curiosity about the mushrooms. When the fungus is not fruiting, the area around even the most heavily mycorrhizal trees is empty and unpromising; suddenly and unexpectedly mushrooms spring up. What factors control when mushrooms appear? Moore knew various contradictory rumors about this question, but there seemed to be no solid, experimental knowledge. So he decided to start his own experiment. Because other pickers did not intrude on his haven, he was able to mark all the spots where matsutake appeared. Then he was able to keep records of exactly when they appeared, how many, what weight, and their price. These records could be correlated with rainfall, temperature, and other factors.

Moore did not have either training or mentoring for his experiments. He simply started doing them. Later, he worked with U.S. Forest Service researchers on their projects and became a coauthor of several papers. But in those circumstances he was an assistant, without the ability to frame questions or suggest methods. On his own, he was forced to invent science using his own means. Obscure terminology, standardized scales, and sophisticated testing procedures hardly seemed necessary to him. Instead, he started with the questions pickers want to know: when and where do the mushrooms appear?

With some startling results in hand (his mushrooms responded to temperature not rainfall), Moore decided to make his results public. In 1998, Moore opened the Matsiman.com website. The site was not, however, designed to be Moore's personal blog; instead, he facilitated the making and exchange of knowledge. Everyone, the site suggests, can do research; all it takes is curiosity. The site poses the question, "Who is Matsiman?"

Anyone who loves hunting, learning, understanding, protecting, educating others, and respects matsutake mushroom and its habitat is matsiman. Those of us who can't get enough understanding, constantly trying to determine what caused this or that to happen, or not happen. We are not limited to nationality, gender, education, or age group. Anyone can be a matsiman. There is at least one in every picking community.

To appreciate the extraordinary nature of this public knowledge, it is important to allow Moore his eccentricities. His forest-caretaker position has ended, but he has found a job as a campground host, which allows him to live year-round in a motor home as a steward of public lands. To live in the woods and never pay rent!

He tries out various mushroom-based commodities, such as smoked mushroom seasoning and dried mushroom snacks. It seems unlikely that such experiments generate much of an income, but they keep Moore's exuberance for mushrooms high. Meanwhile, there is nothing proprietary about any of the many ideas he generates. He believes that all knowledge should be accessible; the Matsiman site builds a community of knowledge. Moore loves nothing better than to introduce new people to the world of matsutake, whether through his site or as a visitor to the forests he knows well. I spent a very happy time learning about Moore's matsutake under tanoak, Shasta red fir, and pine.

Conjuring Matsutake Worlds: Toward
More Inclusive Modes of Well-being

Now consider a different mushroom-based project of inclusion: an appeal to matsutake to help us build models of well-being in which humans and nonhumans alike might thrive. The charismatic and energetic organizer Fumihiko Yoshimura has been studying and working with matsutake for most of his life. As a scientist, Dr. Yoshimura conducts some of his work in laboratories and forest field sites. But he is also founder of the Matsutake Crusaders, a Kyoto-based citizens' initiative to revitalize Japan's matsutake forests. The Matsutake Crusaders are volunteers; their job is sculpting the forest to bring back the health of red pine with its associate, matsutake. Matsutake here is not just a delicious food; it is also a valued participant in a world of ecological well-being. The Crusaders' motto is "Let's revitalize the forest so we can all eat *sukiyaki*." *Sukiyaki* (a meat and vegetable stew best made with matsutake) is a popular and traditional food. Sometimes *sukiyaki* is eaten on festive occasions and sometimes during outings in which urbanites enjoy the fresh air. Eating together in appreciation of the natural world, people revitalize their selves as well as their forests. Dr. Yoshimura's movement brings participants into the countryside to offer new vitality to the world.

Dr. Yoshimura draws on a long legacy of applied matsutake science in Japan. Minoru Hamada deserves credit for making matsutake an object of modern science in the twentieth century. Dr. Hamada designed matsutake research to address basic biological questions while simultaneously promoting the production of a valued economic product. After World War II, Dr. Hamada trained a cohort of matsutake researchers who in turn trained many of today's researchers. Makoto Ogawa, one of Dr. Hamada's students, was particularly effective in spreading matsutake research by convincing the government to send matsutake researchers to every prefectural forestry station.[7] Dr. Yoshimura spent most of his career in Iwate prefecture conducting matsutake research and promoting matsutake.

While researchers have successfully grown matsutake mycelia and even matsutake-pine mycorrhiza in laboratories, no one has succeeded in getting these cultivated stocks to produce a mushroom. The focus in promoting matsutake, therefore, has been to make the kind of forest where matsutake likes to live. In Japan, matsutake associates with red pine, *Pinus densiflora*, a pioneer species of disturbed areas. For many centuries, villagers in Japan have created disturbed forests by shifting cultivation and selective harvesting of broadleaf trees that are used for firewood and charcoal. Villagers have traditionally also collected herbs and grass, and raked leaves for green fertilizer. These practices left bright, open hillsides of exposed soils—the conditions preferred by red pine and its partner, matsutake.

All this changed after World War II. Villagers started to use fossil fuels for heating and tractors instead of oxen for plowing. People no longer collected firewood to make charcoal, or gathered leaves and grass. Young people moved to the city, and village forests were neglected. Broadleaf trees grew back with a vengeance, shading out pines; furthermore, pines were weakened by a wilt disease spread by an imported nematode. In the deep shade of the neglected broadleaf forests, pines died. Without their hosts, matsutake also expired. Many matsutake lovers described hillsides they had seen white with mushrooms when they were children, now without a single host pine.

By the 1970s, urbanites became nostalgic for the village forests of their youth—places to see wildflowers in spring, fireflies in summer, and the leaves changing in autumn.[8] Citizens' movements emerged to address the impoverished environment of modern Japan. Unlike wilderness advocates in the United States, many Japanese focused on the lively ecologies of sites that had long experienced human disturbance: the verges of roads, the flood plains of rivers, village irrigation networks and rice paddies—and the open village forest. In these disturbed sites, something that might be called a sustainable relationship between humans and nonhumans could be imagined. Preservation came to mean not human withdrawal from nature but rather guided disturbance. In the process of studying ancient methods of disturbance, modern citizens educated themselves about being in nature.

It was from this milieu that Dr. Yoshimura's Matsutake Crusaders emerged. The name of the group is derived from the popular mobilization effort of the 1980s, known as the Woodland Maintenance Crusaders, in which student volunteers removed grass and weeds that were choking the forest.9 Dr. Yoshimura's group has the added excitement of not just fixing the forest but also, possibly, producing tasty mushrooms. His methods are to promote the growth of pine by removing evergreen broadleaves completely, thus opening hillsides to light. As the pines come back, the hillsides become open forests where wildflowers, rabbits, and hawks can find niches. But no one can guarantee mushrooms. The volunteers must do the work for the love of nature, not just for matsutake.

All of this leads me to a Saturday in June 2006, when my research collaborator Shiho Satsuka and I joined the Crusaders for a day of forest work and play. The site was a steep hillside that had become choked with young evergreen broadleaves. The many slender trees were so close together that a person could not peer very far into the forest, much less walk through it. Our task, Dr. Yoshimura explained, was to clear the land so that only red pine would grow. When Dr. Satsuka and I arrived, a group of men were busy removing trees and shrubs. Surprisingly, to me, they were even digging out the roots of the broadleaf trees. It was labor-intensive work, all done with hand tools, and I realized it would take years to clear even this one mountain. Still, everyone there was cheerful and full of enthusiasm.

Dr. Yoshimura showed us the adjoining hillside, which after much work was open, bright, and green with pine. "This is what our hillside might have looked like in earlier days," he explained. Animals and birds had settled in—and there was hope for mushrooms. Meanwhile, other projects were underway: a garden; a charcoal-making kiln; and a beetle-breeding mound for hobbyists. At the base of the hill was a place to eat, relax, and talk. At lunchtime, the workers sweating on the hill came down. Their colleagues had been constructing a long bamboo aqueduct for serving a special summer dish: noodles in the stream (or "flowing somen"). At the high end of the aqueduct, we poured hot steaming noodles into the cool running water. Everyone gathered around the bamboo "stream" and grabbed the flowing noodles with their chopsticks, mixing them with sauces in ready bowls. There was much joking and laughter. I met rural landowners and urban housewives, and even an anthropology graduate student. Someone offered an amusing haiku about coming from America. Someone else showed off the ingeniously handcrafted crabs he had made. A landowner showed pictures of his property, which he hoped to revitalize using Crusader techniques. We lingered long together before going back to work. This was a revitalization not just of the hillside but of our senses.

Loving in a Time of Extinction

The forms of love I have called up in this paper are diverse, even contradictory. Despite the fact that Andy Moore and Dr. Yoshimura are both concerned with matsutake mushrooms, they might find each other's practices strange. The sciences—and the social and natural ecologies in which they participate—are linked but not continuous in any simple way. I have written elsewhere about the glancing relationship between "forest ecologies" as observed and interpreted in Oregon and Kyoto (Tsing and Satsuka 2008; Tsing 2010). Here, I introduce these separate regions only to the extent that they inform our appreciation of each creative intervention. For Moore, the wild mushroom economy, with its encouragement of participation by people who love the woods, creates the possibilities for vernacular science. He works to free knowledge production from the rule of experts; anyone with a passionate curiosity can contribute. For Dr. Yoshimura, citizens' interest in environmental remediation offers the chance to build connections between human and nonhuman well-being. For him, efforts to re-sculpt forest landscapes make the volunteers happier and healthier, as they work for a more hospitable multispecies environment.

Both interventions contrast with the hegemonic, extinction-oriented practice of what might be called "plantation science." Plantation science teaches us to strive for control of human and nonhuman landscapes. For those who love wild mushrooms, full mastery is not the goal; *indeterminacy* is part of the point. Wherever volunteers gather to promote disturbance forests, or matsutake pickers stop to ponder why the mushrooms come up, plantation science loses a little authority.

In plantation science, managers and specialists make decisions; harvesters are never consulted about the crops. In plantation science, well-being is a formula defined at the top, and no one stops to ask, "Well-being for whom?" In plantation science, experts and their objects of expertise are separated by the will to power; love does not flow between expert and knowledge-object. In contrast, my stories describe how advocacy for mushrooms can lead to projects for building democratic science and publicly inclusive well-being. It's the passion for the mushroom—in all the details of its social-natural ecology—that makes these projects possible.

At the intersection between the sciences of nature and the sciences of culture, a new model is afoot, the key characteristic of which is multispecies love. Unlike earlier cultural studies of science, its raison d'être is not, mainly, the critique of science, although it can be critical. Instead, it encourages a new, passionate immersion in the lives of the nonhuman subjects being studied. Once, such immersion was allowed only to natural scientists, and mainly on the condition that the love didn't show. The critical intervention of this new form of science is that it encourages learnedness in natural science *along with* all the tools of the humanities and the arts. The objectives of those of us in this field are to open the public imagination to make new ways of relating to nature possible. For this, we need to summon the unexpected talents others—whether scientists or nonscientists—have brought to this task. My stories of mushroom lovers and their projects are a small contribution.

REFERENCES

Arora, David. 1986. *Mushrooms Demystified: A Comprehensive Guide to the Fleshy Fungi*. Berkeley: Ten Speed Press.

Blacker, Carmen. 2000. "Minakata Kumagusu, 1867–1941: A Genius Now Recognized." In *Collected Writings*, 235–247. New York: Routledge.

Blyth, Reginald H. 1973. "Mushrooms in Japanese Verse." In *Transactions of the Asiatic Society of Japan*, Third series, 11(December):93–106.

Fries, Elias. 1955 [1857]. "A Short Account of My Mycological Study." Translated by Ib Magnussen and Annie Fausboll. *Friesia* 5(2):135–160.

Hansen, Lise, and Henning Knudsen, eds. 1992, 1997, 2000. *Nordic Macromycetes*, vols. 1, 2, and 3. Copenhagen: Nordsvamp.

Nakagawa, S. 2003. "Nationwide Partnerships for Satoyama Conservation." In *Satoyama: The Traditional Rural Landscape of Japan*, edited by K. Takeuchi, R.D. Brown, I. Washitani, A. Tsunekawa, and M. Yokohari, 111–119. Tokyo: Springer.

Tsing, Anna. 2010. "Worlding the Matsutake Diaspora, or, Can Actor-network Theory Experiment with Holism?" In *Experiments in Holism: Theory and Practice in Contemporary Anthropology*, edited by Ton Otto and Nils Bubandt, 53–76. Oxford: Wiley-Blackwell.

Tsing, Anna, and Shiho Satsuka. 2008. "Diverging Understandings of Forest Management in Matsutake Science." *Economic Botany* 62(3):244–256.

"Who Is Matsiman?" n.d. Accessed September 20, 2010. www.matsiman.com/matsiman.htm.

NOTES

1. Jacob E. Lange, *Flora agaricina danica,* Volume 1, plate 7A,C. Published under the auspices of the Society for the Advancement of Mycology in Denmark and the Danish Botanical Society, Copenhagen, 1935–1940.

2. Lise Hansen and Henning Knudsen are coeditors of the three-volume *Nordic Macromycetes* (1992, 1997, 2000).

3. Alan Christy, personal communication 2008. See Blacker (2000).

4. Minakata Kumagusu, in *Minakata Kumagusu Kinrui Zufu: Colored Illustrations of Fungi.* Watariumu Bijiutsukan and Hiromitsu Hagiwara, eds. Tokyo, Shinchōsa, 2007, p. 76 (original 1921).

5. Mushroom-related sections of *Indeterminacy* can be found by going to www.mundusloci.org/fungus/culture/cage2.htm. Also see the site www.lcdf.org/indeterminacy/index.cgi by Eddie Kohler. Since the stories are gathered from various Cage books and performances, put back together in new performances, they thwart the determinacy of standard citation practices.

6. Translated and published by Reginald Blyth (1973). For Cage performing a different matsutake haiku, see www.youtube.com/watch?v=XNzVQ8wRCBo.

7. See Tsing and Satsuka (2008) for citations and fuller treatment of this history.

8. The distinction between two kinds of broadleaf trees—deciduous and evergreen—is important in central Japan. Deciduous broadleaves are preferred for

firewood and charcoal. Villagers selectively weeded out the evergreen broadleaves. Meanwhile, the deciduous broadleaves grew back from coppice shoots after harvesting, thus establishing their dominance in the forest architecture. This helped to keep forests bright and open. In the late twentieth century when no forest management was being done in many areas, evergreen broadleaves, no longer cut back, became the dominant forest vegetation. Besides discouraging pine and its associates, these new dark forests do not allow the familiar wildflowers, birds, and insects associated with earlier village forests. They also do not offer autumn colors.

9. See Nakagawa (2003, 114) for a discussion of these earlier Crusaders.

About the Contributors

Robert Bringhurst is the author of a three-volume study of Haida oral culture. The first volume, *A Story as Sharp as a Knife* (1999), won the Edward Sapir Prize, awarded by the Society for Linguistic Anthropology, and was chosen by the *Times* His *Selected Poems,* published in Canada by Gaspereau in 2009, has recently been issued in a shorter form by Jonathan Cape, London. Counterpoint recently published two volumes of his lectures and essays: *The Tree of Meaning* (2008) and *Everywhere Being Is Dancing* (2009). His books include *The Solid Form of Language* and *The Elements of Typographic Style.*

Calvin Collins is a visual artist who obtained a bachelor's of fine arts degree from the San Francisco Art Institute and a master's of fine arts degree from the University of Hawai'i at Mānoa. His work can be seen at calvin-collins.com.

Andrew Lam is a syndicated writer and editor with the Pacific News Service. He is the author of two books of essays: *Perfume Dreams: Reflections on the Vietnamese Diaspora,* which won the Pen American Beyond the Margins Award in 2006; and *East Eats West: Writing in Two Hemispheres* (2010). His collection of short stories, *Birds of Paradise,* is set for publication in 2011. Lam was featured in the 2004 PBS documentary *My Journey Home*, and his writing has been covered frequently on National Public Radio's *All Things Considered.*

Leo Litwak is the recipient of John Simon Guggenheim and National Endowment for the Arts fellowships. He has published two novels, a collection of short stories, and two books of nonfiction. His novel *Waiting for the News* received the National Jewish Book Award; his short fiction has appeared in *Best American Short Stories* and *O. Henry Prize Stories*. His articles have appeared in such publications as the *New York Times Magazine,* and *Esquire*. A professor at San Francisco State University for more than thirty years, Litwak lives in San Francisco.

Barry Lopez is the author of eight works of fiction, including *Light Action in the Caribbean* (2000) and *Resistance* (2004), and two books of essays. He recently edited, with Debra Gwartney, *Home Ground: Language for an American Landscape* (2006), a reader's dictionary of regional landscape terms. His most celebrated work, *Arctic Dreams* (1986), received the National Book Award; *Of Wolves and Men* (1978), a National Book Award finalist, received the John Burroughs and Christopher medals. He lives in rural western Oregon and is a *Mānoa* corresponding editor.

Manjula Padmanabhan is an Indian writer and artist-cartoonist. *Harvest,* her fifth play, won the 1997 Onassis Award for Theatre. She has illustrated twenty-four children's books. Her comic strips appeared weekly in the *Sunday Observer* from 1982 to 1986 and daily in the *Pioneer* from 1991 to 1997. Her most recent novel is *Escape* (2008), set in a dystopian future.

Donald Richie is the foremost American scholar of Japanese film. His first major book on cinema, *The Japanese Film: Art and Industry,* coauthored with Joseph Anderson, was published in 1959. He has since published over forty books of fiction, translation, and nonfiction. He has written and directed dozens of experimental films, and authored hundreds of book, film, and arts reviews for the *Japan Times* and other publications. *The Donald Richie Reader,* comprising fifty years of his writing about Japan, was published in 2001.

Deborah Bird Rose is a professor of social inclusion at Macquarie University, Sydney, where her research focuses on multispecies inclusion in this time of extinctions. Her recent books include the prize-winning ethnography *Dingo Makes Us Human* (2009) and *Reports from a Wild Country* (2004). Her newest book, *Wild Dog Dreaming: Love and Extinction,* is forthcoming from University of Virginia Press as part of the series Under the Sign of Nature: Explorations in Ecocriticism.

Anjoli Roy is coeditor of the online journal *Vice-Versa: Creative Works and Comments.* A writer of creative nonfiction, fiction, and poetry, she graduated with a master's degree in English from the University of Hawai'i at Mānoa, received the Myrle Clark Award for creative writing, and was awarded a Grace K.J. Abernethy publishing apprenticeship.

Andrew Schelling is a poet, translator of the lyrical verse of ancient India, essayist, and editor. His book *Dropping the Bow: Poems from Ancient India* (1991) received the Harold Morton Landon Translation Award from the Academy of American Poets. His other translations include *For Love of the Dark One: Songs of Mirabai* (1993; 1998) and *The Cane Groves of Narmada River: Erotic Poems of Old India* (1998). A collection of essays and poems, *Wild Form, Savage Grammar: Poetry, Ecology, Asia,* was published in 2003. He also recently edited and co-translated a comprehensive anthology of South Asian *bhakti* poetry, forthcoming in 2011 by Oxford University Press, India. He teaches at Naropa University.

Kazuko Shiraishi is one of Japan's foremost writers of avant-garde and experimental poetry. She has published over twenty books of poetry, which have been translated into many languages, and has won all of the important literary awards in Japan. Her most recent books translated into English include *Let Those Who Appear* (2002), which received the Yomiuri Literary Award and the Purple Ribbon Medal from the Emperor of Japan, and *My Floating Mother, City* (2009), which received the 2003 Bansui Poetry Award and a Cultural Award from the Emperor. Shiraishi lives in Tokyo.

Arthur Sze is the author of eight books of poetry, including *The Ginkgo Light* (2009), which received the 2009 PEN Southwest Book award for poetry and the

2010 Mountains & Plains Independent Booksellers Association Book Award in poetry. He is also a translator and the editor of the collection *Chinese Writers on Writing* (2010). He lives in Santa Fe, New Mexico.

Fiona Sze-Lorrain writes and translates in French, English, and Chinese. Co-director of Vif Éditions, an independent French publishing house, and an editor at *Cerise Press*, she is the author of a book of poetry, *Water the Moon* (2009). Her translations with Ye Chun of poet Hai Zi are forthcoming in 2012. She has coauthored with Gao Xingjian *Silhouette/Shadow* (2007). She is also a *zheng* (Chinese zither) concertist; her CD *In One Take* will be released this fall. She lives in Paris, France.

Anna Tsing teaches anthropology at the University of California, Santa Cruz, and currently writes about recuperation and nature in the shadow of global capitalism. She is the author of *In the Realm of the Diamond Queen: Marginality in an Out-of-the-Way Place* (1993) and *Friction: An Ethnography of Global Connection* (2004). Her essay in this issue of *Mānoa* draws upon her collaborative research with the Matsutake Worlds Research Group.

Yumiko Tsumura was born and educated in Japan. She received a master's of fine arts degree in poetry and translation from the University of Iowa and is a professor of Japanese language and culture at Foothill College in California. With her late husband, Samuel Grolmes, she collaborated on the translation into English of two volumes of poetry by Kazuko Shiraishi and the collections *Tamura Ryuichi: Poems 1946–1998* (2000) and *Poetry of Ryuichi Tamura* (1998).

Melissa Tuckey is the author of the chapbook *Rope as Witness*. She is a recent recipient of a Fine Arts Work Center fellowship and is a founding member of Split This Rock Poetry Festival in Washington, D.C.

Thom van Dooren is an environmental anthropologist-philosopher whose current research involves human relationships with plants and animals, globalization, climate change, and species extinction. He is a chancellor's postdoctoral research fellow at the University of Technology in Sydney, and with Deborah Bird Rose he co-edits the ecological humanities section of the *Australian Humanities Review*.

Yang Zi is the author of a dozen books in China, including *Border Fast Train* (1994), *Gray Eyes* (2000), and *Rouge* (2007), and is cofounder of the literary journal *Big Bird*. In 1990, he became an alderman of Tahaqi Village. At present, he is vice chief editor of the *Nanfang People Weekly*. He is a prolific translator into Chinese of such Western writers as Osip Mandelshtam, Paul Celan, Fernando Pessoa, Gary Snyder, and Charles Simic.

Ye Chun writes and translates in English and Chinese. She is the author of *Travel over Water* (2005), a book of poetry, and cotranslator with Fiona Sze-Lorrain of Hai Zi's book *Wheat Has Ripened,* forthcoming in 2012. Her poetry and translations have appeared widely in American literary journals. Also a visual artist, she lives in Virginia.